MELANIE HARLOW

MH PUBLISHING

For my girls, sisters and best friends

I must be a mermaid ... I have no fear of depths and a great fear of shallow living.

ANAÏS NIN

ONE

MAREN

Soft female voices drifted through the haze.

"Is she breathing?"

"Yes."

"Are you sure? Because she looks dead."

"Aren't you supposed to look dead doing Corpse Pose?"

"Not *that* dead."

"Mildred Peacock kicked the bucket during yoga at the center last year, remember?"

"That's right. She was wearing those awful purple leggings."

"And that rubbish pink lipstick."

"I don't think the teacher's dead. I think she just fell asleep."

I opened my eyes and saw the nine students from my Friday morning Yoga for Seniors class standing above me. I was lying flat on my back, legs extended, arms at my sides, palms up.

"Oh my God." I sat up. "Oh my God, I'm so sorry, ladies. I must have dozed off. This has never happened to me before."

"We thought you were dead," said one white-haired woman wearing a T-shirt that said "My Grandma is a Hooker" above a picture of a crochet hook and a ball of yarn.

"You looked good dead." Another old lady nodded enthusiastically. "Much better than Mildred Peacock."

Embarrassed, I scrambled to my feet. "Forgive me, please. I haven't been sleeping well, and it's catching up with me." For weeks now, I'd been having this recurring nightmare about being locked in a room with a big snake. I'd tried everything I could think of to ease my subconscious mind—meditated, detoxed, cleared my chakras—but nothing had worked.

"That's all right." The Hooker patted my shoulder. "Happens to everyone. Try some warm milk."

"Put some whiskey in it," suggested a salt-and-pepper-haired woman with a smoker's voice.

"Thanks, I'll try that." I glanced at the clock and saw that I'd been out for the entire last ten minutes of class. "The bus is probably here to take you back to the senior center, ladies. I'll see you next week. Thanks for coming."

Several of them told me to get some rest before shuffling out of the studio, toting their rolled-up mats and water bottles. Over in the corner of the room, I turned off the music and looked at my reflection in the mirror. Bags under my bloodshot eyes. Paler-than-usual skin, especially for July. Worry lines creasing my forehead. I tried to relax my face, but the lines didn't disappear.

Great, now that stupid nightmare was giving me wrinkles. Pretty soon I would look just like those old ladies in my class. I *had* to get some sleep.

Allegra, the instructor for the next class and an old

friend from ballet school, came into the room. "Hey, Maren. How's it going?"

"Other than the fact that I just dozed off while I was teaching?"

Her jaw dropped, then she smiled. "You did not."

"I did. They thought I might be dead."

She laughed and rubbed my upper arm. "You poor thing. Still not sleeping at night?" Allegra knew about the nightmare.

"No," I said. "And I have no idea what to do."

"You need to take some time off, Maren. A few days for mental health."

She was probably right, but it was hard for me to take days off. I owned the studio, taught several classes a day, and often worked the desk, too. "I'll think about it."

"I can help cover for you. Just say the word."

I gave her a grateful smile. "Thanks. The room's all yours."

Grabbing my water bottle and mat, I headed for the lobby and went behind the desk. I tucked my mat out of sight, checked email and phone messages, and put a load of towels in the laundry. Then I texted my sisters, Emme and Stella.

Me: You will not believe what I did this morning.

Emme: WHAT?

Me: I fell asleep while teaching Yoga for Seniors.

Emme: HAHAHAHAHAHA

Me: They thought I was DEAD.

Emme: OMG that's even funnier!

A moment later, my phone rang, *Emme Devine* flashing on the screen.

"Hello?"

"I'm driving now so I had to call you," she said, laughing. "But that's hilarious."

"It wasn't hilarious, it was mortifying," I whispered, smiling at a few women who passed by the front desk on their way to the dressing room. "I'm the teacher. I'm supposed to set a good example."

"I bet those blue-hairs didn't even notice. Half of them were probably asleep too. For Christ's sake, *I* struggle to stay awake during yoga."

I sighed, tipping my forehead onto my fingertips. "It's that stupid nightmare, Em. I'm not getting any sleep."

"You're *still* having it?"

"Yes."

"The same one? About the giant snake and the door with no handle?"

"Yes."

"You need to google that shit, Maren. Figure out what it means."

"No. I told you, I don't believe in seeking wisdom on the Internet. Google doesn't have any insight into my consciousness. I have to find the answers within." I looked up and saw new faces heading for the desk. "I gotta go. I'll see you tomorrow."

I'M in a room full of people, but they can't see me.

I keep trying to talk to them, but I can't speak. I can't even open my mouth.

I look down and notice I'm naked.

That's when I see the snake.

Slithering through the crowd along the dark wood floor, it's heading straight for me.

Panicked, I start running for the door at the end of the room, but my progress is hampered because I'm carrying a clock in my arms, the old-fashioned kind that used to sit on top of my grandparents' piano. It's ticking loudly.

Eventually, I reach the door but discover there is no handle. And it won't budge.

The clock ticks faster and faster. I look down and notice the second hand is moving backward. It's counting down, like a stopwatch.

I bang on the door, too scared to turn around and see how close the snake is.

It hisses behind me, and then—

I sat up in bed, gasping for air and damp with sweat, the sheets tangled around my legs. My heart was thundering in my chest. Sliding out of bed, I went over to the window. It was open, and a soft summer breeze blew through the screen, cooling my arms and chest. Taking a few deep breaths, I listened to the chirp of the crickets and inhaled deeply—fresh cut grass, the Forget-Me-Nots blooming in the window box, the lingering whiff of charcoal from someone's backyard grill. I centered myself in the moment and focused on the way the air felt moving in and out of my lungs. Within a few minutes, my pulse had slowed and the trembling in my limbs ceased, but I couldn't shake the anxious residue the dream had left behind.

It had to mean *something*, so what the hell was it?

Giving up on sleep for the time being, I left my bedroom, which was at the back of my ground-floor flat, and walked through the dark to the front. After making sure the curtains were closed, since I wore only a tank top and undies, I switched on a lamp. My laptop was sitting on the coffee table where I'd left it, and I scooped it up. I'd meant what I said to Emme earlier—normally, I didn't believe the Internet could enlighten people about their own minds—but at this point, I was desperate for a clue.

Settling cross-legged on the couch, I set it in my lap, opened it up, and typed "dreams about snakes" into the search box.

The results, as I had expected, were all over the place.

Freud (of course) viewed the snake as a phallic symbol. Since there was a distinct lack of phalli in my life, I didn't really see how that would make sense, unless my subconscious was bemoaning that lack. If that was the case, my subconscious could line up right behind the rest of me. I hadn't had sex in two years.

The Dream Maven posited that a snake could represent something that tempted you, possibly something you felt guilty about. Well, damn, that could be any number of things.

Vodka, leather shoes, frosted strawberry Pop-Tarts, gay porn. The list seemed endless. But ninety-nine percent of the time, I didn't indulge in those things, so I didn't really think it was one of them. (Except for maybe the gay porn thing. That had real possibilities.)

According to another site, running away from a snake that's chasing you might symbolize someone or something you're afraid to face. Again, I couldn't really think of anything I feared. Of course, I had *questions* about life—was I on the right path? Would I ever find love again? Did I have a higher purpose? But those weren't exactly fears.

Occasionally, I struggled with feeling like I had given up my ballet career too soon and missed the feeling that performing in front of an audience gave me. But I'd taught myself to find validation from within, and the truth was, I hadn't liked living in New York City at all. I had left my apprenticeship with the American Ballet Theater after just one year.

But I didn't think that was it, either. When I searched my soul, I felt no regret about leaving the ballet world, with its constant pressures, strict hierarchy and intense competition. It wasn't for me. I much preferred the inner peace and harmony I got from yoga, and running a successful studio afforded me a good enough income to live on my own, travel a little, and treat myself to the occasional luxury. I was happy. Healthy. Balanced. Fulfilled.

At least, I had been before the nightmares. Now I was exhausted, irritable, off-kilter, and full of doubt. Was the universe trying to warn me about something?

I googled a few more things—being naked in a dream (did I feel vulnerable? Had I been caught off guard?), the clock in my hands (was I concerned about time running out?), the locked door (did I feel confined by something?)—but felt no closer to decoding my psyche than I had before. With a frustrated sigh, I closed my laptop and set it aside. It wasn't helping. What I needed was some deeper self-reflection.

Yawning, I rose to my feet, switched off the lamp, and promised myself some extra meditation time tomorrow. It was late, after 3 a.m., and I had to teach class in the morning, which would be followed by an afternoon shopping excursion with my sisters to look for bridesmaid dresses for Emme's wedding. She'd gotten engaged a few weeks earlier to a great guy, a single dad who adored her. I was thrilled for her—this was her dream come true. As girls, when I was filling my scrapbook with pictures of ballerinas and pointe shoes, she was filling hers with brides and bouquets. It was no surprise to anyone that she grew up to be a successful wedding planner.

I got back in bed and eventually managed to fall asleep, but it felt like I had barely closed my eyes when my alarm went off three hours later.

Groaning, I dragged my ass out from beneath the sheets and went to work. I was uncharacteristically grouchy at class—at least three people asked me if I was feeling okay—but at least I stayed awake through it. When I got home afterward, the only thing I felt like doing was stuffing my face with bad-for-me food and taking a nap. But I didn't ever buy any bad-for-me food, which made me even angrier with myself, and I stood in front of the open snack cupboard muttering curse words and willing a box of frosted strawberry Pop-Tarts or at least a bag of Fritos to appear. When the universe failed to deliver, I had to settle for Craisins.

Fucking *Craisins*.

After polishing off the entire bag standing at the kitchen counter, I stuffed it into the trash and stomped down the hall to my bedroom. I pulled down the shades, kicked off my flip-flops, and crawled beneath the covers, pulling them over my head.

"YOU OKAY?" Emme frowned at me in the mirror of our huge dressing room at the bridal store. "Or do you really hate the aubergine?"

I looked down at the deep purple dress I wore, which had to be the ninetieth one I'd tried on in the two and a half hours we'd been here. On my best day, shopping wasn't my thing. Today, it was akin to torture. "No, the color's fine. I don't hate it. I think I'm just done trying on dresses. They're all looking the same to me."

"Hey, what about this one?" Stella breezed into the room holding up a long, one-shouldered dress in navy blue.

"I think Maren might have reached capacity." Emme shook her head. "I don't know how we have a little sister who doesn't like to shop."

"Sorry. Can I take this off now?" I was already slipping the heavy dress over my head.

"Go ahead." Sighing, Emme handed me a hanger. "I guess I've seen enough for today. Let's go get a drink."

We left the dressing room, and Emme thanked the saleswoman who'd been helping us, telling her we'd probably come back another day to try on some more. I hid my grimace as well as I could.

It was a beautiful summer night, warm and clear, and I tried to let the fresh air and pretty sunset cheer me up as we walked, but my spirits dragged. Less than half a mile up Old Woodward, Emme led us into a wine bar called Vinotecca, and we found three seats at the bar. I sat in the middle.

"Ooh, I want bubbly," Emme said, clapping her hands. "I'm going to have a glass of Prosecco."

"I'm not supposed to have any alcohol," I said glumly, eyeing the bottles of wine behind the bar.

"Why can't you have alcohol?" Stella asked.

"I'm detoxing my pineal gland."

"You have a penile gland?" Emme blinked at me.

"*Pineal* gland, not penile."

"Why on earth would you need to detox your pineal gland?" Stella wondered.

"Because it's the third eye chakra," I explained, sorry I'd mentioned it. "Some people believe the pineal gland is the source of human intuition. Poor diet and exposure to toxins can calcify it, causing us to lose perception. I'm trying to get some insight into why I might be having that stupid snake nightmare." I sighed and stared longingly at a bottle of zinfandel, my favorite. "But I think I'd rather have a glass of wine."

The bartender came over and we each ordered a glass of wine—Prosecco for Emme, pinot noir for Stella, and zinfandel for me. I figured it couldn't do any more damage than an entire bag of Craisins, which probably had a shelf life of about a thousand years.

"Tell me again what the nightmare is about," urged Stella, a therapist whose favorite activity was probing people's minds, even when she wasn't in the office. She'd put on what I called her Therapist Face, which said *you can trust me*, and touched my arm. "Maybe I can help."

Taking a deep breath, I described the crowded room, my inability to be seen or heard, my nakedness, the snake, the clock, and the locked door. They listened, rapt with attention. "And then I wake up," I finished, "right as the snake is about to bite me."

The bartender brought our wine, and I took an eager sip.

"And you can't fall back asleep afterward?" Stella asked.

I shrugged. "Sometimes, not always. Not last night." From the corner of my eye, I glanced at Emme. "Last night I got out of bed and googled the dream."

Emme beamed and puffed out her chest. "And?"

"Let me guess." Stella held out a hand. "The Internet thinks the snake is a penis."

I pointed at her. "Exactly."

Stella rolled her eyes. "Good old Freud."

"Is there a penis in your life we don't know about?"

Emme gave me a pointed look over the rim of her narrow glass.

I shook my head. "Nope. Not one that isn't battery-operated, anyway."

She snorted. "Maybe you need a real one."

"Maybe." I swallowed some more wine. "But I don't really think the dream is about sex."

"Let's think about one of the other things from your dream," Stella suggested. "Like the clock."

"Maybe it's a biological clock," Emme said. "Maybe you're subconsciously thinking about getting married and having kids, and worried about waiting too long."

"But I'm not even thirty," I protested. "I don't feel any pressure whatsoever to get married. And I could always adopt if I wanted kids."

"How about the door?" persisted Stella. "What do you think that means?"

"I'm not sure," I said. "The Internet thought maybe I was feeling confined by something. But I can't think what."

"The door was closed, so maybe you need *closure* on something." Emme sipped her Prosecco. "Or someone."

"That's a good point," said Stella. "Can you think of anything in the past you might have unresolved feelings about? Your ballet career maybe?"

I shook my head. "It's not that."

"Mom and Dad's divorce?" Emme suggested.

"No, that never bothered me either. They were obviously unhappy together."

"A relationship?" asked Stella.

Something twisted in my gut.

"No," I lied.

I couldn't go there. I never went there.

Emme went there. "What about Dallas Shepherd?"

My stomach hollowed.

Dallas Shepherd.

My first crush, my first kiss, my first everything.

He'd had the body of an athlete, the hands of an artist, the face of a god, the charm of a fairy tale prince, and the sense of a cinder block.

Not that he wasn't smart—he was. He used to amaze me with all the things he could memorize. Random things I said offhand he could repeat back to me almost verbatim. And he was so damn talented—he could draw anything. I never understood why his grades were so terrible, or why he made such bad decisions. He was *always* getting in trouble at school. Fights. Pranks. Smoking in the bathroom. He didn't even *like* cigarettes! It drove me crazy, all the dumb stuff he used to do—but he couldn't stay out of trouble, and I couldn't stay away from him. It was like trying to fight gravity.

"Come on, that was twelve years ago," I said, attempting to laugh. I'd been seventeen the last time I saw him, not that I had known it was going to be the last time. He'd made sure of that. "I think I'm over him by now."

"I don't know about that," Emme said. "You haven't really dated anyone seriously since then, and you were pretty wrecked after he left."

I shifted in my chair. "No, I wasn't."

"Yes, you were. Stella, remember that pillowcase she had with his face on it?"

Stella laughed while I huddled in humiliation, remembering all the tears I'd cried on that pillowcase. "I never saw it, but you told me about it."

Emme was delighted. "She would put it on every night and take it off every morning to hide it. I only know because

I caught her doing it once. She made me swear not to tell Mom."

"Okay, enough," I snapped.

"You shouldn't be embarrassed about your feelings, Maren." Emme patted my shoulder.

"I don't have feelings about Dallas anymore," I insisted.

"You never think about him?" Stella pressed.

I shrugged and took a few swallows of wine. "Not really." Another lie.

I thought about him every time a man disappointed me in bed and left me wondering if I'd ever feel that *thing* I'd had with him again—that insatiable desire between us. *I can't get enough*, he used to tell me, his ravenous mouth seeking every inch of my skin.

I thought about him every time I drove past the house on the lake where he used to live, or the high school we'd both attended, or the dark church parking lot he'd driven to that final night, where he'd gone down on me in the backseat of his Jeep before pulling me onto his lap and whispering that he loved me, that he wanted me, that he needed me, as he slid inside me, slow and deep. He'd been uncharacteristically broody and intense that night, and I'd been so lost in my own feelings I hadn't thought to ask him why.

I thought about him every time I saw someone sketching, remembering how he was constantly drawing things—with a pencil on the back of a test he'd failed, with a pen on a paper napkin at a restaurant, with a Sharpie on people's arms at parties. One time he'd spent all night "tattooing" my left arm in gorgeous, scrolling mandala designs that stretched from my hand almost to my shoulder. My mother had been furious and my ballet teachers appalled, but I'd loved the idea that he'd created something so beautiful on my skin, as if I were his canvas. I'd wished it was a real tattoo, and he'd promised someday it would be. He'd promised a lot of things.

But it turned out he was better at sex than promises, and his sudden vanishing act had left a bruise on my heart that had never completely healed. To make peace with it, I'd simply come to accept that tender spot as part of me, and I avoided pressing on it.

Could the dream be about Dallas? But why now, twelve years later, when I'd already moved on? Sure, it had taken me a long time, but I'd gotten there. I dated occasionally. It wasn't *my* fault I'd never fallen head over heels for someone again. It wasn't like you could choose your soulmate—either you felt that *thing* or you didn't. And I'd just never felt it for anyone else. What was I supposed to do, fake it? I'd rather be single.

The three of us were quiet for a moment before Emme spoke again. "Why does it have to mean anything? Maybe it's just a random bad dream."

I shook my head. "I don't believe anything is random. But let's talk about something else, okay? I'll figure it out. Deciphering messages from my subconscious is not your problem."

"Well, what's your subconscious saying about that dark purple dress?" Emme asked.

I laughed and shook my head. "Nothing yet, but I'll let you know if I hear something."

"Good. We're now thinking October or November up at Abelard, and I'm envisioning kind of a soft autumn color palette—eggplant, heather, thistle, sangria, eucalyptus." She ticked the colors off on her fingers.

"That's going to be beautiful, Emme," I said. Abelard Vineyards was the winery our cousin Mia and her husband

Lucas owned up on Old Mission Peninsula. It would be gorgeous that time of year.

"I agree," said Stella. "But can you really plan a wedding that fast? That's only a few months away."

Emme rolled her eyes and sighed dramatically. "I'm a wedding planner, Stella. That's what I *do*. We'll get better prices in the off-season, and besides ..." Her cheeks went pink and her shoulders rose. "We don't want to wait. We want to be married *yesterday*."

Now it was Stella who sighed. "Must be nice to be so in love. How's it going living together?"

"Fantastic. I've never had so much sex in my life," Emme whispered excitedly. "And it's better every time. Nate is just ... so generous. And talented. And well-endowed." She shivered. "It's mind-blowing."

I peered into my empty glass, wondering if a second glass was a horrible idea. I didn't drink much and had a pretty decent buzz from the first.

Emme looked across me to Stella. "What about you? Things still strictly platonic with Buzz?"

I nudged Emme with my foot. Buzz was our nickname for Stella's psych professor boyfriend, Walter. We called him that because he was so passionate about his beekeeping. What he *wasn't* passionate about was Stella—at least not sexually. Emme and I remained perplexed about their year-long relationship, which seemed more like a friendship than anything else, or maybe like a brother and sister hanging out together. But Stella claimed to be fine with that.

"Yes," she said. Then she looked around, like she was trying to find something she'd lost. "Is there a menu anywhere? I'm getting kind of hungry."

"I'm up for some food," said Emme. "I'll flag down the bartender." But beneath the bar, she nudged me back, and I knew she'd noticed, just as I had, the way Stella had avoided any further discussion about her and Buzz.

I understood completely. Who'd want to follow up Emme's dreamy rhapsodizing about Nate's sexual prowess and their mad rush to the altar with anecdotes about holding hands at the movies and listening to endless stories about pollination on their Sunday morning jogs? I didn't want to talk about my sex life either. Two-year dry spell aside, it was pretty depressing that I was twenty-nine and the only guy I'd ever experienced mind-blowing sex with was my high school boyfriend.

Stop thinking about him.

I put him from my mind and did my best to focus on what Emme was saying about centerpieces and seating arrangements.

Dallas Shepherd was nothing more than a memory.

TWO

DALLAS

"I really think you should reconsider, Lisa." I handed back the picture of Tweety Bird to the eighteen-year-old girl sitting in the chair across from me. "My gut feeling is that you'll regret getting this tattoo."

"How do you know?" Lisa pouted, which made her look even younger.

I shrugged. "Just a hunch. Let's talk about another design, okay?"

"But I love Tweety Bird. And I want it to say 'You're my Tweety Pie' above and then my boyfriend's name below."

"Then I'm definitely not doing it." I sat back in my chair and crossed my arms. "I have a strict rule about tattooing names on people. I won't do it."

"Why not?"

"Because I've never known anyone who had that done and wasn't sorry later on. I'm all about having no regrets in life."

"I won't regret it," she insisted. "Rocky and I are in love. That's forever."

"A tattoo is forever. Love, not necessarily. Either way, I won't put your boyfriend's name on your arm."

"How about his face?" She began scrolling through pictures on her phone. "He's really cute."

"No."

"His real name is Rockton. Would you put that?"

"Not a chance."

"Haven't you ever been in love?" she demanded.

"Once," I told her.

"What happened?"

"That's complicated. And private."

She rolled her eyes.

"Suffice it to say, I fucked up. I was young."

She gave me the side eye. "You don't look that old."

"I just turned thirty. I was seventeen then."

"Oh." She nodded, confirming that thirty was definitely old. "So what did you do?"

I cocked my head. "Didn't I just say it was private?"

"Look, I paid a hundred-dollar deposit to get this appointment with you."

"For a tattoo. Not a true confession."

"You won't even give me the tattoo I want. My dad's a lawyer, you know."

"Is he aware that you're here with a picture of Tweety Bird?"

She fidgeted in her seat. "Just tell me what you did. Then I'll pick a different design."

I sighed heavily and checked the clock on the wall. It wasn't even six yet, but this day had been long enough already. I had the same dull ache in my head I'd had for the last four months, and I still had to call my older brother, Finn, at some point. I wasn't looking forward to it. Maybe if I told her the story, she'd get bored and move on. "Senior year, I was getting in trouble too much and my parents sent me away."

"What kind of trouble?"

"Dumb shit."

"Where'd they send you?"

"To obedience school."

My humor was lost on her. "Was the girl upset?"

"Probably. I left without telling her."

She gasped. "Why?"

"I didn't want to say goodbye."

"She must have been *so* pissed at you."

"She probably was."

Lisa's eyes went wide. "You don't know? Like, you never talked to her again?"

I shrugged and checked the clock again. "Told you I fucked up."

"But...but why?" Lisa seemed genuinely distressed at my assholery. "If you loved her, why leave her like that?"

"Because she was better off without me and I knew it. Now let's talk about another design."

She brought out her phone and showed me a Pinterest board she'd created with tattoo ideas. Most of them were pretty terrible, but I got the feeling she liked birds and flowers, so I got out a pencil and sheet of paper and sketched something for her—a small bird standing on a little branch with flowers at both ends. It was feminine but not cutesy, a classic subject with an abstract feel. She loved it.

I pulled on some gloves and got to work. I wasn't much for conversation while I was tattooing someone, but I was used to people wanting to talk to me. It always amazed me the way some people treated their tattoo artists like therapists. Maybe it was just that they wanted to talk through the pain.

Maybe it was the fact that I was entirely focused on them and they weren't used to having someone's full attention. Maybe the fact that they had to trust me with their skin made them feel like they could trust me with their feelings. Whatever. It was fine with me—as long as they didn't expect me to reply— and if they found something therapeutic about getting a tattoo, well, good. God knows I'd worked through some emotional shit with ink. Sometimes it was all you could do.

Lisa got queasy about halfway through, so I decided we should take a break. While she relaxed with a bottle of water and a few deep breaths, I peeled off my gloves and checked my messages. My doctor's office had called to confirm my films had been sent to Boston, as requested, and my brother had called—again—but didn't leave a message this time.

My friend Evan, whose station was next to mine, knocked on the half-wall separating us.

"Yeah."

He pulled back the black velvet curtain above the wall. "Hey. Beer after work? Widmer?"

"Sounds good."

"How much longer will you need?"

"Probably an hour or so."

"Okay. I'm done, so I'm gonna run home and eat dinner with Reyna. Text when you're ready and I'll meet you."

"Will do."

An hour and a half later, Lisa was the proud bearer of her first tattoo. Her complexion had lost most of its green tinge, and she was all smiles as she studied it through the protective plastic bandage. "I love it," she said. "You were right, this is much better than Tweety Bird."

"Told you so."

"Am I done?"

"Yes, but sit tight for a minute. It's not good to get up too fast, and we need to go over aftercare instructions."

"Okay." She was silent as I handed her a sheet explaining when she should remove the bandage, how she should wash and dry it, and what to put on it to help her skin heal.

"No sun, no swimming, no soaking for two weeks," I warned. "And after it's healed, make sure you use sunblock on it."

She nodded. "I will."

I stood up and offered her my hand. "Thanks for coming in."

"Thank you." She rose and shook my hand. When she let go, I waited for her to leave so I could start cleaning up, but she continued to stand there, looking at me curiously.

"Something else I can do for you?" I asked.

"I want to know what happened to the girl. The one you loved."

My heart stuttered a little. "I don't know."

"Well ..." She fidgeted impatiently. "What was her name?"

"Maren." I hadn't spoken her name out loud in years. Feeling it on my lips again made my chest go tight.

"Do you ever think about her?"

Every day. "From time to time."

A smile snuck onto her lips. "You still love her."

"Goodbye, Lisa. Thanks for coming in." I turned my back to her and texted Evan that I would be out of here shortly.

She laughed. "See? Sometimes love *is* forever. Even if you don't want it to be. You should go see her."

"It's too late."

"It's never too late."

I ignored her and she finally walked away, but as I finished cleaning up, I kept hearing her words in my head. *You still love her.*

The vise on my heart contracted. Of course I still loved her. I'd never tried not to love her. No matter what I had done, or how long it had been, or how many other women had tried to take her place in my heart, she was always there, as permanent as any tattoo on my body.

I'd been thinking about her a lot lately, too. My memories of being with her were so fucking vivid these days. They hit me out of nowhere, as if someone had pushed a button in my brain. The colors were so vibrant, from the sapphire blue of the lake we used to swim in to the golden flecks in her brown eyes. If I took a deep breath, I'd smell the lotion she used to wear that made me want to lick her skin. I could hear her laugh as if she was in the same room with me.

But it wasn't just the memories getting to me—it was the thought of her *now*. I wasn't on social media, because fuck that shit, but I'd been drunk and curious enough times late at night to look her up. I knew she still lived outside Detroit not far from where we grew up, I knew she had quit ballet and opened up a yoga studio, and I knew she grew more beautiful every single year, so beautiful it hurt.

You should go see her.

My stomach muscles tightened. The truth was, I'd been thinking about it. Ever since the test results came back.

On my way out of the studio, I stopped to talk to Beatriz, the owner of the shop, who was wiping down the glass case of body piercing jewelry in the lobby. Her long, blue-tipped braids swayed in front of her shoulders as she worked.

"Hey," I said, "got a second?"

She looked up at me and smiled. "Sure thing. How did it go with Tweety Bird?"

"I talked her out of it."

"Good man." She straightened up and set her rag aside. "What can I do for you?"

I rubbed the back of my neck with one hand, wondering how to approach this. I hadn't told her about my head yet. "Remember when I said I might need some time off for a family thing?"

Beatriz nodded. "Yeah."

"Looks like I might have to go back east for a few weeks. Maybe even a couple months."

Her dark eyes were concerned. "Everything okay?"

"I'm not sure yet. I hope so. I know that's a long time, and I don't expect you to keep my position open—"

She held her hand out to silence me. "Your position is here whenever you get back. I won't say we won't miss you since you're so damn popular, but your job is safe, Dallas. You're wickedly talented and professional as fuck."

That made me smile. "Thanks."

"When do you need to take off?"

"I have to call my brother back tonight. I'll know more after I talk to him."

"Okay. Just let me know. You've got appointments on the books but I'm happy to call them and reschedule for when you get back, or suggest another artist."

I nodded. I hated to lose business to another artist because I had worked hard to build up a clientele over the last few years, but the truth was, I wasn't sure if I'd be able to work again anyway. And it wasn't like I needed the money. "Thanks, I appreciate it."

She narrowed her eyes. "Are you okay? I know you said

this thing with your family is stressing you out, but I feel like there's something else. Some kind of inner turmoil."

Beatriz was good at reading people. In fact, she claimed to be a little psychic. "Maybe you can tell me," I said. "Did you bring your crystal ball today?"

She reached over the counter and gave me a shove in the chest. "Crystals are not the same as a crystal ball, asshole. And it's not my psychic powers telling me something is off with you, it's your face."

I looked down at my reflection in the mirror standing on the counter. Same dark hair with a cowlick that wouldn't behave. Same stubbly jaw that could probably use a razor. Same scars above my eyebrow and beneath my chin. And if I smiled, I'd see the tiny chip in one front tooth my mother always wished I would get fixed. "What's wrong with my face? I don't see any turmoil. Looks the same as always to me."

Beatriz sighed heavily. "There's nothing *wrong* with your face, Dallas. You're gorgeous. You know that. If I liked men and I wasn't your boss, I would totally want to bang you. It's your expression, the vibe you're putting out there, your soul. It's *full* of inner turmoil."

"Hm. Well, maybe it's just been a long day, and my soul needs a beer."

She shrugged. "There's that."

"On that note"—I turned and headed for the door—"I'm out. See you tomorrow."

Widmer Brothers was just a couple blocks away from

the shop. As I walked over, I debated calling my brother and getting it out of the way. While it would be nice to have the buzz a couple of beers would give me to dull the edges of what was sure to be a tense conversation, I knew I'd feel even less like making the call once I'd knocked them back. Knowing me, I'd blow it off again. It's not like I had made a decision yet.

Finn wouldn't get that. He thought he knew best, just like always, and he was going to pressure me to do what he said. Well, it was my fucking life and I'd make my own damn decision when I was good and ready. Maybe he needed to hear that, and maybe provoking a fight would let me blow off a little steam. Pulling my phone from my pocket, I stood on the sidewalk in front of the brewery and made the call.

It was nearly eight here, which meant it was just before eleven p.m. in Boston. Maybe he was already sleeping because he had to get up early, although I had no idea what a neurology professor's schedule was like during the summer.

Yes, my older brother is a neurologist as well as an associate professor at fucking Harvard Medical School.

That's right, Harvard.

As you can imagine, Finn was the pride and joy of my family, always had been. Excelled at everything he'd ever done, from academics to music to running track. When he graduated from high school, class president and valedictorian (naturally), and proud holder of not one but two state records in track and field, he had already accepted his full ride to study chemistry at Harvard, although it had been very difficult to turn down his scholarship to study piano at the San Francisco Conservatory. My mother practically cried every time she told the story.

I was the other son.

When I entered high school two years after he left, teachers were expecting another Finn Shepherd, Wonder Boy. What they got was me. I didn't blame them for being disappointed—plus I was used to it. I'd been disappointing my parents for fourteen years. What was another four years being a disappointment to strangers?

"Hello? Dallas?" Finn sounded anxious.

"Yeah, it's me."

"Why didn't you call me back yesterday?"

I'm fine, thanks. How are you? "Sorry. I was busy."

"I fail to see how anything could take priority over this."

Of course you do. We've never understood each other. "I told you I needed time to think."

"And you haven't called Mom yet. Do you know how uncomfortable it makes me to have to hide this from her?"

"Again. Sorry."

"I got you an appointment with Dr. Acharya at Mass General. He's the surgeon I told you about. The best."

"I haven't made my decision yet."

"It's just a consultation. But Dallas." He paused. "You don't have a lot of time to waste. Please take this seriously."

I exhaled, looking at the darkening eastern sky. "When's the appointment?"

"Tuesday. Eight a.m."

Today was Wednesday. I had to work tomorrow, so that gave me only five days to get from Portland to Boston. "That's not really enough time for the drive."

"For Christ's sake, Dallas, you can't drive that distance. Get on a plane. You shouldn't be behind the wheel at all."

My doctor here had said the same thing, but I'd ignored him. And I actually hated flying. I didn't like any situation where I wasn't in control.

But I wouldn't admit that to Finn. And I wouldn't let him tell me what to do. "I want to drive. I need the time alone to think about all this."

Finn sighed heavily. "Whatever. You do it your way, like you always have. But I cannot stress enough how important it is that you are here for that appointment. I had to call in a lot of favors to get it. And for God's sake, be careful."

"I will." Evan approached on his bike and I lifted a hand in greeting, then held up one finger to let him know I'd only be another minute. He nodded and began locking up his bike.

"Are you taking the Depakote?"

"Yes." But I wasn't, not regularly. It made me feel dizzy and tired, and I wasn't convinced I needed it.

"Good, you need to. Especially if you're driving. What about the eye doctor? Did you go back?"

"Yeah. She changed my prescription."

"Did it help with the headaches or vision issue?"

"Some."

"Good. Please call Mom and Dad, okay? I know things aren't easy with them, but this isn't just about you."

I laughed. I couldn't help it. "See, that's where you're wrong, Finn. In fact, this *is* just about me. It's my head, my future, my decision. And I will deal with the consequences of whatever action I choose to take. Wasn't that the whole point of Mom and Dad sending me away? So I could learn the hard lessons?"

"Christ, Dallas. Why do you have to be such a defensive asshole all the time? They tried everything they could to get through to you, to ensure you'd have a good future, and you kept fucking up. What were they supposed to do?"

Accept me for who I was, I wanted to say. *Better yet,*

except me for who I wasn't—you. But he would never understand.

"Nothing, Finn. Forget it. I'll see you next week."

Another heavy sigh from my brother. "I'm sorry. I know this isn't easy for you. And ... I'm glad you reached out."

"Yeah, well ..." I looked at Evan, who jerked his head toward the door, signaling he'd go in without me. I nodded. "Listen, I gotta go. I'll be in touch." I ended the call, slipped my phone into my pocket, and went into the brewery. Spotting Evan at the bar, I made my way over and took the seat next to him. "Sorry about that."

"No problem. Your brother?" Evan was the only person I'd told about what was going on with me.

"Yeah."

"You didn't have to cut the call short."

"I was pretty much done. There's only so much fake concern I can take."

"Come on, man. They're your family. Isn't it possible they are actually concerned about you?"

"It's all fake with them. Or it's just because I'm their blood relative. It's not because they care about me. There's a difference."

"You don't think it's possible for them to come around? Maybe they didn't get you as a kid, but—"

"Because they never made any effort to get me. They expected a certain kind of son, and I was never going to be him. So they got rid of me."

Of course, that was a bit of a simplification. I was leaving out the parts where I failed classes on purpose, got into fights that had nothing to do with me, mouthed off when I felt like it, and pulled some pretty ridiculous pranks. But all these years later, it still made me angry that they'd attended every single one of Finn's endless piano recitals, but they'd never once come to an art showing of mine.

It's not a performance, Dallas. It's just a drawing, I can see it at home. It's not like you'd actually be doing anything while we were there.

After a while, I didn't even invite them anymore. It's not like they'd have appreciated it anyway. One Christmas I gave my father a sketch I'd done of his childhood home. He'd studied it critically and said, *You got the windows wrong.*

I shook my head. "You know what? It was better that way. I'm just different from my family. I'm sure they were happier when they didn't have to deal with my shit anymore, and I was glad to get out of their house. There's a reason they're all on the East Coast and I'm in Portland."

"I get it, man." He shrugged. "You're just so laid back about every other thing in life except your family. Seems like, with everything happening, this might be a good opportunity to—"

"I don't really want to talk about it."

Evan held up his hands. "Okay. No problem."

The bartender came over, and after we placed our orders, I asked Evan how his wife, who was nearly nine months pregnant, was doing. He groaned and launched into a huge diatribe against pregnancy in general and his wife in particular. Our beers arrived and I listened to Evan talk, but my mind wandered. I couldn't stop thinking about Maren.

Out of nowhere, a memory surfaced—our first time. It was so intense, I felt paralyzed by it. I could see her face in the dark, smell the rain on her skin, hear thunder outside my bedroom window, feel her hands on my back. She'd whispered in my ear, *Don't stop this time. I want it to be you.*

And our last time, in the backseat of my car.

The taste of her on my tongue. The sound of my name on her lips. The feel of her on my lap, sliding down my cock.

The agonizing weight of knowing it was the last time, and keeping it from her.

Did she hate me for it? Would she ever forgive me? Did it even matter to her anymore?

All these years, I'd told myself I'd done the right thing by staying away, that she deserved better than me. I still believed that.

But now ... I wanted to see her again. I wanted to know she was happy. I wanted to tell her I was sorry for what I'd done. Was it too late?

It's never too late.

Maybe it wasn't.

By the time I went to bed that night, my mind was made up. Instead of driving to Boston, I'd fly to Detroit on Friday. Then I'd rent a car and go see Maren, or at least try to see her. After that, I'd drive to Boston. That would still give me plenty of alone time to think about my decision.

I wouldn't do exactly what Lisa had said—I wouldn't tell Maren about my feelings. That was too fucked up after all this time. But I could see her again and apologize for what I'd done. Even if she refused to forgive me, asking her to would ease my conscience.

It might be the last chance I got.

THREE

MAREN

After talking to my sisters about the nightmare, I felt better.
I even thought it might go away.

It didn't.

In fact, it got worse. By the middle of the following
week, I was so sleep deprived I was starting to imagine
snakes everywhere. My heart would pound every time I had
to open the trunk of my car or a closet door or the lid on the
washing machine. I kept expecting a fucking Burmese
python to jump out at me and sink its fangs into my skin.
And I fell asleep two more times teaching class.

On Friday morning after Yoga for Seniors, Allegra came
into the room and asked how I was doing, and I broke down
in tears, weeping into my hands.

"That's it," she said, setting her mat aside and rubbing
my back. "I'm sending you home on mandatory leave. Go
get some rest. I don't want to see you here until Monday at
the earliest. And if you need another day, you call me."

Under normal circumstances, I might have tried to
argue with her, but I was so tired I couldn't think straight.
And maybe she was right. Maybe I had been working too

hard, and this was my body's way of telling me to slow down and hit reset. Put my own needs first—physically, mentally, spiritually. "Okay," I agreed, sniffling. "You win. I'll take a few days for myself."

"Good girl. This is the right decision, you'll see."

On the drive home, I tried to think of ways I could treat myself that would contribute to an improved sense of well-being. Should I get a massage? A couple spa treatments? Have my hair done? I wasn't into fussing with my appearance too often, but a trip to the salon might be just what I needed. A little pampering. A little indulgence. Some guilty pleasure.

But first … an epic nap.

I went straight to bed when I got home, practically asleep before my head hit the pillow.

THE DOORBELL WOKE ME UP.

I sat up, groggy and stiff, and checked the clock. Whoa —it was after four already. I'd slept for almost five hours straight and hadn't even dreamed. Even my subconscious must have been wiped out.

Whoever was at my door knocked on it loudly three times in a row.

"Okay, okay. I'm coming." Tossing the covers aside, I got out of bed and went to answer it, wondering who it could be. I wasn't expecting a delivery or a visitor, and my sisters both had a key. Yawning, I turned the lock and pulled the door open.

My heart stopped.

It had been twelve years, but I recognized him instantly. That unruly hair. The square jaw, now covered with scruff.

That dimple in his chin. Those deep-set eyes, somewhere between sage green and cerulean blue. The sculpted lips, curving into a smile at the sight of me.

The memory of those lips on mine clutched at my throat—I couldn't breathe.

Fuck you, universe.

"Hey, stranger." Dallas's voice was a little deeper. His chest a little broader. He wore dark jeans and a black T-shirt that fit him like a snakeskin—I mean, a second skin. Tattoos were scattered along his forearms, and on his wrist was a thick black watch.

Tick, tick, tick.

I swayed, a bit unsteady on my feet, and braced one hand on the doorframe.

"Maren? You okay?"

"Yes." My voice cracked, and I cleared my throat. Forced my shoulders back. "I'm fine. What are you doing here?"

"I wanted to see you."

"Why?"

"To apologize. Can I come in?"

"No." It surprised me how raw my anger felt, given how much time had gone by. Like fresh blood spilling from an old wound.

He nodded slowly, sticking his hands in his pockets. "Fair enough. I know it's probably a shock to see me."

"To say the least."

"I probably should have called you first."

"You probably should have called me twelve years ago."

He nodded. "You're right. I should have."

"Why didn't you?"

"What can I say? I was a kid. It was a dick move."

"*That's* your apology?" I stared at him for a moment

longer, then I shut the door in his face. He blocked it, keeping it from closing all the way.

"Hey, wait." He pushed it open again, but he didn't try to come in. "Look, I'm sorry. I don't know what else to say. I was seventeen, and I didn't know how to say goodbye."

I crossed my arms over my chest. "Maybe you were too busy fucking me to remember."

"What can I say? I like sex better than talking. And I'm *much* better at it."

"Not. Funny."

He took me by the upper arms, which were bare in my yoga top. Warmth pooled at my center, and I felt lightheaded. His touch had always done that to me. "Maren, I'm sorry. Really and truly sorry for leaving that way. My parents sprung it on me less than twenty-four hours before they put me on a plane. After fighting with them, I went right to you. I have no excuse other than I didn't want to spend our last night together being sad."

"That was selfish of you. Maybe *you* didn't want to say goodbye, but I would have liked the chance."

"I should have given it to you. The truth is ..." He took his hands off me. Ran one over his stubble, which distracted me, because I'd always loved his hands. "I thought you'd be better off without me."

"That wasn't your decision to make."

"I know. I'm sorry."

"Is that why you never answered my texts or calls?"

"Yes." His dark eyes were solemn. "I knew I had let you down, and I was ashamed of myself for it. Can you forgive me?"

I exhaled, biting my lip. Could I? I liked to think of myself as a forgiving person. I certainly didn't believe in holding grudges, and anyone who knew me would say I was a peacemaker, not a fighter. But I also felt like I'd earned the right to get a few things off my chest.

I forced myself to look him in the eye. "It took me a long time to get over what you did to me, Dallas."

He nodded, letting me speak.

"My entire senior year, I was lonely and miserable. I kept waiting for you to get in touch and at least tell me you were okay, that *we* would be okay no matter what, just like you'd promised." I shook my head, feeling my throat close up. "Was everything you said a lie?"

"No," he said seriously. "I never lied to you, Maren. I was an immature asshole, and I made stupid decisions, but I never said anything I didn't mean."

You said you loved me, I almost shouted. *You said you needed me.* But I pulled myself together. What good would it do to throw that in his face at this point? Did I really want to hear him say he'd been just a kid who didn't know what love was? Would that honestly make me feel better after all this time?

"You promised to take me to the senior prom," I said instead. "You know what I did that night?"

"What?"

"Nothing. I sat home, and not because no one asked. A few guys did."

His hands flexed at his sides. "Why didn't you go?"

"Because I knew I'd only spend the evening missing you. It wouldn't have been fun for my date or me. But you know what?" I stood a little taller. Puffed up my chest. "I should thank you. I never made the mistake of trusting someone too easily again."

"Well ... you're welcome." One side of his mouth hooked up in a sexy crooked grin that made me feel seventeen again.

"Stop that. I'm still mad at you."

"You are?"

"Yes." I gave him my meanest stare.

His grin widened. "Is that your evil eye? Fuck, that's cute."

"My anger is cute?"

"No. Yes. Wait, is that a trick question? *You're* cute. Your anger is not. And I hate that I caused it. You were the last person on earth I ever wanted to hurt."

"You were the last person on earth I ever thought would hurt me."

He accepted that with a slow nod. "I'll always be sorry for that. I deeply regret it."

His eyes held mine, and I felt in my heart he was being sincere. It would feel good to forgive him, wouldn't it? The past belonged in the past; the present was what mattered. And in the present, I was not a lovesick seventeen-year-old girl pining after a guy who'd left her behind, and Dallas was no longer that irresponsible, impulsive seventeen-year-old boy. He was a grown man who wanted to apologize for his thoughtless actions so long ago. Most guys probably wouldn't have bothered.

Which made me wonder.

"I'm curious," I said, folding my arms over my chest again. "Why now? After all these years?"

He looked down at his boots. "I don't know. It just felt like it was time."

Something told me that wasn't the whole truth, but I didn't press him. Maybe it had taken him this long to grow tired of carrying the burden of his guilt. Who was I to insist he keep doing it?

"Okay, Dallas," I said, letting my arms drop. I imagined

myself letting go of all the hurt like a child releases a helium balloon into the sky. "I forgive you."

His shoulders relaxed as he exhaled. "Thank you."

"Feel better?"

"Yes. Do you?"

"Yes." It was the truth. I hadn't realized how much I'd needed to hear him say those words, even after all that time. Maybe now my nightmares would stop. This had to be what the universe was warning me about, right?

"Well, it was good to see you," he said, pulling keys from his pocket.

"You too," I admitted, and suddenly there was a part of me that didn't want him to go so quickly. "Do you ... do you want to come in?"

He smiled. "Sure, thanks."

My heart beat erratically as he followed me into the front hall and shut the door behind us.

"So are there two apartments in this house?" Dallas glanced up the stairs to the upper flat.

"Yes." I opened the door to the lower, which led into my living room. "This one's mine. How did you find out my address, anyway?"

"It wasn't that hard."

"That's actually kind of scary." I shut the door behind him.

"You live alone?" he asked.

"Yes."

He wandered over to the bookcase along one wall and studied my framed photographs. "These are your sisters, right?"

I walked over and stood next to him, shoulder to shoulder. Or rather shoulder to bicep, since I was a good five inches shorter than he was in my bare feet. "Yes. That's Stella, the oldest," I said, pointing to her in a photo of the three of us taken at Emme's engagement dinner a couple weeks ago. "And that's Emme, my middle sister. She's getting married this fall."

"Everyone looks happy."

"We are."

He glanced down at me. "I'm glad to hear that."

Our eyes met, and something happened in my chest that made me back away and head for the kitchen. Put a little distance between us. "I'm thirsty. If I go into the other room to get us something to drink, are you going to leave without saying goodbye?"

"Depends. Are you gonna keep giving me shit about what I did?" He trailed me into the kitchen, which was small and narrow.

"Maybe." I took two bottles of water from the fridge and handed him one. "You'd deserve it."

"Fair enough." Leaning back against the counter, he twisted the cap off the bottle and drank.

Standing across from him, my back against the fridge, I watched, mesmerized by the motion of his throat as he swallowed. When I caught myself staring, I looked down at my water and unscrewed the cap. "So where do you live now?"

"Portland."

"Wow. That's a ways from here. What do you do there?"

"I'm a tattoo artist."

I had to smile. "Of course you are."

He smiled back, and the first genuinely warm current passed between us. "And you have a yoga studio?" he asked, gesturing toward my clothing.

"Yes." For a moment, I was self-conscious about my appearance. I touched my messy bun, wishing I'd taken a moment at the studio to redo it. "I taught this morning. Then I came home and took a nap, so I'm —" Then I realized something. My arm dropped. "Hey. How do you know what I do?"

"Um." He looked at the ceiling, laughing a little. "I may have drunk-Googled you once or twice."

I gasped. "What? That is so unfair! You're not even on social media, so I had no clue about you."

"Does that mean you drunk-Googled me, too?"

"*No.*" I sniffed and drank some water before going on. "I *sober*-Googled you."

He laughed again. "I think that might be worse."

I kicked him gently in the shin with one bare foot. "At some point, I just wanted to know you were still alive, you big jerk."

"I'm alive."

"I can see that." Now that we were through the heavy stuff, I wanted to know more about him. "So fill me in on the last twelve years."

"Not much to tell. I graduated from boarding school. Tried college for a year or so but didn't take to it. Drifted a while. Ended up in Portland and apprenticed at a tattoo shop there. Liked it well enough to stay. The end. Now what about you? You quit ballet?"

"Yes. I went to New York after high school, had an apprenticeship with ABT, which was—"

"You did? Maren, that's fucking amazing. That's exactly what you wanted."

"Thanks." I tucked a strand of hair behind my ear. "It *was* what I wanted, but it turns out I wasn't really suited for that life. Or life in New York City."

"Too cutthroat?"

"I guess. I came back to Michigan and went to college.

Got my degree in kinesiology and health with a minor in business and opened the studio a couple years later. The end."

"Never been married?"

"Not even close. But I like being a free spirit."

"Me too." He studied me for a moment, that crooked grin taking over his mouth, almost like he couldn't control it. "You look good, Maren."

My face warmed. "Thanks, but I'm kind of a mess right now. Obviously, I wasn't expecting you."

"Yeah, I thought about calling first, but I was afraid you might not want to see me."

"I'm not sure what I would have said, to be honest. But now that you're here, I will admit to being glad you came."

"Good."

"So how long are you in town?" I lifted my water to my lips.

"Not long. Really I'm just passing through on my way to Boston to see my brother."

"Finn?"

"Yeah. He's a neurosurgeon, teaches at Harvard Medical School." Dallas's tone was flat, as if he wasn't happy about his brother's impressive credentials. I remembered how he'd always felt that Finn was his parents' favorite and figured some of that resentment still lingered.

"That's nice," I said carefully.

"Yeah." He swallowed the rest of the water in his bottle in long gulps and put the cap back on it.

"Here, I'll take that." I reached for his empty bottle, and when he gave it to me, our hands touched. I might have done it on purpose.

Turning my back to him, I opened the pantry door and tossed both empties in. My stomach was doing something dangerously twisty, and I put a hand over it. Took a steadying breath. When I turned around again, he was looking at me with a gleam in his eye.

"What?" I asked, immediately on guard. I recognized that expression. It said I've Got an Idea.

"You should let me take you out for dinner tonight. For old times' sake."

I shook my head. "I don't think so."

"Why not? Do you have a hot date?"

"Uh ... no."

"Do you have something against dinner?"

"No."

"Do you have something against *me*?" He touched his chest with his hand. God, those hands got to me. Somehow they were strong and graceful at the same time. Masculine, yet elegant. So much talent in them—it was sexy as hell.

And he'd certainly known how to use them on me.

Something fluttery happened between my legs, and I squeezed my thighs together, crossing my arms over my chest. Briefly I wondered if I'd plugged my vibrator in to charge. I was going to need it tonight. "No. It's nothing against you."

"Then what's the problem?"

The problem is that you still do something to me. But I couldn't say that out loud.

"Come on," he cajoled. "I'm only in town one evening, and I've got no one to spend it with. I'll probably never be back this way, so what do you say you and I catch up a little over dinner? And tomorrow, I'll be out of your hair." He opened his arms as if to show me he had no secret weapons or tricks up his sleeve.

I wavered. After all, he wasn't suggesting anything other than dinner. I had the whole weekend off, and it's not like I had any firm plans. Plus, spending time with him might be just what I needed. If the nightmare truly was related to unfinished business between us, then maybe I should take this opportunity to consciously say goodbye. Maybe then the door would open, and I'd be free to move through it.

He'd have his redemption, and I'd have my closure. The end.

"Okay," I said.

His grin widened. "Great. Where should we go?"

"You can choose, since this is your last Detroit hurrah. I'm sure there will be something on the menu I can eat."

One of his eyebrows cocked up. "Are you a vegetarian or something? Because you used to eat like a hog. I never did know where you put it all."

I kicked him again. "Very funny. No, I'm not a vegetarian, but I eat very clean. You know, organic if possible, non-GMO, whole foods."

"I get it. Portland is full of people like you."

"I take it you're not particular about what you eat?"

He shrugged. "A burger is a burger to me. As long as it tastes good, I'm happy. I'm easy like that."

"I guarantee a burger made from grass-fed, free-range, locally-sourced beef tastes better than one made from animals pumped full of hormones and antibiotics kept in feedlots full of their own excrement and processed in filthy industrial meatpacking plants."

Dallas held up his hands in surrender. "You win. Now please stop talking or I will never enjoy a hamburger again."

I smiled sheepishly. "Sorry. I studied nutrition in college and learned a lot about the benefits of responsible, sustainable farming versus industrial agriculture."

"You can tell me all about it over our responsible, sustainable dinner. I'll pick you up around eight?"

I glanced at the digital clock on the stove. It was just after five, which gave me plenty of time to get ready and maybe sneak in some meditation. I wanted to feel completely at ease with myself going into tonight. "Sounds good. I assume casual?"

"Considering I haven't worn a tie in about eight years, that's a safe assumption. I don't even think I own a pair of pants that aren't jeans."

I was curious. "What happened eight years ago?"

"My grandfather died."

"I'm sorry. I know you were close."

He shrugged. "He was a good guy, the only one in my family I could talk to. He understood me, for some reason. Or at least he didn't judge me for being unlike my father or my brother."

I nodded slowly, picturing the silver-haired man I'd met a couple times. "He was the gunpowder guy, right?"

"Sort of. That's how his family made their fortune, anyway, but he'd sold that business before my father was born, and invested all his money in the stock market."

"Smart."

"He left me a lot. Of money, I mean. Much more than he left anyone else." All the light had gone out of Dallas's eyes. "I don't really get it."

"He must've trusted you to do the right thing with it."

"Or he thought I needed it more than anyone else because I wouldn't ever make anything of my life."

Our eyes met, and for a moment I saw the boy that he'd been, always so hurt by his family's disapproval. "I don't believe that for one second."

"Yeah, well, you were like him. Always thought the best of me."

I tried again, like I always had. "Let me ask you this.

Did he put up a lot of barriers between you and your inheritance? Put a lot of conditions on it?"

Dallas shook his head. "Not one. It was mine almost free and clear."

I lifted my shoulders. "There you go. He trusted you."

"Thanks." He smiled and pushed away from the counter. "I should get going. See you at eight?"

"Sounds good." I walked him to the front door, and he gave my upper arm a squeeze before heading out to his rental car. I watched him get behind the wheel and pull away, still a little in shock.

Dallas Shepherd, after all this time.

I walked back into my flat, closing the door behind me. Grabbing my phone from my purse, I floated, trancelike, through the living room, down the hall, and into my bedroom. I'd planned on calling one or both of my sisters, but instead I lay on my back on top of the covers, set my phone aside, and placed my hands on my stomach. My body had that fluttery, weightless feeling I used to get before going on stage, a combination of nerves and excitement. But I didn't have anything to be worried about, did I? Tonight wasn't going to be a performance. I didn't need to impress him. And it was only natural that a little desire for him lingered. I'd always liked his light eyes. And his agile hands. And his full mouth. His muscular body. His sense of humor. His dimpled chin.

But it wasn't a big deal. I wasn't concerned that he would take advantage of it. He hadn't even tried to give me a hug.

I frowned. Maybe he didn't find me attractive anymore. Maybe he had a girlfriend. He'd said he wasn't married, but he never said he was single. A sudden rush of jealousy stole my breath.

Which was ridiculous.

Dallas and I hadn't been together in twelve years. Did I think he'd been celibate all that time? Of course not. I hadn't, either. But I didn't like thinking about him with anyone else, so I made up my mind not to do it.

I wouldn't think about him with me, either. I wouldn't think about his hands or his lips or his tongue or his cock, the way he'd touched or tasted or moved, the words he'd whispered in the dark.

Let me do this to you.

God, I can't get enough.

You know I love you.

But of course, then there were the words he should have said but didn't.

I'm leaving tomorrow.

I don't have a choice.

This is goodbye.

For a fleeting moment, my throat was tight, and I was that seventeen-year-old girl again. Left behind. Confused. Broken.

I swallowed hard and closed my eyes, forcing myself back to the present.

Tonight wasn't about rehashing the past; it was about making peace with it, so I could stop having that stupid dream. We weren't rekindling an old flame. We were reconnecting as friends.

I wouldn't let him get to me.

FOUR

DALLAS

I lay on the bed in my hotel room, staring at the ceiling but seeing only her.

She was even more beautiful than I'd remembered, and yet she looked exactly the same. Huge brown eyes, porcelain skin, a dusting of freckles across her tiny nose, adorable heart-shaped face, that perfect round mouth that used to drive me wild. When we started dating, at sixteen, she claimed she'd never even been kissed.

I'd fixed that in a hurry. And then some.

She might have been shy and inexperienced at first, but she had a dancer's intuition and knew how to move her body instinctively. I bet she still did.

Stop it. Don't think about her that way.

I hadn't planned to ask her to dinner. I'd gotten off the plane this afternoon, rented a car, and driven straight to her house without a clue what I was going to say to her except *I'm sorry for being a dick* and *Please forgive me*. All I'd hoped for in return was to hear her say she didn't hate me and that she was happy.

But there was something so damn irresistible about her.

Once I saw her, talked with her, I wanted more. You didn't take one bite of the most delicious cupcake in the world and put it back in the box—you ate the whole thing.

You stay away from her cupcake.

I frowned. My conscience had been sounding all kinds of alarms ever since I left her house. But I hadn't asked her to dinner to get her into bed. I just liked being around her. I mean, yes, I was still attracted to her and wished that things could have been different between us. My feelings for her had never gone away. But things were the way they were, and I couldn't change them. I'd had her. I'd fucked it up.

There wasn't time for a second chance.

Then it hit me—the perfect idea for tonight. I nearly laughed out loud, it was so damn brilliant. But since it would require some legwork to pull off, I needed to get started on it. Propping myself up on some pillows, I reached for my phone and made a few calls.

An hour later, everything was in place. I'd had a stroke of luck in that one of the managers here at the hotel turned out to be a former classmate and football buddy. He was more than willing to help me—for the right price, of course. What I was asking for wasn't easy. It would be a little costly, but it would be worth it, and I couldn't help feeling pleased with myself as I tucked my credit card back into my wallet. While it was open, I pulled out the folded piece of paper I'd carried with me for the last twelve years and opened it up.

I remembered the night I'd drawn it like it was yesterday. It was fall of our senior year, right before my parents made the decision to send me away. We were sitting in my car in her driveway, and she was upset with me because I'd been suspended from school and wouldn't be allowed to attend the homecoming dance, which would have marked our one-year anniversary.

I didn't really give a shit about the dance, but it was important to her, and she was important to me. The disappointment in her face was like a knife to the heart. She sat there trying not to cry and asking why it was so hard for me to stay out of trouble, her lower lip trembling. I said I was sorry and promised to make it up to her, but secretly I was thinking how pretty she looked when she was sad. I'd just picked her up from the ballet studio, and her hair was up in a bun. Her shoulders were bare. As she talked, I probably should have been listening to what she said more closely, but I found myself memorizing the angle of her jaw, the shape of her head, the curve of her mouth, the fullness of her lashes.

Later, I went home and stayed up half the night drawing her in my sketchbook, trying to capture the perfect blend of beauty and heartbreak I'd seen in her expression, almost as if she already knew I was a lost cause. I'd planned on giving the drawing to her as a gift, but the next day my parents informed me of their decision about boarding school and I forgot about it.

Twenty-four hours later, I was gone.

Sighing, I folded the drawing up and replaced it in my wallet. I couldn't turn back time. There was no use regretting what was never meant to be. Tonight, I'd do my best to put a smile on her face and make up in some small way for what I'd done back then. Then I'd say a proper goodbye like a mature adult and take off for Boston tomorrow. I didn't belong in her life.

I had no illusions about that.

I KNOCKED on Maren's door a few minutes after eight.

When she answered it, my jaw dropped. "Jesus Christ, Maren. I'm an old man. Are you trying to kill me?"

She laughed and looked down at her legs, most of which were visible below the hem of a very, very short skirt. "You're only thirty."

"I know, but ..." I clutched my heart. "Have mercy." My eyes roamed over her body from head to toe. Her blond hair swung loose around her shoulders, with just a few strands pinned back around her face. Just like when we were young, she hardly wore any makeup. Above the skirt she wore a loose white blouse that draped softly over her curves and somehow managed to be elegant and provocative at the same time. On her feet she wore high-heeled sandals that laced up her calves, and I had a sudden urge to untie those laces with my teeth.

Tonight would be a test of my willpower for sure.

She came out onto the porch and pulled the front door closed behind her. "Listen, I don't go out for dinner that often. I work a lot of evenings and haven't gotten dressed up in a long time. So no mercy for you."

I sighed heavily. "Fine. As long as you're okay with me staring at you all night."

She shrugged and smiled up at me. "As long as you're okay with a strict look-but-don't-touch policy."

"I promise to be on my best behavior tonight." I offered her an arm. "Shall we?"

"Yes." She looped her hand around the inside of my bicep and we walked down the porch steps together. "So where are we going?"

Trying to ignore the thump in my chest, I led her to the silver Range Rover I had rented earlier today and opened the passenger door. "I'm not telling."

"A surprise? Really?" She looked up at me and smiled

brightly. "I love surprises." The look on her face made me think that no one had done something like this for her before, and I wondered what kind of dickheads she'd dated after me.

I shut the door, then walked around to the driver's side and got in. Buckling my seatbelt, I stole one more look at her legs before starting the car. The scent of her filled my head. My cock stirred, and I shifted a little in my seat, attempting to casually adjust my jeans.

On the drive downtown, we talked more about our families and what everyone was up to. I told her Finn had a wife and two kids, that my mom and dad were doting grandparents who made the trip from West Palm Beach to Boston often to see them, and that I was perfectly happy living on the opposite coast, although I did like being an uncle and Skyped with my niece and nephew at least once a week.

"How old are they?" Maren asked.

"Olympia is eight and Lane is six. They're awesome. So smart and funny."

"I bet they adore you."

"Only because I send them tons of junk food and presents." I signaled and exited the highway at Bagley Avenue. "And they send me pictures they've drawn and tell me I should tattoo people with them."

Maren laughed. "That's cute."

"I should visit them more often, but I usually only get there once a year. You see your family much?"

"My parents don't live around here anymore, but I see my sisters at least once a week. It's hard because we all work a lot. Stella is a therapist with her own practice. She also runs marathons, so she trains a lot. Emme is a wedding planner, so her weekends are usually booked. Plus now she's planning her own wedding, and the guy she's marrying has a six-month-old baby." She was quiet a moment. "Stella also has a boyfriend, or at least a guy she's been seeing for a year or so."

I glanced over at her. "What about you? Are you seeing anyone?"

"No," she said. "To be honest, I can't seem to meet anyone I really connect with."

I tried not to feel good about that. "I wonder why."

She shrugged. "I'm not sure. And you? Are you seeing anyone?"

"Nope. I learned a long time ago that I make a shit boyfriend."

"Oh yeah?" She folded her arms across her chest. "And why is that? Because other than your failure at goodbye, I remember you as a pretty great boyfriend. When I wasn't mad at you for getting in trouble."

I smiled as I turned left onto Michigan Avenue. "That was a long time ago." *And no one ever compared to you.* "Mostly, I've just never been that into anyone. I moved around a lot in my twenties, and now I work long hours doing something I enjoy. I don't take a lot of time off, and when I do, I'm selfish with it."

"What do you like to do?"

"I like to be outside. Biking, hiking, climbing, skiing in the winter, swimming in the summer. And I love road trips." I pulled up to the valet at the Westin Book Cadillac Hotel.

Maren noticed where we were for the first time and gasped. "Oh my God! Are we having dinner at Roast?"

I grinned and shook my head but said nothing more as I unbuckled my seatbelt.

"Oh, come on. We're here, you can tell me now." The

valet opened the passenger door, and she poked me on the shoulder before getting out of the car.

But still, I kept the secret. It was too good, and I'd worked too hard to arrange everything on short notice to give it up so easily.

I walked her into the hotel, and when she paused in the lobby, looking toward the entrance to the restaurant, I took her by the hand and tugged her toward the concierge. "This way."

She followed me, but seemed a little hesitant. I wondered if I shouldn't have taken her hand. Truthfully, it had been sort of instinctive, but maybe it was too romantic a gesture. Not in line with the look-but-don't-touch policy I'd agreed to. I let go of her hand as we waited behind another couple at the desk.

"Um, Dallas?" She turned and looked at me uneasily. "We aren't going up to a room, are we?"

"No." I didn't even tease her. "I promise we aren't. But that's all I'm saying."

"Okay." She looked relieved, which reinforced my plan not to touch her. It was clear she didn't want me to.

The couple in front of us moved away, and the concierge, a young woman, smiled at us. "Good evening. Can I help you?"

"My name is Dallas Shepherd."

Her smile grew wider, and she winked at me. "Of course. Mr. Young has everything set up for you, Mr. Shepherd. Just give me one moment and I'll let him know you're here." She picked up the phone on her desk and discreetly made the call. After hanging up, she told us, "He'll be out in a moment and meet you at the elevators. Enjoy your evening."

I thanked her and placed a hand on the small of

Maren's back, guiding her at my side toward the elevators. When I realized what I was doing—touching her again—I dropped my arm.

We reached the elevators, and she turned to me, suspicion in her eyes. "What is this?"

"You'll see."

"Shepherd!" A voice boomed behind us. I turned to see Aiden Young coming toward us, buttoning his suit coat. He offered me his hand, and I took it.

"Aiden, do you remember Maren Devine? She went to school with us."

"Of course I do." He offered her his hand as well. "Welcome."

Maren shook his hand, looking back and forth between the two of us. "Thanks," she said. "I'm not sure what I'm doing here, but it's beautiful. You're a manager at the hotel?"

Aiden nodded and punched the elevator button. "General Manager, which means I can only get away for a moment, but I'll take you guys up."

When the doors opened, we let Maren step in first, and he and I exchanged a look. *Thank you*, I mouthed behind her back. Not that he was doing this solely as a favor to an old friend, but still, I was grateful. I wouldn't have been able to do this without his help.

When the doors closed, Aiden stuck his key into the number panel, turned it, and hit a button. The elevator began to ascend.

"So," he said. "I'll tell you a little bit about the building history. When the hotel was completed in 1924, it was the tallest building in Detroit as well as the tallest hotel in the world. For decades, it was the city's most luxurious hotel, its twelve hundred rooms, three ballrooms, restaurants, lounges, and shops catering to affluent visitors from all over the world. In 1939, the hotel became part of baseball history. On May second, New York Yankee Lou Gehrig collapsed on the grand staircase. In the hotel bar, he told his manager he was taking himself out of the starting lineup against the Tigers, breaking his string of two thousand one hundred thirty consecutive games played."

"God, I haven't been to a Tigers game in forever," I said.

Maren looked up at me with a sympathetic smile. "Too bad your trip is so short."

"Yeah." For a crazy second, I thought about saying it didn't have to be that short and asking her to come to a game with me tomorrow. Thankfully, Aidan spoke up again before I opened my mouth.

"The hotel also appeared in the 1947 movie *State of the Union*, starring Katherine Hepburn and Spencer Tracy, and they stayed at the hotel, as did Martin Luther King Jr., the Beatles, Elvis Presley, Frank Sinatra, Presidents Franklin D. Roosevelt, John F. Kennedy, and Ronald Reagan, among others. The hotel closed in 1984, was in danger of being demolished for years, was robbed of its copper piping and chandeliers, vandalized, spray-painted, and left to rot."

"So sad," Maren said, shaking her head. "How could something so beautiful be abandoned that way?"

"Luckily, it was given a second chance." The elevator stopped, and the doors opened. Aiden placed a hand over them to keep them open, and I followed Maren into a dimly lit hallway.

When the doors closed, Aiden motioned for us to follow him. "Once again, it's one of the most opulent, romantic places in the city." At the end of the hallway, he pushed open a door that led to a stairwell. "Up we go."

Maren glanced back at me, more puzzled than ever, but

she started up the cement stairs. I couldn't take my eyes off her legs in front of me. Her calf muscles were insane from all the ballet training. I remembered how flexible she'd been and felt my dick start perking up.

"In addition to all the history I just gave you," Aiden said, his voice echoing off the walls, "this hotel was also the site of a certain prom a few years back."

All of a sudden, Maren stopped moving and looked down over her shoulder at me. "No way." The stunned, joyful expression on her face was worth every penny I had to pay to make this happen.

Goose bumps rippled down my arms inside my jacket. I smiled at her.

Her jaw dropped, and she continued up the stairs. At the top, Aiden moved ahead and opened the door to the rooftop. "Ballrooms were not available tonight, but when Dallas asked if you could have the roof to yourselves, I had to admit no one had booked it. In fact, no one has ever even asked to book it." He laughed.

Maren stepped over the threshold onto the rooftop. "Dallas is definitely one of a kind."

The three of us moved away from the door, and I saw the table that had been set for us, complete with white linens, flower centerpiece, and candlelight. Luckily, the air was warm, and the wind was soft. The sun was still setting beyond the skyline to the west, and to the east the Detroit River was visible; a little to the south was the Ambassador Bridge, and beyond the river, Canada. The view was breath-taking on all sides.

After turning around in a full circle, Maren looked at me with shining eyes. "Dallas. This is incredible."

"You'll have your own server for the night, and he should be up shortly," Aiden said, checking his watch. "I should get back downstairs. Dallas, you have my cell if you need anything. Maren, good seeing you again, and I hope you enjoy your evening." He gave us a smile before heading back to the stairwell door.

As soon as he was gone, Maren turned to me. "I cannot believe you did this."

I shrugged. "I felt pretty bad when you said you'd missed the prom because of me. I figured I owed it to you."

She laughed and rolled her eyes, which were filled with tears. "You didn't, but whatever. I'll take it." Opening her purse, she hunted around in it for something. "God, I don't even have tissues. I didn't know you were going to make me cry."

"No crying allowed at the prom. And I hope it's okay I'm wearing jeans."

"It's fine." She sniffed and closed her purse. "I'm not that dressed up either."

"You're perfect." Our eyes met, and the air between us suddenly felt full of hope and possibility. In any other circumstance, I'd have kissed her.

But I couldn't do that tonight.

"Oh, I almost forgot." Reaching into the inside pocket of my jacket, I pulled out a wrist corsage. "Sorry if it's a little smashed. I had to get rid of the plastic container to hide it from you."

She giggled and held out her arm. "That's okay. It's beautiful."

"Good." I slid the elastic band with three deep red roses attached to it along with some other green stuff onto her wrist. "I told the lady at the florist to make it a prom corsage. Pretty sure she thought I was crazy. Or creepy."

"You might be crazy. But I love it. Thank you for this." Then she rose up on tiptoe and pecked my cheek. When she lowered her heels, she stood there for a moment, her hand on my arm, her mouth so close I could have simply tipped my head down and my lips would be resting on hers.

My heart stumbled over its next few beats. I wanted to do it so badly, but I'd promised her I'd behave. I'd promised myself I'd behave. There were so many reasons why I shouldn't be here tonight, standing so close to the only girl I'd ever loved, tempted beyond reason by her legs and her lips and her laugh and her eyes and her ability to make me feel like I fucking *mattered* in the universe.

What was the right thing to do?

If only—

The door from the stairwell opened, and we moved apart.

FIVE

MAREN

The server, whose name was Jason, pulled out my chair, and I sat down across from Dallas. Then I listened to Jason go over the menu, but he might as well have been speaking another language. I didn't comprehend one word he said.

My heart was still hammering—Dallas and I had almost kissed. And I'd wanted to. Like really, really wanted to. I thought he'd wanted it too, but we'd been interrupted before I could tell for sure.

Was the *thing* between us back? Or was I imagining it?

Maybe this whole "old times' sake" business was getting to me. But it sure did feel nice.

"Maren?" Dallas's voice pulled me into the moment. "Something to drink?"

"Oh. A glass of wine, please." I looked up at Jason. "A sauvignon blanc maybe?"

He nodded. "Absolutely. One sauvignon blanc and one old fashioned. I'll be right back, and I apologize that service might be a little bit slower than usual tonight. We're quite a ways from the kitchen and bar."

"That's okay," said Dallas. "We're not in a rush."

"Very good." Jason headed for the stairwell door, leaving us alone again.

"Good thing he's young and looks in good shape. He's going to be up and down the stairs all night." Dallas picked up his water and took a sip.

I shook my head. "I still can't wrap my brain around this."

He shrugged and sat back in his chair, looking smug and mischievous and way too handsome. "Don't think. Just enjoy yourself. Pretend you're in high school."

"This totally reminds me of something you would have pulled back then."

He laughed. "You're right. Although this is more romantic than the pigs."

I groaned. At the beginning of our senior year, Dallas and his football buddies had been suspended for letting three pigs loose in the halls at school. They'd spray-painted numbers on the pigs: one, two, and four. It had taken hours for school officials to realize there were only three pigs. "Where did you guys even get those pigs?"

Dallas shook his head. "I don't remember. I think someone's uncle had a farm? God, that was hilarious."

"Poor little piggies. I felt sorry for them, being painted-on and then chased all around school."

"It was non-toxic paint. I promise you, no pigs or humans were harmed in that prank."

"Unlike the Slip'N Slide episode at the end of junior year." In order to "claim" the senior hallway as their own, Dallas and his friends had turned it into a giant Slip'N Slide.

The crooked grin broke out on his face. "Oh yeah, Hagerman broke his nose, that asshole. It was his own fault.

No one told him to dive face first toward the lockers. He overshot the tarp by a mile."

"And how about parking your car in the school courtyard?"

He held up one finger. "That was in protest over them denying us parking passes senior year. It was us exercising our right to free speech."

I rolled my eyes. "They denied you parking passes because of all the shit you guys had pulled the year before."

"Whatever, that one wasn't even my idea, but I got all the blame for it."

"Because it was *your* car! I told you that you were going to get blamed for it."

"I know. Holy fuck, you were mad about that." He was laughing again. "You didn't have sex with me for a week."

"I didn't *talk* to you for a week."

He cocked his head. "You didn't?" But his foot nudged mine under the table, so I knew he was joking.

I leaned my elbows on the table. "And then, of course, there was the letter."

He sighed, the smile sliding off his face. "Yeah, I know."

Shortly after the parking incident, Dallas and his friends had written a letter on school letterhead from the principal to all the new freshmen that the school was implementing mandatory "penis inspections." While several senior guys had been behind the prank, Dallas had taken full blame for the idea and its execution, resulting in a long-term suspension, which his parents viewed as the final straw. They sent him to boarding school right before our one-year anniversary.

But of course, I hadn't realized that until after he was gone.

"What can I say?" he asked. "It seemed funny at the time."

"It was kind of funny," I admitted. "But you had promised me you weren't going to get in any more trouble."

"Did I promise that?"

"Among other things."

Dallas looked at me like he had something more to say, but a second later Jason came through the door with a tray carrying our drinks. He set them down and asked if we were ready to order, and I had to admit I hadn't even looked at the menu yet.

"Just give me a minute," I said, opening it up and scanning it quickly for something I'd like. Only the steaks had descriptions that included the name of the farm where they came from, but I wasn't sure I felt like steak tonight. I bit my bottom lip as I read through the entrees, wondering if the rest of their meat was organic.

"Let me know if I can help," Jason said.

"I have a few questions," Dallas said. "The roasted half chicken. Is it organic? Locally sourced? Cage-free? Was the chicken joyful while he was alive? I can't eat a sad chicken."

"Um ..." Jason looked a little uncomfortable. "I'm not exactly sure where the chickens come from."

Laughing, I kicked Dallas under the table and said, "I'll have the lobster spaghetti."

"And I'll have the New York strip. Medium rare." Dallas handed the menu over to Jason with a grin. "Sorry, man. Didn't mean to give you a hard time."

The waiter smiled. "No problem. I'll put this right in."

When we were alone again, I picked up my wine glass and stuck out my tongue at him. "Meanie."

"Sorry. Couldn't help it. I felt like I knew what you were thinking. Was I right?" He took a sip of his drink.

I looked off to one side, took a drink of wine. "Maybe." When I looked back at him, the crooked grin was on his face, and my heart was zinging around in my chest like a pinball.

I wondered if he knew what I was thinking then.

———

Two glasses of wine, one bowl of lobster spaghetti, and half a slice of butterscotch peanut butter pie later, I was pleasantly tipsy, overly stuffed, and not at all ready for the night to end. Two hours had flown by. I couldn't remember the last time I'd laughed so much on a date.

"You mentioned you like taking road trips," I said, setting my fork down and picking up my cup of tea. "Where have you been?"

"Lots of places."

"What are some of your favorites?"

He ate another bite of pie and thought as he chewed. "Zion National Park. Zephyr Cove. Big Sky. The skiing is amazing there."

"I've never been skiing."

"What?" He finished the last of the pie and set down his fork. "What the hell do you do during winter?"

"Fly somewhere warm for a yoga retreat, like Bali."

"I do like beaches. Can't say I've ever been to Bali, though."

"You should go sometime, it's so beautiful. Put it on your bucket list."

"I don't really have a bucket list." He picked up his cocktail.

"No? Nothing you want to make sure you do before you leave this life and move on to the next?"

He thought for a second. "You believe there's a next life?"

I shrugged. "Sure. I don't know what it looks like or how we get there, but I like the Buddhist belief in karma."

"Oh yeah? Tell me about it."

"Well, I'm not an expert, but my understanding is that Buddhists believe our minds are totally separate from our bodies, and when we die, our consciousness continues to a deeper level. But our minds sort of save up positive actions, which sow the seeds of future happiness when you're reborn. Negative actions sow the seeds of future suffering." I shrugged. "That's karma."

"Guess that means I'm fucked in the next life, huh?"

I rolled my eyes. "Stop it. You're a good person. You might have made some questionable decisions in this life, but that's not the same as being cruel."

"Maybe we'll meet again in the next life."

My pulse quickened. "Or maybe we've met before."

"It would explain a lot of things, wouldn't it?" He sipped his drink. "So what's on your bucket list?"

"Lots of things. Ride a camel in the desert. Stand next to the Sphinx. Dive off a yacht into the sea."

"Which sea?"

"I don't know, I'm not too picky about that. Let's say the Aegean."

"Aegean it is."

"But those are more superficial things. I'd really like to make a difference in people's lives." I looked down at the tablecloth. "That sounds trite and silly, but I really do want to help people. I teach free yoga classes for seniors at my studio, and I've done free programs for kids at low-income schools and in rural areas, but I wish there was something I could do on a broader scale." I looked up and saw him smiling at me, but it wasn't patronizing. It was genuine.

"I bet you've helped more people than you realize."

Holding my tea in both hands, I shivered. "Got a little chilly up here all of a sudden, didn't it?"

Immediately, he set down his glass and took off his jacket. Rising to his feet, he moved behind me and draped it over my shoulders. "Here. Can't let my prom date be cold."

I laughed and set the cup down, pulling the jacket tighter around me. It was warm and smelled like him. I sniffed the collar. "What is this?" I inhaled it again, and all my nether regions tingled. It was subtle and woodsy, manly but not overpowering. "I like it."

"It's called He Wood," he said with a grin as he sat down again.

"Of course it is." I looked down at the corsage on my wrist. "I still can't get over all this, Dallas."

"Good." He laughed a little. "Your face when you thought I might be trying to take you up to a hotel room was priceless."

"I bet. Are you even staying here?"

"Yes. It's a nice place."

"So when did you decide to do all this?"

"Today. Your story about missing the prom kinda got to me. I felt bad."

"So this is a pity date? Is that what you're saying?"

"Totally." He grinned at me, and suddenly I knew how he'd felt the night he hadn't wanted to say goodbye.

I didn't want to do it tonight.

But you will, said a voice in my head. *You have to. This isn't real, Maren—it's pretend. Maybe it's not a pity date, but he did all this to be nice, not because he still has feelings for you. You don't really have feelings for him, either. You're just remembering what it was like when you did. And it's making you feel lonely. But he lives in Portland, you live here, and you're most likely never going to see each other again. So feel your feels, get your closure, and go home before you do something stupid. You're strong, but you're not invincible.*

A moment later, Jason returned with Dallas's credit card, waited while he signed the check, and told us there was no rush to leave. When he'd gone, I sat back in my chair and sighed, looking out over the city lights. "Dallas, this is the nicest thing anyone has ever done for me. Thank you for a wonderful night."

He looked surprised. "Do you have a curfew or something?"

"No."

"Good, because we haven't even danced yet."

I laughed. "You want to dance with me?"

"Of course I do. It's the prom, isn't it? Grab my phone in my inside jacket pocket."

I reached into the pocket, pulled it out, and handed it to him. He searched for something, tapped the screen, and set it on the table. A song began to play, and I gasped. It was "Hey There Delilah," a song I'd loved back then.

"You remembered," I said, feeling a lump in my throat.

Dallas pushed his chair back, came around to my side of the table, and held out his hand. I took it and stood up, letting the jacket fall from my shoulders. He led me away from the table and slightly closer to the edge of the roof with a full view of the city beneath us. Without a word, he took me in his arms, and it was like home. Warm, safe, solid, familiar. I laid my head on his shoulder and pressed my body close to his. We swayed slowly, much slower than the tempo of the song, but I didn't care. I wanted to be out of time with the rest of the world, I wanted us to be in a place where past, present, future didn't exist. There was only us, here in this place, holding on to each other as if we'd never been apart. As if we'd never let go.

The lump in my throat grew bigger, and I tried hard to hold back the tears. I breathed in and out, attempting to center myself in the moment and simply be grateful for it. But the scent of his skin only made me want the impossible even more. Eventually, a tear fell. And then another. I sniffled.

Dallas stopped moving and leaned back from the waist. "Hey, you. I told you, there's no crying at this prom."

I laughed and let go of him to wipe my eyes, hoping my mascara hadn't run. "Sorry. I guess this trip down memory lane has me a little emotional."

"It's this song. It's sappy as fuck."

I poked him on the chest. "Stop it. I still like this song."

"I know, but it's making you sad, and I want to remember you smiling tonight. Let's do something else. Something fun."

"Like what?"

His eyes lit up in the dark. "I've got an idea."

"What is it?" I asked suspiciously. Dallas's ideas could be trouble.

"You'll see." He let go of my waist and took my hand, trying to pull me toward the door. "Come on."

"Dallas, my bag!" I cried, laughing as I tried to dig in my heels. "And your jacket and phone."

He hurried to the table, grabbed everything, and bolted for the door again.

"Is this idea of yours even legal?" I asked, trying not to break an ankle hurrying down the stairs in my heels.

"That's debatable. But it doesn't matter, because we're not going to get caught."

I groaned. "You always said that."

"And we never did."

He was mostly right. As a couple, we'd been lucky—our parents had never walked in on us, a cop had never knocked on the window of his car, the condom had never broken.

"Okay, *we* never did, but *you* did," I reminded him. "Half the time, I used to think you *wanted* to get caught, you were so blatant about breaking rules." We exited the stairwell and headed for the elevators. Dallas kept my hand in his.

"That's because I believed that it was more fun to get away with something if everyone knew it was you. Why pull a prank in secret? And I didn't care about the punishment. It was always worth it." He hit the button and turned to face me. "Except the last time."

I sighed. "Just don't get me arrested tonight, please."

"Relax," he said as the doors opened.

"Have you ever been arrested?" I asked as we stepped into the empty elevator.

He hesitated. "Once."

"For what?"

"I got into a fight with an off-duty cop who was being a real dick to his girlfriend at a bar." He shook his head. "That night did not end well for me."

"I can only imagine."

"But I promise, you will not end up in handcuffs tonight." He grinned delightedly and leaned closer to whisper in my ear. "Unless, of course, you'd enjoy that."

Heat bloomed at the center of my body and spread to my extremities like a nuclear blast. "Pretty sure that would violate the look-but-don't-touch policy."

He straightened up. "Oh yeah, that. I promised to behave tonight, didn't I?"

"You did." But I gave him a wicked smile.

"Well, then." He checked his wristwatch. "Good thing it will be tomorrow soon. Is it true what they say about a prom dress at midnight?"

I laughed as the doors opened. "Guess you'll have to wait and see."

———

"DALLAS, THIS IS CRAZY!" I whispered as we ran across the lawn of the huge house on Lake St. Clair where he'd grown up.

"Shh! Don't talk until we get to the water," he whispered back.

I struggled to keep up with him, although at least I'd ditched my heels in the car after he'd warned me there might be running involved with his idea. He'd left his jacket and dress shirt in the car and wore only a white T-shirt with his jeans. He was barefoot, too. The moon shone down on us like a spotlight, and I tried not to think about the signs we'd seen saying PRIVATE PROPERTY NO TRES-PASSING.

"Who lives here now?" I asked as we neared the seawall.

"No idea." He pulled me over to where a dock jutted into the water. A small Boston Whaler bobbed in the water next to it, as well as a wooden dinghy, two oars lying on the bottom. "Holy shit, this is perfect."

I stopped when he tried to lead me onto the dock. "Dallas, no! We are not stealing a dinghy," I whispered. "You said we were just going to go night-swimming at your old house like we used to!"

"We're not stealing a dinghy—we're borrowing it." He looked up at the massive house, which sat back about two hundred feet from the water. "And the house is totally dark. I bet the owners are out of town."

I glanced back at the house, too. It did look pretty deserted, but still ... could we really take a boat that didn't belong to us for a spin?

"Come on." Dallas tugged on my hand. "Live a little. When's the last time you misbehaved, goody two shoes?"

"I can't remember," I shot back. "But it was probably with you."

He moved closer, so close I felt his breath on my lips. "Then come on. Be bad with me one last time."

My insides tightened. The list of ill-advised things I was doing "for old times' sake" was growing longer by the minute, and I was a bit concerned about where it would ultimately lead.

Not concerned enough to go home, though.

"Okay," I told him. "But if we get caught—"

"I'll say I kidnapped you." He jumped into the boat, steadied himself, and reached up for my waist. "Look at all my tattoos, I'm obviously a pirate," he said. "Now come on."

After I let him lift me into the boat, I took a seat on the bench at the back while Dallas untied the ropes tethering it to the dock. I shivered, although the night was warm and I was slightly sweaty from running.

The water was relatively calm but my nerves were choppy as hell as Dallas rowed us away from the dock. What on earth were we doing? And tomorrow, would I be okay with it? Would I have the closure I wanted, or would being with him set me back again?

"You're looking very serious," Dallas said over the wind that whipped my hair around my face.

I opened my eyes and smiled. "Just taking it all in. This is a lot to process."

"What is?"

"Seeing you. The prom. Nautical larceny."

"Ah." Dallas rowed us into a tree-lined cove tucked into the coastline where we used to hang out and swim during the summer we were together.

There was no one around so late at night, and it was much quieter out of the wind, sheltered by trees. Dallas dropped the boat's small anchor into the water as I looked around. "God, I haven't been here in years."

"Me neither. We had some good times here, didn't we?"

"Remember how you guys used to climb those trees and jump into the water?"

He laughed. "Yeah. That was fun."

"I was positive one of you was going to break your neck."

"Nah." He looked up. "Wonder if I could still do it."

"Dallas Shepherd. Don't even think about it."

He stood and whipped off his shirt.

My breath caught at the sight of his bare upper body—he was thicker and more muscular than he'd been back then, and he had tattoos on his shoulders, arms, and the sides of his ribcage. It was too dark to see what they were, but I longed to run my hands over the ink. Ask him about each one. Listen to his stories.

He unbuttoned his jeans and paused with his hands on the zipper. "Close your eyes if you're shy, violet."

I lifted my chin, heart pounding. "I'm not shy."

He grinned and shoved his jeans down. But before I could get a good look at him in his underwear, he kicked them off and dove over the side of the boat. I squealed as the water splashed me.

A few seconds later, he surfaced, tossing his head. "Fuck, that feels good."

"Is it cold?"

"It's perfect. You should come in. Unless you don't want to get your hair wet or something."

I stood up and unbuttoned my blouse. "Please. As long as you've known me, have I ever been that girl?"

"Nope. But I don't really know you now."

I felt his eyes on me as I removed my top and unbuttoned my skirt. My pulse was accelerating rapidly. "So ask me something."

He was silent a few seconds. "Have you spent the last twelve years hating me?"

"I've never hated you."

"Did you ever think about me?"

"You know I did." I stepped out of my skirt and stood there in a nude bralette and panties.

"Christ," he said, staring up at me.

I put my hands on my hips. "Any more questions?"

"Yeah. How serious were you about that whole look-but-don't-touch thing?"

Giggling, I jumped over the edge of the boat. The water was cool but not shockingly cold, and I stayed under for a moment, my feet planted on the sandy bottom. When I came up, Dallas had moved closer to me.

The water was over my head, but he could stand here. His hair looked black, all wet. His eyes shone in the dark.

"I'm trying really hard to behave like I said I would," he said, coming even closer.

I swam backward, giggling. "I can see that."

"But I've got to be honest, I'm not sure I can keep my promise."

"I'll be honest, too. This is one time where I hope you don't."

He reached out and grabbed my arm, pulling me toward him. Giving in, I wrapped my legs around his waist and looped my arms around his neck. My entire body radiated with desire. Anticipation. Heat. Only he could make me feel this alive.

"God, Maren." His voice was low and serious. His arms tightened around me. "I told myself I couldn't do this. But I must have been fucking crazy to think I wouldn't."

"Same," I whispered, longing to feel his lips on mine again. "But I don't care. I want this. Even if it's just for one night, I want this. I want you."

Our mouths came together, and we kissed as feverishly and passionately as if no time had passed at all. We were young and reckless and bursting with need, desperate to satisfy the gnawing hunger inside us that never seemed to go away, no matter how often we fed it. His hands moved beneath my ass, squeezing my flesh, pulling me against him. I could feel his erection through the fabric of his boxer briefs and my underwear, and I moaned when he rocked his hips, sliding his cock along my clit.

He tasted sweet and sinful at the same time—like whiskey and butterscotch, like a memory and a fantasy—and his mouth was familiar but his kiss felt brand new. *The facial hair*, I thought, moving my hands to his jaw as his tongue stroked mine. *He didn't have it back then*. I loved the rough masculinity of it on my palms and against my cheeks and lips. I loved that he was thirty and not seventeen, that his body felt so big and strong, that years had gone by and he'd matured into a man but his desire for me hadn't dissipated.

I reached down into the water between us and rubbed my hand along his thick, hard length, shivering with want. At my touch, he dug his fingers into my thighs. "Maren," he said, his voice gruff. "Come back to my room. Stay the night with me."

"Yes," I whispered, already hating the minutes that stood between now and the moment I'd feel him inside me again. The memory of it had my body tight in its grip. "Let's go."

I didn't want to wait for the next life.

SIX

DALLAS

So much for sticking to the plan.

I wasn't much of a planner anyway, never had been. I liked spontaneity. In fact, I generally had three mottos in life:

1. Rules are made to be broken.

2. You only live once.

3. A tiger doesn't lose sleep over the opinion of sheep.

So if I wanted something, I went after it.

And I wanted Maren. We wanted each other.

Even if it's just for one night, she'd said. *I want this again. I want you again.*

I shut off every other voice in my head.

She was shivering in the passenger seat of the car, her hair messy and damp, her blouse clinging to her wet skin. But her smile was radiant, her laugh intoxicating. "Are you cold?" I reached over and took her hand, moving it into my lap. "I'm sorry. I promise to warm you up soon."

She giggled. "You better. But I hope no one sees us running through the lobby of the hotel like this." She tucked her hair behind her ear.

"I don't give a fuck who sees us."

"That's because you look dark and sexy all wet. I look like a soggy golden retriever. When you look back on tonight, I hope you remember what I looked like when you picked me up for the prom, and not what I looked like when you took me home."

I picked up her hand and kissed the back of it, pressing down a little harder on the gas pedal. "First of all, I'm not taking you home anytime soon. Second, you look just as hot to me right now as you did then. Hotter, even. I think imperfection is sexy."

"Then I guess it's your lucky day."

We were both quiet for a minute, and my mind wandered back to the start of it all. "Remember the first time we hooked up?"

She nodded and laughed. "I was just thinking about that night, too. You were having a party at your house after Homecoming our junior year, and you threw me in the pool in my dress."

"You dared me to. I can't resist a dare."

"I was trying to get your attention. I couldn't wait around forever for you to notice me."

"It wasn't that I hadn't noticed you. I just thought you were too good for me. Honor roll student. Teacher's pet. Ballerina. Sweet little Maren Devine."

"Oh, stop."

"I'm serious. I had no idea you were into me until one of your friends said something. Then I couldn't stop thinking about you."

She giggled. "My date was not amused."

"Your date was a jackass."

"He was. He spent the entire night talking about his

new Mustang. But at least he *asked* me to the dance." She poked my shoulder.

"I remember I pretended to feel all bad after tossing you in the water. I took you upstairs to my room to give you a towel."

"You took me upstairs to kiss me."

"Fuck yes, I did. Not sorry."

"My first kiss."

I glanced at her. "I remember."

She sighed. "My poor date didn't stand a chance."

"Nope. Because then I offered to drive you home, so you wouldn't get the seats in his new Mustang all wet."

"Pretty sure everyone saw right through that, including my date."

"I didn't fucking care. That thirty minutes we spent parked down the street was worth it. Even if I did come in my pants."

She burst out laughing. "Did you? I don't think you ever told me that."

"I did. When I walked you to your door, I tried to hide it by untucking my shirt, but I was terrified you were going to notice and be all grossed out."

"And I was terrified I was doing everything wrong, because I had zero experience."

"You did everything right. I promise." Turning right onto Washington, I pulled up at the valet stand.

"I don't think I slept at all that night."

I put the car in park and looked over at her. "Babe, you're not gonna sleep much tonight, either."

She grinned. "My heart is beating so fast right now."

Hand in hand, we raced through the hotel reception area and dashed into the elevator. Thankfully, we had it to ourselves, but I didn't even wait for the doors to shut before

I kissed her, pushing her back against the wall and running my hands up the sides of her ribcage. She threw her arms around my neck, her fingers sliding into my damp hair. When the doors opened on my floor, I backed out and she clung to me, her chest pressed against mine. I lifted her up and she locked her legs around me again like she had in the lake, and I managed to walk down the hall toward my room. At my door, I had to fumble for the card in my wallet, but she stayed right where she was, the strength in her legs holding her up.

It took a few tries, but eventually the door swung open and I walked us inside the room. As soon as it slammed shut behind us, Maren released her legs and put her feet on the floor. I reached for the buttons of her blouse, but she stopped me. "Wait," she said breathlessly. "I've been in the lake. I feel like I need a shower."

"Good idea," I said, pulling her into the bathroom and switching on the light.

Two minutes later, our clothing and shoes littered the bathroom floor and we stood kissing beneath a stream of hot water, the steam rising around us. Her body was perfection —tight and toned, with curves in all the right places. Her skin was like satin beneath my hands. She had three tattoos, a lotus flower on her inner arm, three little birds on the front of one shoulder, and a hand of Fatima on her upper back. They were all beautiful, but I wished I'd been the one to do them.

She wanted to wash her hair, and I thought I'd go out of my mind watching her rinse out the shampoo, her back arched in a mouthwatering curve, her nipples taut and tempting, her eyes closed as the water ran down her body. My dick was so hard I lasted about five seconds before taking it in my hand and lowering my mouth to one of her breasts. She moaned, and it was the sweetest sound I'd ever heard.

"Wait," she pleaded, reaching for the soap.

"Let me," I begged, taking the bar from her. "I need something to do with my hands before I get myself off just watching you."

She laughed, deep and throaty. "That could be hot, too."

"Another time." I lathered her up from head to toe, willing myself to finish the task without losing control. I wanted my mouth on every inch of her body.

When she'd rinsed off, she reached for the soap. "Want me to do you?"

"Uh, that's always a yes," I said, closing my eyes as her soapy hands moved over my chest and shoulders.

"I love your tattoos." She moved around me, lathering my back and sides. "I want to hear about them."

"Tomorrow." I grabbed the soap back from her. "Let me finish this. I'm going to fucking explode in a second, and I'd like to preserve my dignity tonight." Quickly, I finished up, set the soap aside and dropped to my knees in front of her.

She gasped when I grabbed one leg and kissed my way up the inside of her thigh, and reached out to catch her balance, one hand on the tile wall. "What are you doing?"

"I don't think I got enough dessert." I dragged my tongue up the center of her pussy, slow and soft. "I'm in the mood for something sweet." I did it again, and again.

"Oh, God. That feels ... so good." Her other hand slipped into my hair as I circled her clit and sucked it gently into my mouth.

She tasted even better than I remembered—more like a dream than a memory. I slung her leg over my shoulder and slid one finger inside her, then two. She was hot and tight and slick. My cock twitched in jealous agony, and I pulled my fingers from her and wrapped them around my erection, fucking my fist for a moment of relief.

"Oh fuck, that's hot," she whispered. "And you're so good with your tongue. Oh my God, Dallas, I'd forgotten—what this is like—I'm going to—"

The leg she stood on began to tremble and her cries grew incomprehensible. I took my hand off myself and used my fingers inside her again, pushing in deeper, seeking out all her hidden pleasure spots, and paying close attention to the way she responded to each flick and stroke and swirl of my tongue. I wanted to give her exactly what she needed to fall apart above me. I wanted her leg to buckle. I wanted to make her scream.

A second later, her body tightened around my fingers and her voice echoed off the tiles as the orgasm ricocheted through her. I felt her clit pulse against my tongue, and my body surged with adrenaline. Lust. Greed.

I rose to my feet and she threw her arms around my neck, crushing her lips to mine. Once more, I lifted her up and she twined her legs around me. Reaching between us, I positioned my cock beneath her and hesitated. "Is it okay? Do you want me to get a condom?" The last thing I wanted to do was leave that shower, but if she asked me to, I would. "I don't mind. I always use one, although I haven't been with anyone in a long time."

"How long?" she asked.

"Almost a year."

"I win. It's been two years."

"Let me go get a condom," I said, starting to lower her.

"No!" She clung to me with her arms and legs. "No. Don't leave. It's okay," she murmured against my lips. "I'm on the pill, and I trust you."

Of course she did. She always had. Was I violating that trust now? Wouldn't she be angry if she knew what I was keeping from her?

For fuck's sake, don't think about that.

I shoved every thought from my head and focused on what it felt like to ease into her body again, to watch her face reflect the pain and pleasure of taking me in deep, to hear her strangled breaths and anguished sighs, to feel her fingers clutching at my shoulders.

"I forgot how big you are," she whispered. "But I love the way it hurts. I missed it. I missed you."

Holding back as much as I could, I went slow until I felt her body relax and she began to issue breathless commands against my lips that had me driving into her with deep, rhythmic strokes. *Fuck me. Yes. Right there. Don't stop.*

It was unbelievable—I was with Maren again, I was inside her, nothing between us. It couldn't be real. It was too good to be true. For a moment, I was terrified my head was messing with me. Was I hallucinating? Was I conscious? Was this some kind of altered state? Was she only a ghost? A memory?

I opened my eyes. No, no—she was here. I could see her, I was holding her. She was gorgeous flesh and blood in my arms. I was kissing her and touching her and moving inside her. I heard my name on her lips.

Dallas...oh God...Dallas...it's happening again...yes, yes, yes...

I began to let go, bracing her against the wall and pounding into her so viciously I was sure her back would bruise. And I liked it—I was such a fucking dick that I liked the idea she'd leave here tomorrow with black and blue marks on her unblemished skin, something more than an insubstantial memory. I wished it were permanent, a tattoo.

She came a second time, her cries even louder, her hands fisted in my hair, her body clenching tight as my cock surged inside her. I thought my legs would give. I thought my heart would explode. I thought my life would flash before my eyes.

When it eventually became clear that I wasn't going to die right here in the shower at the Westin, I started to breathe again. Our foreheads rested together. Her arms and legs were still wrapped around me, and I didn't want her to let go.

Ever.

She picked up her head. "My God. It's true."

"What's true?"

"A woman can have two. *In a row.*"

"Two orgasms, you mean?"

"Yes! That's never happened to me before."

I felt like a hero. "Good."

"And you know what else I just realized?"

"What?"

"We never did this before. Took a shower together."

"Probably because we lived with our parents, Maren."

"True." She looked down at our bodies, still joined. "I like it. I like being able to see you. We were always in the dark, half-dressed or something. Nervous about being too loud or getting caught. We never really got to take our time."

"I don't think I was capable of taking my time back then." I kissed her lips, her cheek, her throat. "But tonight is a different story."

"Or at least another chapter in the same story." She brushed the hair off my face. "We never really felt finished to me."

"Me neither."

We were both silent then, even though there were a hundred things I wished I could say.

I still love you. I never stopped. Run away with me. Let's go, just the two of us. We'll rewrite history, give ourselves a different ending this time.

But deep down, I knew that was impossible.

———

WHEN OUR FINGERTIPS started to shrivel, we got out of the shower and dried off. I couldn't take my eyes off her, as if I was afraid she was going to disappear.

She looked around at the clothing scattered on the bathroom floor. "I should probably hang my stuff up. I'm going to have to walk out of here in it eventually."

I didn't like thinking about her walking out. "I'll hang it up for you." Tossing my towel onto the vanity, I leaned down and picked up her blouse and skirt.

"Thank you." She grabbed my towel, hung it on the back of the bathroom door along with her own, and scooped up her undergarments. "I'm just going to rinse these out real quick."

I left the bathroom and hung her clothing in the closet next to a couple shirts of mine. Then I stood there for a moment. I'd never lived with anyone, so I'd never shared a closet before. It sounds stupid, but there was something I liked about seeing our things hanging side-by-side like that. I shut the closet door and caught Maren's reflection in the full-length mirror on the back of it. She stood naked at the sink, rinsing out her things. My chest felt tight. *This is what it would be like. We'd do little things for each other, we'd observe one another doing insignificant, routine tasks, we'd walk around naked with no shame.* For a moment I let myself imagine it, a life together without the tick of the clock in my head, counting down the hours we had left.

But that was pointless. Time was not on my side.

She caught me looking at her in the mirror and smiled over her shoulder. "Hey."

I went into the bathroom and wrapped my arms around her waist from behind, pressing my lips to her shoulder. I needed to make the most of every moment we had. "Hey."

She wrung out her things and spread them on a hand towel to dry. "There. That's a little better. Want me to rinse yours?"

"No. I don't give a fuck about them." I kissed the back of her head. "Your hair smells good."

"Thanks." She rested her arms on top of mine, leaning back into my chest. "You feel good." Then she turned to face me, ran her hands up my chest and down my shoulders. "Tell me about your tattoos now."

"That could take all night, and I have better ideas." Already my dick was showing interest in how close her hips were to mine.

She smiled as she traced the Arabic lettering on my left deltoid. "Indulge me a little. What's that say?"

"It says, 'I have found both freedom and safety in my madness; the freedom of loneliness and the safety from being understood, for those who understand us enslave something in us.'"

"That's beautiful. But also sort of sad. What is it from?"

"*The Madman*, by Khalil Gibran. He actually wrote it in English, but I liked the look of the Arabic better." I also liked that most people couldn't read it. My connection to the sentiment wasn't something I enjoyed explaining to anyone.

"Did you design it?"

"I draw all my tattoos. But someone else does them."

"What about this?" Her hand moved over the tiger on my left forearm. "Why a tiger?"

"I like the way they move."

She nodded, running her palm over the ink covering my right shoulder and upper arm. "And this one?"

"A Maori tribal design."

She drew a line with her finger down the center of my chest and over to the side of my rib cage, where I had decided to put the one tattoo I thought of as hers. It was an abstract drawing of a mermaid, done in sweeping minimalist curves. She'd once told me her name meant *sea* and she thought of mermaids as her spirit animal. "Ooooh, I love this. Did I ever tell you how much I love mermaids?"

"I don't remember," I lied.

"Does it mean anything?"

It means part of you is always with me. "No. I actually drew it for someone else, but he decided on a different design, something more traditional. So I kept it for myself."

She bit her lip, nodding slowly as she studied it. "It's beautiful." Then she looked up at me wistfully. "Maybe you'll design a mermaid tattoo for *me* someday. Maybe you'll even do it."

I swallowed hard. Heard my neurologist's voice.

You should be prepared to lose some fine motor control on your right side.

She focused on her fingers moving across my chest again. "I could come visit you in Portland or something."

I didn't say anything, and she looked up again.

"Would that be okay? To come visit you sometime?"

Words refused to form. I knew my silence was worse than a lie, but I couldn't speak.

Her cheeks went pink. "Sorry. That's probably too forward of me."

"I just—can't make any promises," I managed, hating myself.

She put on a face so brave it nearly broke my heart. "I get it. Really. And if all we have is tonight, so be it. I'll think of it as an unexpected gift. A second chance for the goodbye I wanted back then."

Because I didn't trust myself with words, I kissed her, and felt desire stir inside me again. Heat spread from the center of my body. My heart began to pump harder. My cock began to stiffen, tapping against her thigh.

She smiled and reached down, taking it in her hand. "Already? I'm impressed."

"Good." And because I didn't want to spend the entire night fucking her in my hotel bathroom, I took her by the shoulders and steered her out into the room. Then I swept her off her feet and carried her over to the bed, laying her on top of the sheets where I'd rested earlier. The bedside lamp was on, and I reached to switch it off, but she grabbed my arm.

"Leave it on," she whispered, reaching for me. "I like seeing you."

I stretched out above her, settling my hips between her thighs, sealing my lips over one perfect breast, kneading the other with my hand. She gasped when I circled her taut little nipple with my tongue and dug her heels into the back of my legs when I sucked it into my mouth. Vowing I'd spend more time on her now that the first orgasm was out of my system, I lavished attention on every inch of her skin, and I didn't let her put her hands on me. I kissed her in places I'd never kissed anyone—the inside of her elbow, the back of her knee, every single one of her toes. I swept my tongue across her collarbone, up the top of her spine, along the crest of her perfect round ass. I touched her in places I knew she liked and discovered new ways to make her moan and sigh and plead, her body quivering beneath me.

"Dallas, I need you inside me," she said. This time when she reached for my cock, I let her have it, groaning at her touch. She grasped it firmly, working her hand up and down my shaft before teasing the slick crown with her fingertips. "Now. Please."

I did as she asked, sliding inside her in one smooth stroke. Her hands moved to my ass, and she pulled me tight to her body, rocking her hips and grinding against me. I braced myself above her, shifting my weight to give her the angle she needed.

"Yes," she breathed. "Deep like that. God, you're so perfect. No one has ever made me feel this way."

"Come again for me," I whispered, unable to stop the speeding freight train inside me. I fucked her hard and fast, every nerve ending of my body on fire, praying she was with me. "I want to feel you."

A moment later, neither of us could talk as the untamable need to possess each other fully took over and carried us off the edge of tension into the free-fall of release. As our bodies shuddered and stilled, we clung to each other, skin damp with sweat, breath hot and quick, hearts hammering against one another's chests.

When the room came back into focus, I tipped onto my side and gathered her close, breathed her in.

"Oh my God," she whispered. "I had two *again*. I don't even know how you're doing that. It's so good. Why is it so good?"

Because I still love you. "I don't know."

"But ... does this—with me—feel different to you?"

I could hear the nervous tremble in her voice, and it forced me to be honest. "Yes. It does."

"Do you think maybe it's because you were my first or something?"

"Maybe."

She was quiet for a moment. "Remember that night?"

"Are you kidding me?" I pulled back a little and looked down at her. "Of course I do. It was a Thursday night in July. We were in my bed, and there was a thunderstorm going on. I was going to stop, but you said, 'Don't stop this time.'"

She smiled, but there was something sad in her expression, too. "I've never regretted it."

"I'm glad."

"But I always used to wish it was *your* first time, too."

"It felt like it was. It was the only first time that mattered to me, anyway."

She leaned away from me and gave me a dubious look. "Stop it. Do you mean that?"

"Yes." Offering her these little truths about the past made me feel less guilty.

"That makes me happy." She snuggled up to me again, then reached between us and ran her fingertips over the Arabic quote on my shoulder. It was so soothing, I got a little drowsy and probably would have fallen asleep if she hadn't asked a question.

Her voice was soft and curious. "Do you really feel this way? Do you like being lonely because it makes you feel safe?"

"Yes," I said, too tired or too guilty or too in love to lie to her any more tonight.

She sighed and kissed my chest, but said nothing more. A moment later, we were both asleep.

SEVEN

MAREN

Tick.

> *Tick.*
> *Tick.*
> *Out—I have to get out.*
> *Tick. Tick. Tick.*
> *It's coming for me. It's moving too fast.*
> *Why won't the door open?*
> *Tick, tick, tick.*
> *Frantic, I look down and notice the door doesn't even have a handle.*
> *I'm trapped.*
> *Tickticktickticktick*
> *I try to scream, but choke on the sound. I try to bang on the door but can't pry my hands from the clock. I'm sweating and crying, my heart is racing—because it's real this time. It's not a dream, and—*

"Shh, you're okay. You're okay." I heard a man's voice above the out-of-control ticking of the clock. I opened my eyes.

Dallas was on his side, propped on one elbow looking

down at me. One of his hands brushed the hair back from my forehead.

Confused, I bolted upright and glanced wildly around the room. "Where is it?"

Dallas sat up too. "Where is what, babe?"

"The snake." But even as I said it, something in my brain recognized how ludicrous it sounded.

"God, I'm so tempted to make a joke right now." He put an arm around me and kissed my bare shoulder. "But I won't. There is no snake, Maren. You were having a nightmare."

The fog was beginning to clear. The bedside lamp next to me was still on, allowing me to take in my surroundings. King-sized bed. Brown leather chair. Large flat-screen television mounted on the wall. Nothing was familiar. "Where am I?"

"You're in my hotel room."

As my pulse decelerated and reality sank in, the memory of last night came rushing back to me. "Oh. Right. The prom." I looked under the sheet. "Guess it's true what they say about the dress."

He chuckled. "You awake now?"

"Yes." I took a few deep breaths. The scent of sex and Dallas filled my head, grounding me. "Sorry."

"No need to apologize. Can I get you anything? Water?"

I shook my head. "I'm okay. I just need to be still for a minute."

He kissed my temple. "Okay."

Closing my eyes, I concentrated on my breathing, inhaling and exhaling deeply and slowly, letting the ebb and flow of it calm me. Dallas rubbed my back in gentle, soothing circles.

I opened my eyes and looked at him. "Thanks."

"You're welcome. *Now* can I make a joke about a snake in the bed?"

My lips tipped up, but my stomach still felt a little uneasy. "Go ahead."

He sighed. "Nah. Wouldn't even be fun. You sure you're all right?"

I nodded, but I wasn't. Not really. Why wouldn't that stupid nightmare let me be? What if it had nothing to do with closure? What if Dallas and I parted ways tomorrow and I still couldn't sleep at night? I blinked back tears and sniffed.

"Hey. Come here." Dallas lay back on the pillows and reached for me, and I molded myself to his side with my head on his warm, broad chest. He wrapped his arms around me and kissed the top of my head. "Talk to me. Do you have nightmares a lot?"

"Lately, I do. The same one." I described the dream to him in full detail. "It sounds so stupid. But it feels so real while it's happening. And I don't know what it is or how to stop having it. I've tried everything."

"Like what?"

"Meditation. Yoga. Detoxing. Melatonin. Clearing my chakras."

"Your *what*?"

Laughing a little, I looked up at him. "My chakras. They're sort of like spiritual focal points in the body. Energy flows through them, and if they're blocked or cluttered with ... stagnant baggage like fear or pain or negativity, you don't feel right. You have to clear that stuff to reconnect with your inner wisdom and allow your consciousness to grow and guide you."

"Not gonna lie, that sounds a little strange to me, but you do you."

I clucked my tongue. "Dallas, have you been neglecting your chakras?"

"Safe to say I have."

"They're probably a mess. I should teach you how to clear them."

"Thanks for the offer, but we're focused on you, remember? What can I do to make you feel better?"

Sighing, I put my head on his chest again. "I don't know. I actually thought just being with you would help."

"With me? Why?"

"Okay, this might sound sort of strange too, but I believe dreams deliver powerful messages from the universe to our subconscious mind. When you showed up yesterday, I thought maybe the dream had been a warning."

"Am I the snake? That's kind of badass."

"Hey!" I slapped him lightly on the chest. "That snake is seriously messing with my mental and physical well-being. It's not a good thing."

"Sorry, sorry." He squeezed me. "Go on. What did you think it had to do with me?"

"I thought maybe ..." I focused on my fingertips against his skin. "It was about getting closure on my relationship with you. To be honest, that was really the only thing in my life I had unresolved feelings about. I've been having the nightmare for a few weeks now, and then you showed up out of nowhere, and in my head, the message was clear: this is the opportunity for resolution. So when you asked me to dinner, I said yes."

"Wait a minute. That's the only reason you said yes? For closure? I'm a little offended you weren't thinking about my good looks and sparkling personality, Maren. I feel used."

"Okay, it was a little bit about those things. You're still sort of charming, and you do have a cute butt. But mostly it was about me."

"*Sort* of charming?" He flipped me onto my back, pinning my wrists to the mattress above my head.

I giggled. "Didn't you hear the part about your cute butt?"

He glanced over his shoulder. "It is pretty cute."

"And I like other parts of you, too."

One eyebrow cocked up. "Oh yeah? Which ones?"

My entire body tingled as he lowered his mouth to my neck. "Give me my hands back, and I'll show you."

"I don't think so." He worked his way across my throat, his lips and tongue warm on my skin. "I want to hear you tell me about them."

"I like your smile and the little chip in your tooth."

He picked up his head and eyeballed me. "This is not a promising start." But he lowered it again and kissed a path from the base of my throat down the center of my sternum.

"I like your chin. It has a dimple I always want to kiss."

Against my thigh I could feel his erection growing harder.

"I like your nose. It's just the tiniest bit crooked."

He looked up at me and dragged his scruffy jaw across my chest. "It's taken a few punches."

"Did you deserve them?"

"Probably." He took one nipple between his teeth and flicked it softly with his tongue.

"Mmm." I arched my back. "I love your mouth. Your lips. Your tongue."

"Getting warmer." He worked his way back up my neck

and kissed me hard and deep. I opened my knees and he settled his hips between my thighs. Then somehow he shackled both of my wrists with only one of his hands, and reached between us, guiding himself inside me.

I moaned as he slid in deep and reached over my head again. But this time, instead of grabbing my wrists, he locked his fingers with mine, clasping our hands together.

"I love your hands," I whispered as he began to move, his body undulating slowly and sensually over mine. "And the way you touch me. I love your tattoos, because they tell me pieces of your story. I love your skin, because it smells so damn good. I love being this close to you. I love thinking that we've met somewhere before and we'll meet somewhere again."

I wanted to go on, but I was losing focus, and my ability to speak was diminishing as the storm inside me grew. It gathered hot and strong at my center, twisting and whirling upward like a cyclone until I was breathless and dangling and frantic to feel our bodies sharing the same erotic pulse. But I managed one last little detail. "And I love your cock," I whispered as he pushed me even closer to the edge. "Because it makes me *come so hard*."

Dallas groaned as his orgasm hit, and I came the moment I felt him throbbing inside me, my body on fire, the world around us melting away. I never wanted the feeling to end.

Somewhere inside my head, I began to wonder why it had to.

This was *good*. We were good together—better than good. I knew he felt it, too. Why was he so against giving us another chance? Why did it have to end when he left? He hadn't really given me a good reason. He'd just said, *I can't*.

And I'd backed down—it wasn't really in my nature to push people, and he must have his reasons.

But what were they?

He let go of my hands so he could prop himself up, lifting his weight from my chest. "That was a good list."

I smiled. "Do you feel better about yourself?"

"Much."

"Good. Hey, what time is it?"

He glanced at the clock next to the bed. "Going on two."

"Can I get up for a minute?"

"No. I like you right here where you are."

"I have to take my pill."

He rolled off me immediately. "Up you go, cupcake."

"That's what I thought." Laughing, I grabbed my purse from the floor and went into the bathroom, shutting the door and snapping on the light. Items of clothing—all his, except for my shoes—were still scattered on the floor. I set my bag on the vanity, next to where my underthings were drying on a hand towel, and cleaned myself up. Afterward, I took a pill from the packet in my purse and swallowed it with some water.

I checked myself out in the mirror, taking in my damp, messy hair, smudged mascara, and a faint rash around my mouth. What the hell was that? I leaned closer, touching it with my fingertips. Then I smiled—it was from Dallas's scruff rubbing against my sensitive skin. I looked down at my body and noticed it on my chest, stomach, and inner thighs too. Grinning, I splashed some cold water on my face. I'd forgotten how aggressive Dallas could be. How hot-blooded. It was sexy as hell.

But he was playful too. And generous. And sweet. I still couldn't get over what he'd planned for me tonight. A guy who would go to all that trouble was a romantic at heart. Combine all that with the package it came in, and any woman would swoon. It was seriously amazing that he was still single.

Then it hit me—maybe he wasn't.

Maybe the real reason why I couldn't come visit him was that he had a girlfriend—or even a wife! My God, he could have kids! A wave of nausea struck me, and I swayed forward, bracing my hands on the sink as my face dripped.

Oh, God. Oh, God. I didn't want to believe it, but it made total sense to me. Total, heartbreaking, stomach-turning sense.

I grabbed a towel and mopped off my face. Out of the corner of my eye, I spied his travel kit on the vanity. It was olive green twill, unzipped, and two seconds later my hands had seized it. If he was hiding a wedding ring, this would be the place, right?

I felt horrible as I rummaged through it. Criminal. I'd never been the kind of person who snooped in other people's things or opened their medicine cabinets at parties or eavesdropped on their restaurant conversations. Now here I was with my hands in someone else's personal business, hunting for a sign that he was scamming me and cheating on someone back home. I was disgusted with myself. But I didn't stop until I'd taken everything out of that bag—toothbrush, toothpaste, mouthwash, comb, hair product, razor, shaving oil, tweezers, deodorant, lip balm, condoms, ibuprofen, a bottle of prescription pills—and held it upside down, shaking it as if a platinum band might slip from the lining.

When it was obvious there was nothing else in there, I dropped the bag and put my hands on my face. My cheeks were flaming hot. I peeked through my fingers at my reflection, and a deranged naked woman peered back at me.

That's it—I was losing my mind. This whole nightmare thing was making me *insane*. Dallas wasn't married. He just didn't want to lead me on. He liked being single. In a way, it would have been easier if a ring *had* been hidden in the bag. At least I would have had some concrete reason why he didn't want to see me again.

Angry with myself, because I'd known right from the start what tonight was—and what it *wasn't*—I began putting everything back in the bag. Out of curiosity, I glanced at the label on the prescription bottle. Depakote. I'd never heard of it before. The bottle was pretty much full. I tucked it back inside the bag and tried my best to make it look like nothing had been disturbed. But I felt terrible.

I went back into the room, where Dallas was stretched out on his back, hands behind his head, sheet pulled to his waist. He smiled at me, and I felt even worse.

"Come back to bed," he said.

Ignoring my guilty conscience, I crawled under the sheets, and he pulled me on top of him, my head on his chest.

For a couple minutes, we lay like that, the length of my body along his as he slowly ran his hands up and down my back and I listened to his heartbeat. Our breathing synced, and I felt peaceful inside.

"I was thinking," he said softly.

"'Bout what?"

"I don't have to be in Boston right away."

I opened my eyes. "No?"

"No. And I was also thinking about what you said earlier. Catching a Tigers game tomorrow, if they're playing at home."

I picked up my head and smiled. "That would be fun. I love Comerica Park."

"Let me grab my phone." He slipped out from beneath me and walked over to the door, where his jacket lay in a heap on the floor. "Probably I should hang this up."

I watched, admiring his naked form as he hung his jacket in the closet and shut the door. He came back over to the bed with his phone in his hand and sat down, frowning at the screen.

"No game tomorrow?" I asked.

"No. I mean, I don't know. I haven't looked yet. But I have a bunch of texts from my brother I'm going to ignore."

"Why?"

"Because he bothers me. Okay, let's see ..." He typed and scrolled. "Aha! Oh *hell* yes, this is perfect." Looking at me over his shoulder, he grinned. "Tigers vs. Boston Red Sox at Detroit."

I laughed. "But who will you root for?"

"You know what? I'm gonna get my niece and nephew a bunch of Tigers shit just to bug my brother. He *loves* the Sox."

"You're terrible."

"I know. I'll get tickets tomorrow." He set his phone on the nightstand and plugged it in before snapping off the light. "We should probably get some sleep. I just need to take my contacts out." He leaned down and kissed me, then headed into the bathroom, closing the door behind him.

I couldn't believe it—he wasn't going to leave tomorrow! That could mean he'd changed his mind about seeing me again, couldn't it? Or at least that he might be willing to consider giving us a chance? Otherwise, why bother? If tonight was really only about having some fun "for old time's sake," he could've simply dropped me off tomorrow morning and been on his way to Boston. Instead he wanted to stay.

I smiled in the dark.

This was only the beginning. A new beginning. A second chance for a first love.

There was hope for us.

EIGHT

DALLAS

I'd forgotten about the pills.

I stood in the bathroom and stared at my travel bag, which I could have sworn I'd zipped, but was now open, and the bottle of Depakote was plainly in sight.

My stomach went a little queasy at the thought of her seeing it, although it was highly unlikely she would have known what they were for. I took the bottle from my bag and read everything on the label, but there was nothing on it that indicated why someone might take the drug. Still.

Damn it, why had I listened to that neurologist? I didn't need those stupid pills. And damn Finn for guilting me into bringing them on this trip. I wasn't even convinced that those dizzy spells I sometimes got were seizures in the first place. I'd seen one doctor who said they were just "stress episodes."

And I'd only passed out the one time, a *month* ago, and only for like two seconds. I'd probably just been dehydrated. Or hungry. I hadn't even felt the tingling in my hand lately. Half of me was convinced the diagnosis was complete bullshit, and the surgery Finn wanted me to have was just him showing off how much smarter he was than me.

Yes, I'd seen the scans. Yes, I'd read the results. Yes, I'd listened to the opinions of multiple doctors and radiologists, all of whom fired at me with the same bullets.

A 1.2 cm mass. Left parietal lobe. The area that controls upper right side mobility. Probably been there for years. Not on the surface.

And I wasn't an idiot. I knew something was causing the dizziness. The constant headache. The vivid memories. The occasional numb feeling in my hand. The worsening eyesight. But none of those things seemed particularly alarming to me. When compared with the risks of the craniotomy, which included potentially losing motor control and sensation in my right hand (thus ending my days as a tattoo artist—as *any* kind of artist) and some speech or language function, not to mention the rounds of chemotherapy and radiation I might need afterward, well, fuck. A headache, a dizzy spell here and there, and some pleasantly intense memories seemed a small price to pay. And didn't everyone's eyesight get worse as they got older?

Bottom line, I didn't want to be some pitiful, drugged-up, shell of my former self, unable to work or draw or talk, and dependent on others to take care of me. I would never burden anyone that way. And I never wanted anyone to see me as weak. Frail. Vulnerable. Or feel sorry for me.

Especially Maren. No fucking way. I'd rather die than let her see me with a shaved head, staples holding my scalp together, listening to me struggle to speak. And it's not like I could tell her about it at this point, anyway. *Oh, hey, funny thing, I forgot to mention I have a brain tumor.*

I took out my contacts and put on my glasses, frowning at myself in the mirror. It was an asshole move and I knew it, but I had to keep it from her. Not only because she'd be mad, but because she'd pity me. More than anything, I didn't want anybody's pity—not hers, not Finn's, not my parents', not anybody's. I'd always lived my life the way I wanted to, and if this thing in my head was punishment for that, so be it. I'd deal with it my way, in my own good time, and I didn't need to give a shit what my family wanted. It's not as if they'd ever given a shit about what *I* wanted. And I refused to feel guilty about it.

But Maren … Maren was different. She'd never done anything but care for me. I'd come here to put things right, and I was going to end up hurting her again. She was going to hate me for it.

But loving her was the purest, deepest thing I'd ever felt, and I wanted—I needed—to hold on to that for a little bit longer. One more day.

She was already asleep, facing away from me, by the time I got back in bed. I set my glasses on the nightstand and nestled my naked body behind hers, one arm slung over her waist.

I wished I never had to let go.

I WOKE UP ABOUT TEN, and Maren was still asleep. My head was aching, so I went into the bathroom and took some ibuprofen. When I came out, she was awake and sitting up, looking adorably shy as she held the sheet up to her chest.

"Good morning, sunshine," I said.

Her smile lit me up. "Morning. I love that you're wearing glasses but not pants. You look cute in them."

"Thanks. How'd you sleep?" I sat on the edge of the bed.

"Like a baby."

"No more nightmares?"

She shook her head. "No."

"Good." I patted her leg through the sheets. "Are you hungry? "

"Yes. Will you let me take you out for breakfast?"

"No. But I will let you eat room service in my hotel room."

She sighed exasperatedly. "Are you ever going to let me treat you while you're here?"

"Probably not." I got up, pulled on some underwear, and looked around for the menu, spying it over on the desk. "What do you like? Pancakes? Eggs? Bacon? Do you want me to ask if the pig was—" All of a sudden, something about the way the sun was slanting through the window seemed to blind me. Bubbles of light came at me from all directions, and the room faded to white. I stumbled and grabbed the back of the chair.

"Dallas? Are you okay?"

I wasn't. My head hurt. My right hand was tingling and my right arm felt too long for my body. An intense wave of déjà vu washed over me. My stomach billowed up like I was cresting the top of a rollercoaster. I couldn't speak. My heartbeat echoed throughout the room. *Fuck me. Fuck. Me.*

"Dallas?" Maren was standing behind me. Her hand was on my back. "Dallas, what's wrong? Say something."

Suddenly, I realized I was fine again. Mortified and sweaty, but fine.

"Sorry. I'm okay." I looked at her. "I sometimes get … these headaches that affect my vision. I woke up with one."

Her expression was concerned. "Like migraines?"

"Sort of."

"Do they make you dizzy?"

"Sometimes. I think I got up too fast. The room sort of spun." I looked at my right hand, opened and closed my fist a few times.

"What's wrong with your hand?" she asked.

"Nothing. It's just numb. That happens sometimes, too."

"Come sit down. You're all flushed." She tried to lead me over to the bed, but I gently pulled my arm free.

"No, I'm okay. Really. I took something for it already, and some food will make me feel better."

She didn't look totally convinced, but she let me go. My stomach was upset, like it always was after an episode like that, but I pretended everything was fine. I looked over the breakfast menu and ordered some eggs and bacon for myself; fruit, yogurt, and granola for Maren; coffee for me, and tea for her.

"I guess I'll take a quick shower while we wait for the food," I said.

"Okay." She grinned. "I'll get dressed in case I have to answer the door."

I tried to smile back, but the muscles in my face felt strange. Disappearing into the bathroom, I shut the door and got in the shower.

Fuck! Why today of all days? Couldn't this thing in my head leave me alone for one goddamn weekend? Couldn't I feel like myself again for forty-eight fucking hours? I knew it could have been worse, and I was thankful I hadn't lost consciousness, but Jesus Christ. How embarrassing, to be standing there in my goddamn underwear, unable to move or speak.

What if it happened again? What if it happened while I was *driving*? What if Maren was in the car with me? Goddammit! I didn't want to, but after I got out of the shower and dried off, I took a Depakote just in case. I wasn't sure it would help, and it would mean I couldn't drink and I'd probably feel a little shitty today, but I didn't know what else to do.

Moody and frustrated, I came out of the bathroom and got dressed.

Maren was watching me. "You okay?"

"Yeah." I forced myself to smile at her. "Just my head."

Breakfast arrived, and we ate sitting on the bed. If she noticed I didn't eat much or talk much, she didn't mention it. When we were done, I purchased tickets online for the 6:10 p.m. baseball game, and we went down to valet to get the car so I could take Maren home to change.

"Hey," she said, slipping her hand in mine. "What's going on in there? You're so quiet."

"I'm fine."

"Is it the headache?"

"Yeah. The meds I take have a few unpleasant side effects."

She squeezed my hand as my car arrived. "Let me drive, okay?"

I wanted to argue. I wanted to put my fist through a brick wall. I wanted to be someone strong in her eyes, someone who could take care of her, not someone who needed to be driven around like a fucking child. This was exactly why I couldn't tell her the truth.

But my pride wasn't worth her life. I nodded, and when we walked out, I went around to the passenger side, feeling like I'd just taken a punch in the gut.

Maren was all smiles, though, excited about the game, chirping away about how long it had been since she'd taken days off, and how glad she was that she'd done it.

We arrived at her house about twenty minutes later. "I won't be long," she said. "Make yourself at home. Do you want anything to drink? Water or tea?"

"No, thanks, I'm good."

Maren disappeared into her bedroom and I sat on the couch, pulling my phone from my pocket. But instead of checking messages, I looked around at her living room. When I'd been here yesterday, I hadn't really gotten the chance to look at anything besides a few photographs. The room was totally her—feminine and bohemian and colorful. Her couch was a neutral color, but it was covered with pillows in every imaginable hue. In fact, it was clear she was a big fan of pillows. The only other furniture in the room were giant pillows lined up under the window across from the couch. She had a fireplace to the left, but instead of wood, it held candles. In front of the couch was a coffee table that looked sort of Moroccan, and on it sat lots of over-sized books on subjects that ranged from Buddhism to Russian ballet to the pin-up art of Alberto Vargas. It smelled good in here too—like the fancy candles Beatriz sometimes lit at the shop.

I skimmed through the Vargas book for a few minutes before deciding I'd better get the call to my mother out of the way. First, I glanced at my messages—one from Evan checking in, one from a client looking for an appointment, and three from Finn wondering how the drive was going, the last of which was pretty frantic. I hadn't told him I'd decided to fly and was stopping in Detroit. I'd text him back, but first I replied to Evan that all was well enough, to the client letting him know that I was unavailable for a while but to contact Beatriz at the shop. Then I took a breath and pulled up my mother's cell number. But before hitting call, I went outside and sat on the front porch, making sure the door was unlocked behind me. I didn't want to take the chance Maren would hear me.

"Hello?"

"Hi, Mom."

"Dallas?"

"Yes."

"My goodness, I don't remember the last time you actually called me. I usually have to chase you down for weeks to get you on the phone."

Did she have to scold me at the beginning of every conversation? It made me feel ten years old again. "Yeah, I know."

"Your brother said he's been trying to reach you too. Did you change your number or something?"

"No. Just been busy." Unable to sit still, I walked around the side of the house and began to pace up and down the driveway. I could hear the shower running through the open bathroom window.

"Doing what?"

"Working."

"Oh, really? Where?"

My headache intensified. "At the tattoo shop, Mom. Same place I've been for the past few years."

"Oh. When you said *working*, I thought you meant you'd gotten a real job. But what can you expect when you drop out of college?"

I pressed my lips together. In my mother's mind, tattoos were for "lowlifes and inmates" and "people who don't know any better," and *tattoo artist* was not a real profession because I didn't have to wear a suit and tie or even a uniform to work.

But those were not arguments I wanted to have again.

"Listen, Mom. I've got some news."

"What kind of news?"

This was the part I was dreading. I was pretty sure my mother had majored in overreacting at college (with a double minor in snobbery and playing the victim), and I could see her freaking out about this and then throwing a massive fit that I hadn't said anything to her yet, but my brother already knew. I had to tell her *something*, though.

"I'm going to Boston for a consultation with a neurosurgeon Finn knows."

Silence. "A consultation with a neurosurgeon? Why?"

"Because I've been having some headaches."

"What kind of headaches? Migraines?"

"Kind of, but medication hasn't helped. And I had some tests done, which indicated there might be something else wrong."

"Like what? Why do I feel like you're not giving me the whole story here, Dallas? Why do I feel like I'm the last to know what's really going on?"

"Look, I'll know more after I talk to the doctor in Boston, okay?"

"I don't like this. I don't like this at all. How could you just drop this on me right in the middle of a Saturday? I'm supposed to have lunch with a friend today, and now all I'll do is fret about this!"

I bit my tongue and took a deep breath. "My appointment is on Tuesday. I'll let you know how it goes."

"And how long has Finn known about this?"

"A couple weeks."

"And you're just telling *me* now?"

"Like I said, I've been busy, and I really don't want anyone to worry. Everything is going to be fine."

"Something about this isn't right, Dallas. I want to talk to Finn and find out what's really going on."

Because of course, Finn would know more about my own head than I would. But I didn't argue, because I wanted to end this conversation and call my brother before she did. "I'll talk to you soon, Mom."

She was still talking when I ended the call. I hit Finn's name in my recents, glad when he picked up right away.

"Dallas?"

"Yeah, it's me."

"How's the trip going? Are you okay?"

"I'm fine. I decided to fly, and I stopped in Detroit to see a friend. Listen, I talked to Mom."

"Did you tell her?"

"Sort of."

"What do you mean?"

"I mean I sort of told her the truth and sort of didn't. I told her about the headaches and the tests, and I told her that I was coming to Boston to meet with a surgeon you know."

"You didn't tell her about the tumor?"

"No."

"Shit, Dallas, now she's calling me."

"I figured that would happen. Don't tell her anything else."

"What am I supposed to say?"

"Say that it's my fucking business, not yours."

Finn exhaled loudly. "Have you given any more thought to treatment?"

"I haven't decided anything yet."

"I was thinking, if Dr. Acharya agrees to do the surgery,

you could stay with us a few weeks."

"I haven't decided on the surgery yet, Finn. And I don't want you to tell Mom about it because then she'll start pressuring me, too."

"Because she'll want to save your life, like I'm trying to do!" Finn exploded. "This doesn't have to be a death sentence, Dallas. I don't understand you at all."

"What is so hard to understand about wanting to control what happens to my fucking body?"

"Do you want to suffer, is that it? Are you still trying to prove how badass you are? Or do you think you deserve this somehow?"

"Fuck you, Finn," I said, louder than I should have. Some guy was doing yard work next door and glanced over his shoulder at me. But my brother's words were hitting a nerve.

"I'm serious, Dallas. I've been sitting here trying to wrap my brain around this for weeks now. Wondering if you're looking at this as one final 'fuck you' to everyone who cares about you and wants to help, or if beneath all that ink and attitude, you're just scared and don't want to show it."

"Fuck you, Finn!" I was yelling now, but I couldn't control myself. "You don't know anything about me or how I feel!"

"Because you don't talk to me. You treat me like it's my fault I get along with Mom and Dad and you don't. Like I've wronged you somehow by being good at things that mattered to them. You blame me for all the shit that went wrong for you growing up. Those were *your* choices, Dallas."

"You don't get it. Do you know what it was like constantly living in your shadow? You weren't even there and yet you *were*, being better than me at everything in every way. Better at school, better at music, better at impressing adults, better at making good choices. You had done everything so right that there was no room for mistakes. I didn't stand a chance and I knew it, so what was the point of trying? And maybe that's unfair to you, but that's how I felt then and it's a hard thing to get over."

"Don't you think you could be exaggerating things a little bit?"

"Exaggerating! Christ, Finn. Do you know how many times I was asked why I couldn't be more like you? Do you know what it feels like to be told again and again what a disappointment you are? Do you know how it feels to be told your best wasn't good enough?"

"No," he admitted. "Did they really say that to you?"

I laughed. "Are you kidding me? I remember in ninth grade, I worked my ass off and got a B on the math final. Dad said, 'B's are okay, if that's all you can do, but you need A's in math if you want to get into any decent college.'"

"Maybe he thought that would motivate you to try harder."

"Are you even listening to me? I just said I worked my ass off for that stupid fucking B. For *nothing*." I stopped pacing and lowered my voice—this was useless. "But forget it, Finn. I apologize, okay? I apologize that I blamed you for my shit. I apologize for not being a bigger person. I apologize that I'm not acting properly in my current situation. I have no doubt you'd be much better at having a brain tumor than I am. I never do anything right."

"Dallas, come on."

"I'm staying in Detroit another night or two. I'll be there in time for the appointment with the surgeon on Tuesday." I hung up on him before he could get another word in.

Continuing to pace back and forth next to the house, I

fought the urge to throw my phone on the cement and watch it shatter. I felt like destroying something, I was so fucking furious. Why did I let Finn get to me like that? It was so maddening that my family could still rile me up after all these years. I thought about what Evan had said, that I was laid-back about every other thing in life, but my family had the power to drive me insane. It was because they knew exactly how to push my buttons, and they dredged up shitty memories of being not good enough. Just talking to them reminded me I'd been loved less. That love itself was conditional. Was it any wonder I'd distanced myself from them?

I imagined Finn telling my mother the truth and them having a conversation about how fucked up I was. How stupid and selfish. How hard I was making this for *them*.

Do you want to suffer, is that it?

So what if I did? Was it his business, or anyone's? Maybe in some ways Finn was right, and I was looking at this as one last chance to say *fuck you*. To ignore their advice and refuse their help. To be who I was without apology and throw it in their faces. *This is me, this is my choice, deal with it.* God, it had to be driving Finn fucking crazy that I wasn't falling in line to do exactly what he said. But damn if I was going to let him be the hero in my story. I had the power to decide what to do, and I was going to keep it.

Suddenly I noticed that the water wasn't running in the bathroom anymore. *Shit.* I'd been loud. Had she heard me yelling? Had I said anything about the tumor? Or the surgery? What would I do if she asked me about it?

Why couldn't I do anything right?

I slumped back against the brick wall. One thing hadn't changed—she deserved way better than me. Someone who wasn't damaged. Someone who wasn't a liar. Someone worthy of her love. I wasn't even sure someone good enough for her existed, but it sure as fuck wasn't me.

My phone vibrated in my hand, and I looked at it. A message from Finn.

I'm sorry. I'm really sorry.

And then another.

Somehow when we talk, what I want to say comes out all wrong. Bree says I can be insensitive without even trying.

I'd always liked my brother's wife.

Anyway, I wanted you to know I will not betray your confidence with Mom. And when you get here, I'd really like it if we could sit down and talk. I promise to listen.

I frowned at the screen. Did he really want to talk—or listen? Or was this just a ploy to get me to take his medical advice?

Olympia and Lane can't wait for you to arrive. Oly says you can sleep in her room and you can even have the top bunk.

That brought a little smile. I was excited to see the kids, and sometimes it was the thought of them that made me think hard about treatment. It would be nice to see them grow up. But at what price?

Sighing, I pushed myself off the wall and headed for the front door. I wouldn't think about that now. Nor would I worry about mending my relationship with my brother.

Today, the only person I cared about was Maren.

NINE

MAREN

I was so happy, I was tempted to sing in the shower. The only thing that prevented me from doing it was the thought that Dallas might hear me. I am good at many things, but singing is not one of them. Growing up, my sisters always wondered how someone with a gift for dance could be so totally tone deaf.

But I did allow myself to hum "Take Me Out to the Ballgame" as I washed my hair. I knew I shouldn't get too carried away where Dallas was concerned—he was only staying one more day, and it wasn't as if he had mentioned any kind of commitment to seeing each other beyond that. But it was hard not to be hopeful.

The other thing that had me in such a good mood was the long stretch of nightmare-free sleep. It was still a little troubling (not to mention embarrassing) that I'd had the nightmare while sleeping next to Dallas, since I'd thought that forgiveness and making amends would soothe my subconscious, but maybe I had to give it more time. Let the message really sink in deep.

I *was* a bit concerned about what had happened in the

hotel room this morning—for a second there, I'd thought Dallas was going to pass out. He'd seemed to recover quickly afterward, but I'd been relieved when he agreed to let me drive to my house. It was obvious he hadn't liked it, and he'd been a bit silent and sullen during the ride, but he must have known it was the responsible decision. And his Man Ego would survive.

I turned off the water, squeezed out my hair, and grabbed my towel. I had just stepped out of the shower when I heard Dallas's voice coming through the screen. It sounded like he was angry. Yelling at someone. I frowned and moved closer to the window, wrapping my towel tightly around my chest.

"Fuck you, Finn!" He yelled. "You don't know anything about me or how I feel."

I covered my mouth with one hand. I couldn't see him, but his voice was coming from over to the right, as if he had walked into the backyard. A moment later, he went on angrily.

"Do you know what it was like constantly living in your shadow? You weren't even there and yet you were, being better than me at everything in every way. Better at school, better at music, better at impressing adults, better at making good choices. You had done everything so right that there was no room for mistakes. I didn't stand a chance, so what what the point of trying? And maybe that's unfair to you, that's how I felt then and it's a hard thing to get over."

Tears came to my eyes. Poor Dallas. No matter how much time had gone by, no matter what he looked like on the outside, somewhere inside him was the boy he'd been, the one who had never been good enough in his parents' eyes. He'd never talked about it much, but I had always suspected it hurt him more than he let on that they didn't appear to take pride in him. That his brother had clearly been the favorite. That he felt he would never measure up. Hearing him admit it now broke my heart.

"But forget it, Finn. I apologize, okay?" Then he lowered his voice, and a lawnmower came on next door, so it was too hard to hear what he said next. But he wandered past the window a few seconds later, and I heard him say, "I'm staying in Detroit another night or two. I'll be there in time for the appointment with the surgeon on Tuesday."

Quickly, I backed away from the screen so he wouldn't see me.

Surgeon? Goose bumps spread over my skin. Why did Dallas have to see a surgeon? Was it the headaches? And why in Boston? Was it a friend or colleague of his brother's?

I was even more worried now. But I couldn't ask him about it, because that would mean admitting I'd overheard him through the window. He clearly didn't want me to know about it or else he'd have mentioned it already.

After drying off, I hung up my towel and went into my bedroom to get dressed. While I tugged on denim shorts and slipped an embroidered blouse over my head, I wondered what had set off the argument between Dallas and his brother. I wished I could ask him about it, but if he knew that I'd heard him confess how he felt about growing up in Finn's shadow, he'd be devastated. He'd always been so proud. But on the other hand, I wanted him to know he could confide in me. Trust me with his feelings. It must be terrible to hold all that hurt inside. What could I do to help him?

I continued to think about it while I blow-dried my hair. When it was mostly dry, I put in a couple braids near the front and pinned them at the back, leaving the rest down. The only makeup I added was some mascara and lip balm, and rather than perfume, I rubbed a few drops of jasmine oil on my wrists and neck. It was while I was putting the cap back on the bottle that I had an idea about what I could do to help Dallas with both his physical and his emotional pain.

I found him in my living room, sitting on the couch wearing a broody expression. "Hey," I said, sitting down next to him.

When he saw me, his face relaxed. "Hey. You smell good." He reached for me, pulling me toward him so I was lying across his lap.

I looped arms around his head and laughed as he buried his face in my neck. "Thanks. Hey, I have an idea."

"Mmm. Me too." He pressed his lips to my throat and slid one hand up my rib cage, beneath my blouse. "I hope it's the same one."

I giggled. "It's not."

"Then I vote we do mine first." He covered one breast with his hand and nibbled my earlobe. "You'll like it, I promise. It starts by making you come with my tongue and moves on from there."

Between my legs, I felt a pleasant flutter, and nearly gave in to it. "That does sound nice, but first we're going to do something for you."

"What?"

"Clear your chakras."

"I like my idea better."

"I know you do, and I promise we will get there, but first I want to do this for you." I put my hand on his shoulders and pushed back gently, forcing him to look at me. "Please?"

"Why? I'm not having any nightmares, unless I'm in one right now and you're going to make me walk around with this hard-on all day."

"It's not just for nightmares. It's for other things too, and I think it could help you with your headaches." *And your family issues*, I wanted to add. "We have a class on it at the studio, and everyone always says they feel better afterward."

"I already know what will make me feel better."

"Come on, you'll like this. It involves massage." I slid my palms down his chest and spoke seductively. "I'll have my hands all over you. I'll even sit on your lap."

"That's only going to make me want my idea more. I can't promise I'll be able to control myself."

I smiled. "Just try. For me."

He sighed heavily. "I suppose I can't say no to you since I showed up out of the blue and basically kidnapped you for the weekend."

"That's right. You can't." I managed to sit up. "It's going to feel good, I promise."

He stayed where he was while I got everything ready—closing the curtains to block out the light, pouring some rosewood oil into my diffuser dish, lighting the flame beneath it. "What's a sound you like?" I asked him, scrolling through the choices on my Meditation Playlist.

"You screaming my name."

I ignored that. "Waves? Thunderstorm? Ocean breeze? Rainforest? Birds chirping? Babbling brook?"

Another heavy sigh. "Let's go with thunderstorm. They always make me think of you."

A shiver moved through me, and our eyes met in the dim light. "Same."

I selected the track, put it on repeat, and set my phone aside. Then I went over to him and held out my hand. "Phone, please. I can't have any interruptions."

He handed it over, and I made sure the ringer was off before setting it on the mantel. Then I straddled his legs, my knees on either side of his thighs. Since this was going to be a sort of cross between a spiritual and a sensual exercise, I was taking some huge liberties with the practice, but I didn't really care. The idea was to get him to relax, feel good, let go of negative energy, and build trust.

"Wow. This must be a very popular class at your studio." He put his hands on my ass. "I bet you have a lot of male students."

"This isn't what I do in the class, silly. This is something just for you. Are you ready?"

"Yeah. I might like this more than I thought."

I grinned as the sound of thunder rolled gently through the room, taking me back to another summer night, when I'd offered him everything and he'd given it right back to me. "Are you comfortable?"

"Yes. Except that my pants are really tight in the crotch."

I unbuttoned and unzipped his jeans. "Don't get too excited. I'm just loosening these up so I can reach all the places I need to. But I do want you to take your shirt off."

He grabbed his fitted navy T-shirt from the back, yanked it off, and tossed it aside. At the sight of his bare chest, my insides danced around and I was *very* tempted to abandon my idea for his, but I stayed focused.

"Close your eyes, and breathe deeply and slowly," I whispered. Reaching around to his lower back with my right hand, I slid my fingers down to the tip of his tailbone. "At the base of the spine is your root chakra. It houses your sense of safety and security. It relates to basic needs and physicality. I want you to imagine the color red as you think about the words I'm saying and repeat them in your head."

He nodded slightly.

"I am safe," I said softly. "I am grounded. I belong to this world. I have all that I need. I am where I need to be."

Next, I needed to place my left palm on his taut lower abs, beneath his belly button. Since his erection was taking up a fair amount of real estate in that area, I had to concentrate extra hard not to get distracted as I slipped my fingers between his stomach and his cock. He opened one eye and looked at me.

"Sorry," I whispered. "I have to touch you here. But I'll be good."

He sighed and closed his eye again.

"Your sacral chakra is related to emotional and mental acceptance. Creativity. Sexuality. Pleasure and desire."

"I like this one. You should take off your pants."

"Hush." I concentrated on sending energy from my right hand to my left, pausing to take a couple deep breaths. "I want you to imagine the color orange as you repeat these words in your head. I embrace life with passion. I am a beautiful, sensual and creative being. My senses are alive and connected."

After a moment, I moved my left hand up to his solar plexus. "The third chakra connects to your ego, will, power, and self-esteem. Imagine the color yellow as you think about these words. I am courageous and powerful. I accept myself. I make my own choices."

It took me another minute or so before I felt like the energy was flowing freely between my hands, and I wondered if Dallas was struggling with a choice of some kind.

Next, I moved my left hand to his sternum. "The first three chakras were physical. The last four are spiritual. The heart chakra is the center of love, compassion, and devotion. Imagine the color green as you say these words to yourself. I am kind to myself. I am able to let go of the past, to forgive myself and others. I allow love to fill me up and guide me in all my actions. I love without fear."

Dallas's heart beat strong and steady beneath my palm, and I let myself get a little lost in the rhythm of it. His skin was warm, his muscles firm. My breath began to come a little quicker, my pulse kicking up a little higher. I shifted on his lap, and he opened his eyes. The thunder echoed.

"Careful," he warned.

I moved my left hand up to his throat. "The throat chakra is the center of expression, communication, honesty and openness." The muscles in his throat were tight, and I felt him swallow. His jaw was clenched, too. "Relax," I whispered. "Close your eyes and imagine a beautiful vibrant blue. Say to yourself, I have a voice. I speak freely. I speak truth. I speak with love and compassion."

But even as I said the words, I wasn't thinking about speaking. I was staring at Dallas's mouth, anxious to feel it against mine. In fact, before I could stop myself, I'd moved my hand up to his jaw and began rubbing his lips with my thumb. I leaned closer, sliding my right hand farther down the back of his jeans.

"Is there an anal chakra or are you going off script?" he asked quietly. His cock twitched.

"I'm a little off script," I admitted.

He moved his hands to my butt again. "Then I'm going off, too."

"Close your eyes. I'm almost done." Before I completely lost control of the situation, I touched the fingertips of my left hand to the spot between his eyebrows. "This chakra is sometimes called the third eye. It relates to vision, intuition, and insight. It allows us to detach from subjective perception and see truth or symbolic meaning in a situation."

"Right now all I want is to detach you from your clothes."

That was all I wanted too, but I was determined to finish this. I placed my left hand on the top of his head. "The crown chakra symbolizes enlightenment, pure awareness. It brings us knowledge, wisdom, understanding, spiritual connection, and bliss."

"Will it bring you to sit on my face? Because that sounds like bliss to me."

My thigh muscles clenched around his. I had to close my eyes so I wouldn't see him and be distracted. "Dallas. Focus with me. Imagine the energy flowing up through all the points I touched."

"There is definitely something flowing up in me."

"Picture the color violet."

"I'd rather picture my dick in your mouth."

Oh, fuck. I opened my eyes and brought my hands to his shoulders. "You would?"

"Yeah. Does that make me an unenlightened brute?"

"Probably." I kissed him softly, traced his lips with my tongue. "But I'm going to give you what you want."

"You are?" His hands tightened on my ass.

"Uh huh." I slid backward off his lap until I was kneeling on the floor, then pulled his jeans down just enough.

"Oh, Jesus," he said as I took my blouse off and reached behind my back to unhook my bra. "You're so beautiful."

I laughed and ran my hands up his thighs. "You're just saying that because you want to see my mouth on your cock."

"No." He shook his head. "I mean that. It doesn't matter what you do or don't do, you will always be the most beautiful girl I've ever known."

My heart soared. "Really?"

"Yes." His hands fisted in my hair. "Now put your mouth on my cock."

I'D GIVEN Dallas a few awkward blowjobs when we were together, but I never knew what I was doing and I was always scared that he would come in my mouth and not tell me first. It wasn't that I didn't want to do that for him, it was just that the thought of it terrified me. Would I choke? Gag? Make a weird face? Getting something as big as his dick in my mouth was difficult enough, and sometimes when the tip of it hit the back of my throat, there was this terrifying moment when I thought I might suffocate. He never pressured me, and it usually only lasted a few minutes before he wanted to have sex, anyway, and we'd be scrambling to get the condom on fast enough.

This time was different.

I wanted it all—and I wanted him to watch me take it.

So this time when he said *Maren, stop*, I didn't. I pushed his hands away. I went at him faster. Sucked harder. Took him deeper. (I might have quit the stage, but I still knew how to put on a show.)

Dallas struggled to hold back. "Fuck. I'm so close. If you don't want me to come in your mouth—"

"That's exactly what I want," I said, rubbing the tip of his cock over my lips, "so shut the fuck up and give it to me."

"Oh, Christ." He groaned and grabbed my head again, holding me steady and fucking my mouth with zero restraint. I couldn't breathe. I couldn't move. I couldn't believe how much it turned me on to feel him lose control and know that he was watching every second of it. He cursed and moaned and growled and lasted only about twenty seconds before I felt a hot, pulsing stream at the back of my throat.

As soon as he loosened his grasp, I sat back and swallowed. Wiped my lips and chin. Caught my breath. But I only had about three seconds because Dallas launched himself off the couch and came at me like a linebacker, tipping me onto my back and rolling with me to the empty space on the carpet beyond the coffee table. Less than two minutes later, he'd dragged my shorts and underwear off my body and flipped us over again, so I was on top.

"You know what I want," he said. But before I could guess, he slid down beneath me so I ended up kneeling over his face, his arms locked around my thighs. Then he went at me with his unbelievably strong, seemingly tireless, and utterly magical tongue. When I came, I screamed so loud I thought my front windows would shatter, and even when my orgasm was over, he kept going.

"Stop," I begged, trying to lift my hips from where he had me imprisoned above him. "I can't take any more."

"Sorry." He loosened his grip and I wriggled down his body, stretching out on top of him. "But I can't ever get enough."

I laughed, still breathless, and laid my head on his chest. "You always say that."

"But I'm serious. With you, that's how I feel. I'm like an addict." He wrapped his arms around me. "It's a good thing we don't live in the same state. You'd never get a moment's peace."

"Oh, I don't know. I think I'd trade a little peace for more of this in my life."

He was quiet then, and I wondered if I'd said too much. I tried to think of a way to reassure him I wasn't asking for more than he could give, but I couldn't. I tried to think of a way to let him know he could talk to me about his family, but I couldn't. I tried to think of a way to tell him I was falling for him all over again without scaring him away, but I couldn't.

I went for safe instead. "How's your headache? Did the chakra cleanse help?"

"Undoubtedly." He kissed the top of my head. "I'm feeling much better. I also worked up an appetite, so what do you say we head downtown and grab something to eat before the game?"

"Sure. I just need to clean up a little."

We put ourselves back together and headed out to the car, and Dallas tossed me the keys without my having to ask. We parked in a garage downtown, and he held my hand as we walked around Grand Circus Park, finally ducking into Cliff Bell's for something to eat.

We sat at the bar, and Dallas looked around in amazement at the beautifully restored 1930s supper club. "This place is amazing," he said. "How come I never knew about it before?"

"It wasn't open when you lived here. And besides, this wasn't exactly our scene back then." I grinned at him. "Mostly we were looking for places to be alone."

"True." He leaned over and kissed my lips.

I took a breath and decided to be brave. "But next time you're in town, we should definitely come here for dinner and see some music. They have great bands in here. It's really fun."

He nodded, his eyes dropping to his hands on the bar for a moment. "I'd like that."

Victory! I nearly bounced in my seat.

The bartender came over, and I ordered a glass of wine

and a salad. Dallas ordered calamari, and when asked what he'd like to drink, he said, "Just water."

"No cocktail?" I asked, surprised.

He hesitated. "The headache meds I take don't really mix well with alcohol."

"Ah. But they help?"

"A little." His crooked grin appeared. "Not as much as the blowjob."

"Shhhhhh!" I put my hands over his mouth and glanced around to make sure no one heard.

He grabbed me by the wrists. "Hey. You should be proud of that."

"Not in public, thank you. But I'm glad you enjoyed it."

"I did. I don't even want to know why you're so good at it."

I rolled my eyes. "It's not because I've had a lot of practice or anything. I was just really into it."

"Ah."

I leaned closer to him and whispered. "Plus I sometimes watch porn."

He burst out laughing. "Yeah. Me too."

While we ate, we reminisced more about high school and what we knew about where our friends had ended up. I talked about my sisters a little bit, how Emme was driving both Stella and me bananas with all the wedding stuff, and how Emme and I did not understand Stella's strictly platonic relationship with Buzz. "I mean Walter," I said. "Emme and I just call him Buzz because he's obsessed with bees."

Dallas grinned. "That's *buzzarre*."

I laughed and asked him what his friends were like in Portland, and he said he had one pretty close friend named Evan who was married and expecting a baby with his wife.

"That's nice," I said.

"Yeah, it is. I'm happy for them."

I picked up my wine. "Do you want kids someday?"

He shrugged. "I don't think I'd make a very good dad."

"Why not?"

"I'm not...reliable enough. Responsible enough. Mature enough. I'm reckless. Careless. Shortsighted. I don't make good decisions." He looked at me with his water glass halfway to his mouth. "Should I go on?"

I wondered how many times he'd been told those things in his life. Enough to believe them, evidently. "That doesn't sound like you talking. That sounds like someone else. And I don't think it's true."

Another shrug before he looked into his glass like he wished something stronger than water was in it. "It's true enough."

I let it go, although it pained me to hear him talk about himself like that.

"So what will you do with your inheritance?" I asked. His grandfather seemed to be the one person in his family he enjoyed talking about.

"I'm not sure yet. I had a couple ideas at one time, but..."

"But what?"

He shrugged. "Finn talked me out of them. Said they weren't practical. He thinks I should just keep the money invested."

"Well, it's not Finn's money. Tell me about your ideas."

"I thought about opening up my own tattoo shop at one point. But I'm not much of a businessman."

"You could learn. I have faith." *Unlike your family.*

"Yeah, maybe. But I actually really like the shop I work

at now. I guess if I moved somewhere else, it might make sense."

"What was your other idea?"

He rubbed the back of his neck with one hand. "My friend Evan's family has a ranch, and I worked on it this one summer a few years ago and really enjoyed it. It's a working cattle ranch but it also hosts this program for what they called 'troubled youth,' but they were really just mixed up, angry teenagers who felt like they didn't belong anywhere."

"Wow. Did you work with the kids?"

"A little. They had teachers on site for academics, but sometimes I supervised a group of kids working on a ranch project, and a few times I held drawing workshops."

"I bet the kids loved that."

"Some of them did, I think. And I could kind of relate to them because of my background, although a lot of them had it way worse than I did. Some had been abused, some were depressed, some were recovering from addiction. Others were just really fucking mad at the world."

"Must have been tough to see."

"Actually, it was pretty cool to see how working on the ranch helped them. I mean, there was therapy there too, but it seemed like the actual physical work, especially with the animals, really made them feel good about themselves. I was only there for one summer, but I saw some pretty amazing transformations."

"I bet. Are you thinking of doing something like that again?"

He shrugged. "I was, kind of. Evan recently told me his parents are looking to retire, and he and his wife are thinking about buying them out and taking over. He wants to adopt more sustainable practices, but that costs money and he's looking for partners to invest."

"Would you live and work there? Or would you be more of a silent partner?"

"I hadn't really decided that yet. It's a beautiful place, and Evan said he'd even sell me some of the land for personal use. I could build on it if I wanted to."

"Where is it? Near Portland?"

"It's in Lakeview, Oregon. Closer to California, actually."

I nodded, thinking that both states were *very* far away from here and trying not to be sad about it. "What did Finn say about it?"

Dallas exhaled. "Not much beyond, 'A ranch? Are you crazy? You don't know anything about farming.' And he's not wrong, I don't know that much, and I only worked there the one summer. But I liked the work. Evan's wife is in finance and believes the land is a solid investment, and the ranch turns a profit every year."

"Would you miss being a tattoo artist?"

"I don't know. I might. But I think as long as I was still doing something creative, like drawing or painting with the kids, I'd be happy."

"I've heard that therapy is really effective."

"I'm not any kind of therapist," he said quickly. "It would be really informal. But if it did some good..." He lifted his shoulders. "I don't know. It's probably crazy."

"I don't think so at all." I set my glass down. "And don't let your brother talk you out of it if you really want to do it. Those kids need people like you. And the work is reward-ing. I get much more out of the yoga programs I do at schools and women's shelters than I do from teaching at the studio. Not financially, of course, because they're free, but spiritually." I touched my chest. "I feel like I'm doing some good, even if it's just yoga or meditation. Maybe that was someone's only sixty minutes of calm that day, you know? The only time they spent on their body and soul."

He smiled, then leaned over and kissed me. "Yeah. I know."

When we were done, we walked around some more, and finally made our way over to Comerica Park. Dallas held my hand again, and I stayed close to his side. I couldn't say it out loud because he'd have hated it, but I felt so bad for him. The way his family had treated him as a kid—and still treated him, apparently—was so unfair. They focused on all the things he wasn't without noticing all the things he *was*—smart, sensitive, charming, funny, talented, thoughtful, passionate, generous. The kind of person who stuck up for others. The kind of person who remembered your favorite song. The kind of person who knew when you were having a bad day and did his best to make you laugh.

He wasn't perfect. He was stubborn and impulsive and rebellious, he got moody sometimes, and there was obviously something going on with him he didn't want me to know about.

But his heart was huge, and being with him was so easy. It was almost as if we'd never been apart.

I felt myself falling.

TEN

DALLAS

After my phone call with Finn, I wasn't sure anything could put me in a good mood.

That was before I discovered the wonder of the chakra-clearing blowjob by Maren Devine.

Holy. Fuck.

I don't know if it was because she already had me all worked up, what with her sitting on my lap and one hand down the back of my pants and the other one doing all sorts of things to my front and the sound of her voice and the fact that she was devoting all her time and attention to me, or if it was simply the best blowjob I'd ever had—and it was—but I swear to God, I saw stars. Comets. Meteor showers. *Quasars*, and I'm not even sure what a quasar is.

She was just ... incredible. So fearless and unabashed, so eager to please me, so different than she'd been back then. Not that her shyness about it had bothered me back then— when you're seventeen, a blowjob's a blowjob—but there was something so erotic about watching her enjoy it so much today. I felt like she wasn't doing it only for me. (Probably this is something guys tell themselves so they can justify shoving their dick in someone's mouth, but I really did feel like it was turning her on too.)

But it wasn't only the blowjob. Every moment I spent with Maren felt good. I loved that I could still make her laugh. I loved that she wasn't asking me a bunch of questions I couldn't answer. I loved that she still kissed me like she was seventeen and no one was watching. I felt connected to her in a way I'd been unable to connect with any other woman I'd been with. Sex with other women had always left me feeling empty and unsatisfied. Sex with Maren made me feel alive.

The last thing I wanted to do was to say goodbye tomorrow. But I had no choice—this thing in my head wasn't going to magically disappear. I either had to treat it or let it do its worst, and neither of those were journeys I would let her take with me or even see me on.

One night was all we had. Maybe two.

"Do you want a souvenir?" I asked her in The D Shop at Comerica Park. "A shirt? A scarf? A beer mug? A pair of Detroit Tigers Multi-Logo Glitter Flip-Flops?" I held them up in front of her face.

She laughed. "No, thanks. But I'm happy to help you pick something out for your niece and nephew."

"Come on, you need a memento from this weekend. And I want to get you something." *As if anything in here is going to make up for disappearing from her life again.* Ignoring the voice in my head, I set the flip-flops down and picked up a women's navy blue hoodie. "How about this?"

She looked at me like I was nuts. "It's like ninety degrees out."

"Right *now*. But it's Michigan. It could be forty in a couple hours."

"True. But—"

"No buts. It's yours."

She tipped her head onto my shoulder. "Thanks."

For Olympia and Lane I picked out stuffed animals, T-shirts, and water bottles, and for myself I bought a hat. We found our seats and spent the next two hours rooting for the Tigers, booing the Red Sox, cursing the umps, and eating ballpark food—Maren refused to eat a hot dog but she did partake in popcorn, nachos, and even cotton candy. There were plenty of fancy options, but I told her it was sacrilegious to eat something called "Buffalo Cauliflower" at a baseball game, because for God's sake it was *vegan* and came with celery sticks. In addition, I told her anything served with pepper-olive salad, balsamic vinegar glaze, or on a brioche was also out.

When the game was over, we walked back to the parking garage. My head was aching again, but I wasn't ready to go home. The hours were passing too quickly.

"You know what I want?" I said to her as we got in the car.

She laughed. "I have a pretty good idea."

I reached over and tugged on her hair. "Not that. I mean, yes, that, but first I want a Boston Cooler. With real Vernor's."

"Mmmm, those are so good. I haven't had one in years."

"Me neither. Think we can find one?"

She pulled her phone from her purse and googled it. "Corktown. The Burger Bar."

"Let's go."

———

THE BURGER BAR was noisy and crowded, but we managed to find two seats at the bar after a ten-minute wait.

We put in our order, and our floats arrived a few minutes later. "Here you go," said the guy behind the bar as he set them in front of us. "Two Boston Coolers. Made with Vernor's ginger ale and Stroh's vanilla, as authentic Detroit as it gets."

"Thanks." I tasted it, and the flavors took me back years. "Fuck, that's good. I mean, it's not whiskey, but it's good."

Maren sipped hers through the straw. "Tastes like childhood, doesn't it? Delicious."

The guy who'd brought them smiled and nodded. "Glad you like them." Then he looked at Maren a little quizzically. "You look really familiar."

She seemed surprised. "I do?"

"Yeah." He crossed his tattooed arms over his chest. Right away I noticed he wore a wedding band, and he didn't *seem* like an asshole, so I wasn't too concerned I'd have to mess up his face. Still, I sat up taller and listened carefully.

"Do you come in here a lot?" he asked her.

"No," she said with a shrug. "I've only been here once with my sister. She knows the owner."

He grinned. "I'm the owner. Who's your sister?"

"Emme Devine."

"That's it! You look like her. I'm Nick Lupo, Coco's husband." He held out his hand, and she shook it.

"Oh, of course," she said. "I'm Maren, and this is my friend Dallas. He grew up here but lives in Portland now, so we were on a mission to find him a Boston Cooler."

Nick and I shook hands. "Glad you came in," he said.

"Congratulations on the new baby." Maren clapped her hands excitedly. "What's that, your fourth?"

Nick's grin grew even wider. "Yeah. But the first girl."

"You've got *four kids*?" I asked. Damn. He didn't look that much older than me. No wonder he had more gray hair.

"Yep." He looked proud of himself. "I'd have more too, but I'm pretty sure my wife would castrate me."

Maren laughed. "I saw pictures of the baby. She's adorable."

"Thanks." Nick smiled. "I'm totally that dad who shows off pictures to anyone who comes in here, but we're a little slammed so I should get back up front. I was just helping out for a few minutes behind the bar."

"Go on." Maren shooed him away with one hand. "Nice to meet you."

"You, too," he said over his shoulder as he walked away.

"I totally forgot Coco's husband owned this place," Maren said. "He seems like a nice guy."

He did seem like a nice guy. The kind of guy Maren should end up with—successful, friendly, responsible, proud husband and father. More like my brother than me, but with ink.

"They named the baby Frances," Maren gushed. "Isn't that cute?"

"Four kids. Jesus." I shook my head. "I thought one brother was bad. Imagine that poor girl with three."

Maren sipped her float. "Are you looking forward to seeing Finn this week?"

"Not really."

"Want to talk about it?"

"Nah." I shrugged. "Things have always been a little fucked up between Finn and me."

"Because you thought he was the favorite?" She poked around in her drink with the straw.

"Because I *knew* he was the favorite. It's not like it was ever a secret in my family that son number two was not quite living up to the standards set by son number one."

"But is it still that way? I mean, you guys aren't kids

anymore. And your parents have had years to accept the fact that you are not your brother."

I finished my drink, trying not to get worked up about Finn all over again. "Pretty sure I caused them enough disappointment to last a lifetime. And even now when they look at us, they see a clean-cut neurology professor at Harvard, happily married to a fourth-grade teacher and the proud father of two. Then they see me. College dropout. No wife, no kids, no house with a picket fence or a pool in the yard. A drifter with tattoos. A failure on their part to make me into someone better."

"You mean into someone like *them*. Or like Finn." She shook her head. "It's so wrong."

"But it's the way it is, and I'm used to it. It doesn't bother me anymore," I lied, setting my empty mug on the bar.

"Well, it bothers me." She sat up taller on the stool. "I can't imagine what it would feel like if my parents had tried to make me into one of my sisters. Or if they had told me I was a disappointment when I left ABT. Or if they looked down on me for my tattoos or my job or any of my choices. Parents should love their children unconditionally and teach them that it's okay to be who you are. No, that it's *imperative* to be who you are. Otherwise, you're going to spend your life miserable."

God, she was cute. "It's okay, Maren."

"It's not." She sighed and set her half-full mug down. "You should be proud of who you are, Dallas. I'm proud of you."

I frowned. "For what?"

She tossed a hand in the air. "For lots of things. For staying true to yourself. For becoming a tattoo artist. For coming here after all this time just to say you're sorry.

Plenty of guys wouldn't have bothered. I mean, you weren't even eighteen yet. Practically still a kid. What did you really owe me?"

I looked at her in disbelief. "Everything you said I did yesterday. An explanation. The chance to say goodbye. An apology for breaking my promise to stay out of trouble."

"I did say all that yesterday, didn't I?" Her posture deflated a little, then perked up again. "But you know what, I've had a chance to think a little more since then. And I understand better why you did what you did. You thought you were doing me a favor by setting me free."

I nodded. "But I never forgot you."

She blushed and dropped her eyes to her lap. "I never forgot you, either. In fact, I had this"—she squeezed her eyes shut and shook her head—"oh my God, this is really embarrassing, but I had this pillowcase made with your face on it."

My jaw dropped as I turned to face her. "What?"

The pink in her cheeks deepened to scarlet. "After you left, I had a pillowcase made with your face on it because I missed you so much. I used to hide it from my mother by keeping it under my mattress, but every night I would take it out and put it on my pillow. I did my own laundry by then, so she never saw it." She giggled, cringing a little. "My sisters found out, and they tease me about it to this day."

"Do you still have it?"

"No. Eventually, I was too angry to even sleep with your face. And I knew I had to get over you, so I threw it out before I went to New York."

"You threw out my face?" I pretended to be horrified.

"Well, I'm sorry!" She threw both hands in the air, then leaned forward placing them on my thighs. "I had no idea you were going to come back into my life. I would have saved it if I had known."

"Then I win." I signaled the bartender and pulled out my wallet.

Maren sat up straight again. "What do you mean?"

"I mean, I kept *your* face all this time." I opened my wallet, took out the sketch of her profile, and unfolded it. "See?"

SHE STARED at the picture as if transfixed. Her mouth fell open. Slowly, she reached for it, taking it in both her hands. The bartender came over, told us our drinks were on the house courtesy of the owner, and I thanked him, pulling some cash from my wallet to leave as a tip. When I looked at Maren again, she hadn't moved. Tears dripped from her lashes.

"Hey," I said, rubbing her back. "That wasn't supposed to make you sad. It was supposed to prove that I'm a better person than you are."

She laughed, but the tears continued to fall. "I'm sorry, it's just ... You've really carried this in your wallet all these years?"

"Yeah. I drew it the night before I found out I had to leave."

"I remember that night. You picked me up from ballet, and I was mad at you for getting in trouble again."

I nodded. "We sat in my car in your driveway and I remember looking at you and thinking how badly I wanted to draw you."

"So when did you do it?"

"When I got home. I was going to give it to you, but the next morning my parents told me they were shipping me out, and I forgot about the picture with all the chaos." I paused. "And by chaos, I mean frantic sexual acts in the church parking lot."

She sniffed, her lips tipping up. "Yeah, that night was intense. I remember thinking later how it made sense, since you knew you were going. And whenever I started to feel bad about myself and doubt that you'd ever loved me, I would remember that night and tell myself you wouldn't have seemed so tortured if you hadn't really cared."

I stared at her. "You thought maybe I didn't love you?"

Her shoulders rose, and she looked up at me with a helpless expression. "What was I supposed to think? You told me you loved me, but then you were gone without a word. I figured I hadn't meant that much to you."

For a second, I was dumbfounded. Then angry with myself. Then determined to make her understand what she meant to me, if it was the last thing I did.

I grabbed her arm and yanked her off the stool. "Come with me."

"Dallas, what the hell?" She stumbled along behind me, still holding on to the drawing, her feet scrambling to keep up with my long strides. I led her around the back of the brick building, toward where we'd parked, but was too impatient to wait until we reached the car. As soon as we were alone, I swung her around and took her face in my hands. Her skin was luminous in the dark.

"Listen to me," I said. "Not a day has gone by that I didn't think of you and regret what I'd done. Not one fucking day."

"Really?" Her voice was shaky.

"Yes. I walked away because I was young and stupid and ashamed, not because I didn't love you. I did." I hesitated, then thought, *fuck it.* "I still do."

Her eyes widened. "What?"

"I never stopped loving you, Maren. I never even tried."

She started to cry so I crushed my lips to hers and kissed her, deeply, desperately, my tongue sweeping into her mouth, her tears wetting my cheeks. Inside me, something was happening—I could feel my resolve weakening. I wanted this. I wanted it too much.

I broke the kiss, pressing my forehead against hers, my eyes closed tight. "Goddammit. I'm not supposed to be here. I was supposed to ask your forgiveness and let you go. This is all wrong."

"No, no." She shook her head between my palms. "I refuse to believe that. I never got over you, Dallas."

"You should. I'm no good for you."

"You say that because you spent too many years listening to people who were supposed to love you cut you down when they should have built you up." Her tone was fierce. "It's not true."

I pulled back and looked down at her. "You don't understand. I can't give you what you want."

"All I want is you. All I've *ever* wanted is you. And if what you say is true, if you still love me, then we belong together, Dallas. We deserve a second chance."

I felt myself being torn in two. How could I argue with her? How could I destroy this impossible dream she had for us, when I wanted it just as much?

"Let me love you, Dallas," she pleaded, her eyes glittering in the dark. "I know it's not easy for you. I know you don't think you deserve it. But you do. Let me."

God help me, I wanted her love. I wanted to believe what she was saying. I wanted to feel like the man she thought I was, even if it was only for tonight.

"Okay," I whispered.

She threw her arms around me, and I held her tight, lifting her off her feet.

"Take me home," she said softly in my ear. "I need to be close to you."

ELEVEN

DALLAS

We went back to her house, shedding our clothing as we kissed and stumbled from the front door to her room, where we fell into bed, skin to skin, limbs twined, mouths sealed. My need for her was like a living, grasping, starving thing inside me, powerful and wild and all-consuming. I let it take over, let it silence every other voice in my head. She was the only thing in my world, and there was nothing I wouldn't do to make her happy.

Including lie.

"Tell me," she begged breathlessly as I eased inside her. "Tell me we can find a way. Promise me."

"I promise," I said, my heart breaking open. "We can find a way."

Her eyes closed as her head dropped to one side, lips parted. I felt her hands pulling me closer, her heels tight on my thighs. She was warm and wet and soft and beautiful and mine again, mine tonight, mine forever ... I closed my eyes, rocking deeper into her body, feeling her tighten around me, like I belonged inside her, like I was part of her.

"Yes," she whispered, softly at first, but then repeated the word, *yes, yes, yes,* her voice growing louder and louder as we spiraled higher and tighter, and as we exploded together and fell to earth in beautiful fiery pieces, it was like the first time all over again. It was then and it was now and there was never a time when our bodies didn't crave this heat and our hearts didn't share this rhythm and our souls weren't always leading us right back to this place, this feeling, this moment.

I clung to it, as if it could save me from drowning.

"DONE." Maren hopped back in bed and slipped under the covers. She'd gotten up to go take her pill, but otherwise we hadn't left her bed for hours. I was surprised the thing was still standing. I wasn't sure *I'd* be able to stand if I tried getting out of it.

Not that I wanted to leave. On the contrary, all I wanted was to stay here with her for the rest of my life. Or take her back to Portland with me. Or move somewhere new and start over together. Just the two of us, like it should have been all along.

But I knew better, and the familiar ache in my head was a painful reminder that none of this could last. Some ibuprofen might have helped, but I didn't ask her for any. The pain served me right.

Maren stretched out next to me, her head propped on her hand. "Do you have a favorite?" she asked, sweeping her other hand over the ink on my shoulder.

I thought for a second. "The mermaid."

She smiled. "Yeah? Why?"

"Because it reminds me of you."

"So you *did* remember I liked mermaids, you liar." She poked me in the ribs. "You said you didn't last night."

"I think I was trying to be cool."

"I knew something was off about that—your memory was always incredible." She leaned away from me, looking for the tattoo in question. "I can't see it in the dark."

"It's here." I guided her hand to my side, and her fingertips played over my skin. "I got it for you." Another little truth I could offer.

She went still. "You did?"

"Yeah."

It was dark in her room, but I could imagine the pink in her cheeks. "When?"

"Maybe five years ago."

She was quiet for a moment. "Do you like your job?"

"Yes."

"I bet you're really good at it."

"I like to think so. I stay pretty busy." I pictured the shop, wishing I could take Maren there. "My boss is a woman named Beatriz. You'd like her. She believes in all that woo-woo stuff like you do."

She poked me again. "It's not woo-woo stuff. It's real."

"Okay, okay. It's real."

"What's the weirdest thing anyone has ever asked you to tattoo on their body?"

I put my hands behind my head. "I try not to judge people's ideas, but I do think it's fucking strange when they want animals tattooed on their stomach so their belly button looks like the asshole."

"You are kidding me. People ask for that?"

"Yeah. People want all kinds of crazy shit."

"Have you ever refused to do what someone wanted?"

"Sure. If I'm positive they'll regret it. But my only really hard and fast rule is that I won't tattoo names of boyfriends or girlfriends, or even spouses, on anyone."

"Why not?"

"Because in my experience, people always regret it. Feelings change. Couples break up. Marriages end in divorce. People end up hating each other. You think you're going to love one person forever, but history tells us it's not very likely. Tattooing someone's name on your body is like *asking* fate to fuck with you."

She laughed. "You think you can influence fate with your tattoos?"

"I have no idea, but last week this eighteen-year-old girl came in and wanted a tattoo of Tweety Bird with her boyfriend's name—which is Rocky—and the words 'You're my tweety pie' underneath it. I did not want that on my conscience."

"Yikes. Did you do it?"

"Hell no. I told her what I told you. Tattoos are forever. Love, not necessarily. Especially not at eighteen."

She sighed. "I suppose you're right. But I hope you're wrong." She lay down again, her head on my chest, and I wrapped my arms around her. We were silent for a few minutes, and I tried to commit every detail about holding her this way to memory. The scent of her hair. The softness of her skin. The sound of her breath. The memories would have to carry me through.

"Dallas?"

"Yeah?"

"I need to ask you about something."

"Okay."

She took a deep breath. "I overheard you on the phone with Finn. Outside my bathroom window."

My pulse began to pound. I swallowed with difficulty. "Yeah?"

She sat up again. "I'm sorry. I didn't mean to eavesdrop, but I heard you say something about an appointment with a surgeon, and I'm worried. Are you okay?"

I couldn't think. I couldn't move. I couldn't breathe. *Tell her*, said a voice in my head. *Tell her everything. Tell her now.*

"I know it's personal, and you probably don't want to—"

"It's for my dad," I heard myself say out of nowhere. "He was having some, uh, short-term memory problems, and his CAT scan revealed something abnormal. A small mass in the parietal lobe."

She gasped. "A brain tumor? Oh, no."

Oh, *fuck.*

But I kept going. "Finn got him an appointment with a neurosurgeon next week, but he can't be there. So he asked if I would go with my dad. My mom can get a little hysterical in those situations, and she's been very upset."

"Of course. That's so scary. I'm sorry, Dallas. You must be really worried."

Yeah, that a lightning bolt is going to strike me. "I am."

"So he needs surgery?"

"It's an option. But it's risky." And since I was already in this far, I waded deeper. "Apparently that's the part of the brain that controls upper right side mobility ... guess he doesn't want to lose his advantage on the golf course."

My joke fell flat.

"But what happens if he doesn't have surgery?" she pressed.

"They're not sure. Apparently it's acting benign right now. But eventually it would probably ... cause some seizures and other problems."

"So you need to convince him to have the surgery, then."

"That's what my brother wants. But my dad doesn't want to be forced into it. He doesn't like being told what to do. And he's not crazy about the idea of having chemo or radiation. He doesn't want anyone to have to take care of him. He doesn't want anyone's pity."

She made a frustrated noise. "God, men can be so stubborn sometimes."

"Yeah."

"Think you can talk him into it?"

"We'll see. It's, you know, complicated. Because of my relationship with my family."

"Sure. I can understand that." She rubbed a hand over my chest as if to comfort me. "Do you want to talk about it?"

"Not really." What I wanted to do was shut the fuck up. I'd just made things a thousand times worse for myself.

"Okay. Well, I'm here for you. And I'm a good listener."

God, she was so fucking sweet. "Thanks."

"I was really scared it was about your headaches. I mean, I'm sorry about your dad and I hope he'll have the surgery, but I'm glad to hear it's not you."

"Thanks." Was there a place in hell low enough for me?

Smiling, she put her head back down on my chest and held me close. "Night."

"Night."

She fell asleep pretty quickly and rolled away from me, but I lay awake for hours with a pounding head, a churning stomach, and a tightness in my chest. I was scum. Lying, despicable scum. Every shitty thing that happened to me from now until the day I died, I would deserve.

I closed my eyes in agony. How was I going to face her

tomorrow? How was I going to face myself? Was there any way out of this?

Tell her the truth, my conscience pricked. *Tell her the truth or give her up.*

I was trying to decide which one would be best for Maren when she began to murmur in her sleep. A moment later, she started fidgeting restlessly beneath the blankets. I reached over and put a hand on her shoulder. "Maren?"

She stopped moving and quieted down. But soon it began again, and within seconds she was writhing and weeping helplessly like she had been last night. I tried my best to wake her, but she resisted. Then she suddenly sat up, gasping for air.

"Shh," I said, putting my arm around her. "It's okay. You're okay."

She put a hand on her chest. "Oh my God."

"The nightmare again?"

She nodded, a sob escaping.

"Breathe." I rubbed her upper arms. "You're okay, baby. I'm here."

She took some deep breaths. "Thanks. I'm just so tired of this."

"I know."

"Why do you think it's not going away?"

Because I'm the snake that's going to bite you and your mind knows it? "I'm not sure. The mind is a mysterious place."

"Yeah." We stayed like that for another minute or two, and then she yawned.

"Think you can fall back asleep?" I asked.

"I think so."

We lay down again and I held her close. Soon her breathing was deep and even, and I thought she'd fallen asleep until she spoke, drowsily, like she was half in a dream.

"Dallas?"

"Yes?"

"I wish you didn't have to go."

I swallowed hard. My head was killing me. "Me too."

TWELVE

MAREN

I woke up the next morning to the sound of rain beating on the windows. The clock on my nightstand said 9:05 a.m., and for a second, I panicked that I'd overslept and missed teaching my Sunday eight a.m. class. And why was I naked?

Then I remembered I'd taken the weekend off. And the lack of pajamas—as well as the soreness in my muscles—was due to the man sleeping next to me. I rolled over and looked at him, unable to keep a smile off my face.

We could get it right this time, couldn't we? It might not be easy, and it might take a lot of travel or even a move eventually, but we were too good together to be apart. Whatever it took, we could make it work.

Dropping a quick kiss on his chest, I left him sleeping in my bed, slipped into a short white robe, and tiptoed out to the living room. Along the way I saw random pieces of clothing that we'd stripped off each other last night on our way to my room. His jeans, my shorts, my bra, his T-shirt, my blouse, our shoes. Finally, I spotted my purse on the floor near the front door. I pulled my phone out of it to check my messages and saw that I had one from Allegra saying all was well at the studio and she hoped I was resting peacefully, and a ton from my sisters.

I was supposed to be meeting them for brunch at eleven, like we did every Sunday. Part of me wanted to cancel on them since I had a gorgeous, sexy man who adored me in my bed and it was pouring rain, but long ago my sisters and I had made a pact that we wouldn't skip out on each other unless it was absolutely necessary. Plus, I was dying to tell them about my weekend.

How insane that my life had taken such a sharp turn in only two days!

I quickly scrolled through the messages, which were mostly them going back and forth about where we should eat and both of them wondering why I wasn't answering my texts.

Me: Sorry guys, I've been busy.

Stella: Everything okay? We were getting worried.

Me: Yes. I'll tell you all about it at brunch. What did you guys decide on?

Stella: Lady of the House and we have a reservation at 11.

Me: See you there.

I went back into my bedroom and plugged my phone in to charge. As soon as I climbed onto the bed, Dallas opened his eyes. "Morning," I said, sitting on my heels beside him.

"Morning."

"Did you sleep okay?"

His brow furrowed. "My head was bothering me for a while. I don't think I slept much."

"It probably didn't help that I woke up screaming. Sorry about that."

He reached out and put a hand on one knee. "It wasn't that. Did you sleep okay afterward?"

I nodded. "I did. Fell back asleep really easily and slept all the way through until about ten minutes ago."

"Good." His eyes closed again.

"So I have a question to ask you, and you can say no, but I hope you say yes."

"What's up?"

"Every Sunday I have brunch with my sisters at eleven. I won't drag you along, but do you want to wait here for me?"

He opened his eyes. "What time is it?"

"It's only nine fifteen. I'd much rather hang out with you, but I sort of *have* to go to brunch or else they'll harass me."

"Of course." He sat up, but he seemed a little groggy still. "I'll get out of your way."

"No, no. You stay here and sleep. I'll even bring you something back."

"No. That's okay." He looked around and scratched his head. "Where are my pants?"

I giggled. "I think I saw them in the hallway."

"Oh. Right." He swung his legs over the side of the bed and paused.

"Are you dizzy again?"

"I'm fine." But he took another moment before he stood up, and then he moved slowly toward the door.

Watching him, a warning bell pealed in my head. Something was not right. "Can I get you some ibuprofen?"

"Sure." He began pulling on his underwear and jeans with lethargic movements. "Thanks."

I went into the bathroom and took the bottle from a drawer. "How many?" I called out.

"Four."

I shook out four pills and went back into the bedroom, where he sat on the bed wearing only his jeans. "Here," I said, holding out my hand. I was growing more concerned by the minute. "I'll get you some water."

He took the pills from me and I hurried to the kitchen, grabbed a bottle of water from the fridge, brought it back, and watched warily as he swallowed the pills. His color didn't look good.

"Maybe I shouldn't go to brunch today," I said, chewing on a thumbnail. "You don't look like you feel right. I don't think you should drive."

"I'm fine," he said, standing up. "I'm just tired. I can drive."

"Are you sure?"

"Yeah." But he still seemed to be moving sluggishly as he got dressed.

"I'm worried about you," I told him as I followed him to the living room.

"Don't be." He sat down on the couch to tug on his boots. "I'm gonna go back to the hotel and take a nap. Then I need to book my ticket to Boston."

My heart plummeted. "When will you leave?"

"Not sure yet."

"Can I convince you to leave tomorrow? Spend one more night with me?"

He stood up and smiled at me, but it struck me as a sad kind of smile. "Very tempting."

I went to him and slipped my arms around his solid middle. Pressed my cheek to his chest. "We can stay in. I'll cook dinner. We'll just be lazy and hang out, you and me. How does that sound?"

"Like heaven."

I tilted my head back. "Then say yes. Maybe I'll even clear your chakras again."

He shook his head. "You're too good to me."

"Well, I was without you all those years. I'm trying to make up for lost time."

He exhaled and put his arms around me, pulling me close. "Okay. One more night."

I bounced on my toes. "Yay! Thank you."

A moment later, I walked him to the door and pulled it open. Torrential rain poured from an angry pewter sky. "Yikes. Want an umbrella?"

"Nah. I'm okay. See you tonight."

I smiled as he kissed my cheek. "I'll make something nice and healthy and delicious. I bet your diet is part of your problem with your headaches. So much of how we feel is related to what we put in our bodies. You probably don't even realize all the chemicals and additives and preservatives that lurk in everyday foods."

"Probably not."

"I'll text you as soon as I'm home." I realized something. "You know what? I don't have your number."

He pulled out his phone. "What's yours?"

I gave it to him, and he put me in his contacts.

"There. I just called you."

"Thanks. See you later."

He dropped another quick kiss on my lips and took off into the rain.

After he'd gone, I jumped in the shower, grinning like crazy as I imagined the stunned expressions on my sisters' faces when I told them about my weekend. Usually it was Emme who had the dramatic stories about her love life, although since she'd been with Nate, mostly she just rhapsodized about how happy she was.

Today it was my turn.

"WHAT'S WITH YOU?" Emme asked as soon as I dropped into the chair across from her. She and Stella were seated next to each other on the emerald green banquette.

"What do you mean?" I smiled up at the server who poured me some water.

"You look different." Emme eyed me curiously.

"I do?"

"Yes. Doesn't she, Stella?"

Our older sister studied me. "More rested, that's for sure. Are you sleeping better?"

"A little."

"It's more than that," Emme insisted. "I know that look." She leaned closer to me. "You had sex."

I laughed and picked up my water. "Good guess."

My sisters gasped.

"I knew it!" Emme clapped her hands. "With who?"

"You're not going to believe it."

"Tell us anyway," Stella said, wide-eyed.

"Dallas Shepherd."

Two jaws dropped simultaneously.

"Dallas I'm-totally-over-him Shepherd?" Emme blinked at me.

"Dallas   don't-be-ridiculous-that-was-twelve-years-ago Shepherd?" added Stella.

I grinned ruefully. "That's the one."

"Oh my God, Maren." Emme shook her head. "How did this happen?"

"It was the craziest thing," I said. "He showed up on my doorstep out of the blue on Friday afternoon."

Emme gasped again and held up her arm. "I just got goose bumps. Look."

"And said what?" Stella prompted.

"That he wanted to apologize."

"After all that time? Why now?" Her therapist face appeared.

"I don't really know exactly why now." I lifted my shoulders. "I'm a little fuzzy on that, too. I asked him, and he just said he felt like it was time."

"Huh." Stella picked up her coffee and sipped. "Okay, go on."

"He spent a few minutes saying he was sorry and explaining why he left like he did, and—"

Emme held up her hands. "Wait, what was the reason?"

"He was young. Immature. Didn't know how to say goodbye and didn't want to."

"Why not?"

"He said he didn't want to spend our last night being sad. He'd only found out that morning he was being sent away. And he was ashamed."

"Still," Emme said. "Totally shitty. And why not return your messages?"

"He said he'd convinced himself I was better off without him. He thought he was doing me a favor."

Emme huffed. "He should have said that to your face."

"I'm not sure that would have been any easier on me," I told her.

The server came back and asked if we were ready, and I quickly glanced at the menu while my sisters ordered. When she got to me, I asked for the bruléed grapefruit and some tea.

"Okay, go on," Stella said impatiently once we were alone again. "So he thought he was doing you a favor ..."

"Which still sounds like a bullshit excuse to me," said Emme.

"Not to me." Stella touched her chest. "Not if he felt really bad about himself for being sent away."

"He did. And it goes deeper than that." I explained what I knew about the way Dallas had grown up in the shadow of his older brother. "I think he really internalized that. It explains so much about his personality and his choices."

Stella nodded. "Definitely. If it was really that bad, no kid would come out the other side feeling good about himself. I see it a lot in my clients. They think they have nothing to offer, or that no matter what they do, it'll never be good enough for their parents or anyone else."

"Exactly." I nodded. "But anyway, he really didn't try to make excuses, just said how sorry he was, how much he regretted what he'd done, and asked my forgiveness."

"And?" Emme urged.

"And I gave it. Well, first I gave him some shit, told him how I'd felt being dumped that way. But then ..." I shrugged. "It just seemed wrong to hold on to that hurt any longer. I wanted to forgive him. It felt right."

"God, you're too easy," Emme said. "I'd have stood there on that porch yelling at him for days."

I laughed. "Probably. But that's not my thing."

"So how did you get from there to *there*?" Emme leaned forward eagerly.

"That happened later. After the prom."

My sisters exchanged a look. "The prom?"

"Yes." My tea arrived, and I took a sip before telling them about the elaborate date Dallas had arranged because he'd felt bad when I said I'd missed the prom.

Stella sighed. "That is so romantic and sweet."

"It really is," agreed Emme. "I'm totally impressed, and I'd have forgiven him after that for sure."

"I was impressed too, and totally swept off my feet. I was having such a good time, the most fun I've had on a date in years. And at some point during the evening I realized that I still had feelings for him. He asked me if I wanted to go back to his hotel room, and I said yes."

"So how was it?" Emme wiggled her eyebrows.

"Unbelievable. Amazing. *Mind-blowing*."

Emme squealed and clapped her hands.

"And I can confirm Emme's discovery about *two*," I said to Stella. "It's definitely possible."

Stella closed her eyes and sighed. "This is me being jealous."

Emme poked her shoulder. "You need to spice things up with Buzz. He's a smart guy, I bet he's good in the sack. He went to medical school, so he should know where all the parts are, at least."

Stella's expression was dubious. "It's just not like that with us."

"But it could be," I said.

"And frankly, it should be." Emme nodded definitively. "You should seduce him or something. Do you own a sexy bee costume? If not, I think I know where you can get one."

I tried not to laugh because Stella really did look a little upset, but it was hard. Reaching across the table, I patted her hand. "Don't worry about it, Stell. If you don't want to sleep with Walter, don't do it."

She sighed and picked up her coffee again. "Let's talk about you some more. Where did you leave it with Dallas?"

"That's a good question. I'm not exactly sure where we are, but"—I took a breath—"last night he told me he still loves me."

"What?" Emme squawked. "Are you serious?"

"After one date?" Stella blinked at me.

"Yes," I said, laughing a little. "I know, it sounds crazy, but I swear within twenty-four hours, that's how I felt too. It was like our hearts had muscle memory or something. Or a past life thing. It felt so natural being together."

They probably would have given me grief over the past lives comment if our food hadn't arrived right then.

"Okay, keep going," Emme prompted once the server had gone. "What does he do? Where does he live?"

"He's a tattoo artist in Portland," I said.

Emme paused with her fork halfway to her mouth. "God, that's so you. Is he still in town?"

"Yes, but he's heading to Boston to visit his brother's family tomorrow."

"What was he doing in Detroit?" Stella asked.

I took a bite and thought for a second. "I don't really know why he came to Detroit, other than to see me. He's spent all his time with me so far."

"Wow. It must have really been important to him to see you," she said, her eyebrows raised. I could see her therapist wheels turning.

"Is he dying or something?" teased Emme. "Maybe you were on his bucket list."

I put a hand over my heart. "Don't even joke about that. He's got these horrible headaches that make him dizzy and I heard him say something on the phone to his brother about being in Boston in time for an appointment with a surgeon. I freaked out."

"Did you ask him about it?" Emme poured more syrup on her crepes.

"Yes. He said it's for his dad."

"Do you believe him?"

The question struck me as odd. "Why wouldn't I?"

Emme shrugged. "I don't know. I was just connecting dots."

"He gets headaches that make him dizzy?" Stella looked concerned.

I nodded, setting my fork down and picking up my tea. My stomach felt a little weird. "Yeah. Then he had this ... episode yesterday morning at the hotel."

"What kind of episode?"

"He stumbled and bumped into a chair. Stood there like a statue for maybe ten full seconds, not saying anything, not moving. Then his hand went numb or something."

Stella cocked her head. "That doesn't sound good."

"He thought maybe it was a side effect of the medicine he takes for the headaches. It's a drug called Depakote. Do you know of it?"

Stella thought for a second. "It's vaguely familiar, but I couldn't tell you everything it's prescribed for. Meds get approved for new uses all the time."

Emme pulled her phone from her purse. "Let's look it up."

Part of me wanted to tell Emme not to. It felt like I was invading Dallas's privacy again. What reason did I have to doubt his word? But when Emme asked how to spell the drug, I heard myself reciting the letters.

"Found it. It's an anticonvulsant," she said, wrinkling her nose. "What's that?"

"Anti-seizure medication." Stella looked at me. "Is it possible he has epilepsy? Maybe what you saw yesterday morning was a focal aware seizure. Sounds kind of like one."

"Aren't seizures where you can't control your limbs?" Emme asked. "Like your entire body jerks around? Maren said he didn't move at all."

"There are different kinds," Stella clarified.

My heart was beating frantically in my chest, and I grabbed Emme's phone out of her hand. "Let me see this."

"It can treat seizures and bipolar disorder," I read, but my stomach didn't unclench until I read the next sentence. "It can also help prevent migraine headaches."

"Well, then that makes sense," Emme said.

"Can migraines make you dizzy?" I asked.

"Definitely," Stella answered.

I felt better. Not that it would have mattered to me if he *did* have epilepsy, but I didn't want to believe he'd hide that from me. "Anyway, the whole weekend has been wonderful. I'm crazy about him."

"So what happens after he leaves? Are you going to see each other again?" Emme asked.

"God, I hope so. I've never felt this way about anyone."

"Wow. Maybe I'll be planning your wedding next." She nudged me under the table.

I laughed. "We're not racing to the altar any time soon. We're just happy to have a second chance."

"Portland is far away," Stella pointed out. "Are you going to do the long distance thing or will one of you move?"

"We haven't really talked about that yet," I confessed. "It's all pretty new, but"—I put my hand on my chest again—"I feel this, you guys. In my bones. This is the real thing."

Both of them smiled.

"I'm happy for you," Emme said. "Maybe now your nightmares will stop."

"I hope so." I didn't mention that I'd had it both nights Dallas had been with me.

"I wish I could meet him," Stella said.

"Same," Emme added. "When does he leave? Is there time?"

"Tomorrow, I think. Would you guys be able to meet us for dinner tonight?" I felt a little guilty floating the invitation since I'd offered to spend the night in with Dallas, but I really wanted to show him off to my sisters.

"Nate and I can," Emme said. "He'll be back from taking Paisley home by three."

"I could check with Walter." Stella pulled out her phone and began typing a message. "What are you thinking for time?"

"Seven?" I shrugged.

She finished typing and set her phone next to her coffee cup. "He's usually pretty quick to get back to me."

"Hey, I'm going up to Abelard next week to book some wedding stuff. Either of you guys want to go?" Emme looked back and forth between Stella and me.

"During the week?" Stella asked.

"That's the plan. Probably Wednesday to Friday. I've got events over the weekend."

"I took this weekend off, so I don't know about taking days off next week too," I said hesitantly. "But it would be fun. I'll try."

Stella's phone pinged and she picked it up. "Dinner at seven works for us."

I smiled. "Great. Let me run it by Dallas and then I'll text you guys a time and place."

We finished brunch, opened up our umbrellas on the sidewalk, and ran through the rain in opposite directions for our cars. As soon as I was in mine, I pulled out my phone and called Dallas. He didn't answer, so I left him a message.

"Hey. I know I said we'd stay in tonight, but I just saw my sisters and they're dying to meet you. Do you hate the idea of having dinner with them and their boyfriends tonight? Nate and Walter are both really nice, and I think it would be fun. Let me know, okay? Hope you're feeling better." I hung up and dropped my phone into my purse.

On the drive home, I couldn't help thinking about what Stella had said—that what had happened to Dallas yesterday morning had sounded like some kind of seizure. Could she be right? His claim that it was just a dizzy spell had made sense to me at the time, but the more I thought about it, the more worried I became that it wasn't so easily explained. When you're dizzy, you close your eyes, right? His had remained open. And even when you're dizzy, you can talk. Dallas hadn't responded the first few times I'd said his name. Almost as if he hadn't heard me.

It wasn't like me to panic over something like this, but when I got home, I texted Stella.

Me: Hey what kind of seizure did you say that sounded like?
Stella: A focal aware seizure.

I grabbed my laptop and googled it. The first site that came up was related to epilepsy awareness. I read the entire section on focal seizures, and I still wasn't sure if that's what had happened to Dallas. He'd seemed to have some of the symptoms described but not others. And wouldn't Dallas have been diagnosed with epilepsy as a kid?

I researched it a little more, learning that epilepsy could start at any age, and although there was no cure, the seizures could usually be managed with drug therapy, surgery, or changes in diet. Occasionally the condition just went away on its own.

Biting my lip, I set my laptop aside and wondered if that's what was going on with Dallas and he was too proud or embarrassed to tell me. Knowing him, it seemed likely, and I wished more than anything he would open up to me. I didn't want to have such a giant secret between us, mucking up our new beginning. But what could I do?

If I were Emme, I'd probably run right to him and demand to know the truth. But I'd always been more patient and even-tempered than my hot-headed sister. If I were Stella, I'd probably find a way to bring it up in conversation that would naturally lead to an admission. But Stella had training and a way with words that I didn't. She knew how to get people to talk. I was too nervous about saying the wrong thing.

I got up from the couch and checked my phone—no reply yet from Dallas. Disappointed, I decided to spend the next hour meditating.

After changing into more comfortable clothing, I lit some candles, put my phone on Do Not Disturb, chose the sound of ocean waves on my Meditation Playlist, and sat on the rug. I was briefly consumed by the memory of kneeling over Dallas's face yesterday in this very same spot, but I accepted the thought and its accompanying feelings of desire without judging them. Then I closed my eyes and focused on my breath and body awareness.

Sixty minutes later, I felt relaxed, refreshed and rebalanced. I didn't need to panic. I didn't need to confront anyone. Everything happened for a reason, and if there was something Dallas wanted me to know, he would tell me in his own time. Loving someone meant opening your heart to them; it didn't mean forcing them to fill it at the soonest opportunity. Love needed room to breathe, room to grow. I didn't have to behave like either one of my sisters would in this situation. I only had to be me, and trust my instincts.

I checked my messages, and found that I had a text from Dallas.

Dallas: Dinner at 7 is fine. I will be at your house by 6:30.

I was a little disappointed he wasn't coming over earlier, since six thirty wouldn't give us any time together before dinner, but I decided not to ask him. We had the entire night ahead of us, and I didn't want to appear needy.

Me: Great! See you then.

I added a little kissy-face emoji and hit send. Next, I messaged my sisters that dinner was on, and we went back and forth about where to go before deciding on Republic Tavern. I called the restaurant and made a reservation.

After that, I texted Dallas back that since dinner would be downtown, there was no sense in his driving to my house to get me, which was just north of the city. Instead, I told him I'd grab an Uber down to his hotel around five or so, and maybe we could have a drink at the bar if he was feeling up to it.

He didn't answer right away, so I got in the shower. When I was out, I checked my phone and saw his reply.

Dallas: Sorry. I was on the phone with Finn. Are you sure you don't want me to pick you up?

Me: Positive. I'll be there in about an hour. Maybe less.

Dallas: Good. I missed you today.

Relieved, I smiled and texted back.

Me: I missed you too. Can't wait to see you!

I blow-dried my hair and got dressed, choosing a white maxi dress with a deep V-neck and lace panels in its flowing skirt. I applied a little makeup, rubbed some lavender oil into my skin, and pulled on the strappy sandals I'd worn to the prom the other night. When I was ready, I ordered a car and went out on the porch to wait. The rain had stopped, and the sun was finally peeking out from behind the clouds. The temperature was warm, and the light breeze carried on it the scent of mint from my neighbor's herb garden. I turned my face to the sun and inhaled deeply.

It was going to be a beautiful night.

THIRTEEN

DALLAS

After leaving Maren's house Sunday morning, I drove back to my hotel and crashed for five straight hours. I was exhausted. My head hurt. My eyes burned because I'd slept in my contacts. My gut was twisted into knots I knew I couldn't unravel. Barricaded in my room, shades drawn, Do Not Disturb sign on the door, phone off, I pulled the covers over my head and shut out the world.

Except, of course, the world wasn't the problem. *I* was the problem. More specifically, what I'd done was the problem. Looking back, I could see the series of missteps I'd taken, and all of them indicated how weak and reckless and stupid I was.

I'd gone to see Maren and dug up the past when I should have left it buried.

I'd insisted she go on a date with me, swearing not to touch her and knowing full well I wouldn't be able to resist.

I'd slept with her, telling myself it was only for one night.

I'd stayed in Detroit just to be with her when I should have gone to Boston.

I'd told her how I felt and promised her a second chance.

I'd hid the truth from her and then flat out lied when she asked me about the surgeon appointment.

I'd let both of us fall in deep, knowing we would both get hurt.

And now what? Was I supposed to go have dinner with her and her family, spend the evening making polite conversation and pretending nothing was wrong? Spend the night in her bed again, holding her and kissing her and fucking her and making promises and plans I knew I wasn't going to keep?

Miserable and full of contempt for myself, I got out my laptop and did what I'd already done a thousand times in the last few months—researched brain tumors and treatment.

It was all horror stories, and the pictures were even worse. Finn had told me not to do this under any circumstances, and even though I knew he was right, I couldn't help it. I needed to remind myself why I wouldn't let Maren see me that way.

Then I came across something new. A blog by a guy named Chad—an Ironman triathlete with a PhD in chemistry—who'd had a craniotomy to remove a brain tumor followed by radiation and chemotherapy. He had a great sense of humor about it. He claimed his side effects weren't even that bad. Reading his story, I actually began to feel some hope that maybe I could weather this storm, especially if I knew Maren was counting on me.

But then his posts suddenly stopped. After years of updating his readers a few times a month, Chad just disappeared. Months later, his partner posted on the blog that Chad had lost his battle and how hard it had been watching him fight it. How devastating the loss was. How unfair and confusing and painful and sad. How cancer had turned this brilliant, superstar athlete into a shriveled, sickly shadow of his former self. Of course, he went on to say how strong Chad's spirit remained and encouraged all Chad's readers to donate to cancer research.

Angry at the tragic ending to the story and the injustice of it all, I slammed my laptop shut and tossed it aside. A moment later, I opened it back up, got out my wallet and donated to the American Cancer Society in Chad's honor. It didn't make me feel any better, though. If a guy like that— a chemistry genius who could swim 2.4 miles, bike 112 miles, and run a marathon *without a break*—couldn't survive, what were the odds that I could?

Not good.

My room began to feel claustrophobic, so I decided to take a walk. The rain had eased to barely a drizzle, but I didn't care about getting wet anyway. I wandered the wet city streets with no destination, hands shoved in my pockets, head aching, desperately wishing there was a way out of this that wouldn't break Maren's heart and leave her thinking the worst of me. That had been the whole point of my trip here—to redeem myself in her eyes. Atone for what I'd done. But in true Dallas fashion, I'd managed to fuck it up.

After I'd been walking for a while, I ducked into a little jewelry shop.

My conscience taunted me. *You think some kind of trinket is going to make it up to her?*

Ignoring it, I perused what the store had to offer, and when a saleswoman approached and asked what I'd like to see, I pointed out a necklace that reminded me of one of Maren's tattoos. It was a little lotus flower pendant on a delicate gold chain. Delicate, feminine, beautiful. Just like her. I knew she would love it.

I bought the necklace for her and walked back to the hotel, and was about to get in the shower when Finn called. After debating for ten seconds whether or not to answer, I decided I'd better.

"Hello?"

"Hey, it's Finn. You okay?"

"I guess."

"How are the headaches?"

"Shitty."

"Sorry to hear that. How about your vision?"

I pinched the bridge of my nose, closing my eyes. "It's okay."

"Any more episodes?"

"One. Yesterday. Same thing as before."

"Did you lose consciousness?"

"No."

"That's good." A pause. "I wanted to let you know I spoke with Dr. Acharya. He had a chance to look over your films."

"And?"

"He agrees with me about the surgery. The sooner the better."

"Does he think it's benign or malignant?"

"We won't know that until the biopsy."

"Does he think I'll need radiation and chemo?"

"Again, we won't know that until we have all the information. But you need to *have* the surgery to get the information. He'll go over all this with you Tuesday."

"I haven't agreed to anything," I said quickly.

"I know. I just wanted you to hear his opinion." He

paused. "I also wanted to let you know that I feel really bad about our conversation yesterday."

"Don't worry about it. No point."

"Yes, there is, Dallas. You're the only brother I've got. And I haven't done a good enough job seeing things from your point of view or trying to understand your feelings."

I wasn't sure what to say.

"And how can I expect you to listen to me or believe I care when you feel I'm not on your side? But I've never been against you."

"No, you've been *above* me. There's a difference."

"Fair enough. I admit, I have judged your choices because they're not the ones I would have made. But I've been talking to someone about things, and—"

"About my things? Talking to who?" I demanded.

"No. About *my* things," he said calmly. "I see a therapist."

"Oh. You do?" It surprised me. Finn's life seemed fucking perfect. *He* seemed perfect.

"Yes. Everyone's got issues, Dallas. Not just you. But I've been talking a lot about you lately, and my therapist really thinks repairing our relationship is important. I do, too."

"Frankly, I'm not sure what's there to repair," I said. "We've never had much of a relationship. I'm closer to your kids than I am to you. I relate to them better."

"So let's change that. When you get here, let's get to know each other as adults and put the past behind us. Do you think we can?"

"Maybe. Did you ever talk to Mom?"

"Yes."

"Did she ask a million questions?"

"Of course. But I didn't tell her anything."

"I can't believe she hasn't been calling me nonstop."

"I told her not to bother you while you were on vacation and you'd call her from here." Finn's tone was firm.

"Thanks." My phone buzzed, indicating a text message. A quick glance at the screen told me it was from Maren. "Okay. Look, I better go. I'm having dinner with a friend tonight."

"You mentioned seeing someone before. Who is it? Anyone I know?"

A lie was on the tip of my tongue, but at the last second, I decided to be truthful. I wasn't even sure why. "Maren Devine."

"Your old girlfriend, right? Any sparks left?"

I rolled my eyes. "Jesus, Finn."

"Sorry. But I'd like to hear about your visit with her."

"I'll see you tomorrow. My flight gets in around one or two."

"I'm really glad you're not driving. Safe travels."

"Thanks."

We hung up and I read Maren's message saying she'd meet me here at the hotel. Just seeing her name on the screen made my heart beat faster. I replied, offering again to pick her up. I wanted to do things for her.

You could tell her the truth.

Gritting my teeth, I shoved the thought aside and read her response assuring me she didn't need me to come get her and she'd be here soon.

Me: Good. I missed you today.

Maren: I missed you too. Can't wait to see you!

That's because you don't know the kind of person I really am.

Tossing my phone on the bed, I undressed and got in the shower. Being in there reminded me of showering with her, and I recalled the way she'd looked as she stood naked beneath the spray, water streaming down her body. I remembered the way she'd tasted, the way she'd touched me, the way she'd whispered the sweetest things in my ear —*I missed you, I want you, I trust you.*

I was hard in no time, and so fucking tempted to do something about it, but I denied myself. I didn't deserve the pleasure.

After I got out, I dressed in jeans and a dark blue button-down, put in my contacts, and wrangled my hair into something respectable. I glared at the Depakote in my travel bag for a moment, but ended up taking one. The last thing I needed was to have an episode at the dinner table. I was still humiliated by the one Maren witnessed yesterday.

When I was ready, I looked at my reflection in the mirror. It nauseated me.

You're a miserable, lying prick. But you've got one last chance to make this right. Don't blow it like you've done with every other good thing in your life.

I wasn't sure whose voice it was—my father's? Finn's? my own?—but I knew what it said was true.

I had to tell her.

———

SHE KNOCKED on my door just after five. I opened it, unprepared for the way my knees nearly buckled at the sight of her.

"Hi." She smiled and came toward me with open arms. "I missed you."

"Hi." I hugged her close. "You look beautiful. And you

smell delicious. You're probably not even wearing perfume."

She laughed. "Nope. Just a little lavender oil."

I released her and looked her over, head to toe. "God, you're gorgeous."

Her cheeks bloomed with pink. "Thank you. How are you feeling?"

"Better now that you're here. I have something for you."

Her eyes brightened. "You do?"

"Yes." I took her by the shoulders and put her in front of the full-length mirror on the closet door. "Close your eyes."

She did as I asked and I dug the little box with the necklace in it out of my suitcase and opened it up.

"No peeking," I told her, taking it from the box and undoing the clasp.

"I'm not. I promise."

Reaching over her head, I draped the necklace around her throat and fastened it at the back of her neck. "Okay. You can look."

She opened her eyes and gasped. Her fingertips immediately went to the gold lotus pendant, which looked stunning against her skin. "Oh, my God. Dallas."

Our eyes met in the mirror and hers misted over.

"Do you like it?" I asked.

"I love it. It's beautiful." She sniffed. "You're going to make me cry."

I wrapped my arms around her and kissed her temple. "No crying. It's no big deal. I was on a walk today and saw it, and it made me think of you."

"It's perfect." She placed her arms over mine and squeezed. "I'll wear it all the time."

"I'm happy you like it. It reminded me of your tattoo."

She looked down at her arm. "I love this tattoo. It was my first one."

"Yeah? What does it mean to you?"

"I've always liked the symbolism of the lotus flower—rebirth, resurrection, revival. Its roots are in the mud at the bottom of ponds or rivers, and its petals emerge above the water. Every night they close up and duck beneath the surface, and every morning they rise up and open again. I got it at a time in my life when I needed to be reminded of my capacity for resilience. The lotus flower never gives up. It gives me strength when I need it." She twisted in my arms so that she faced me, her arms going around my neck. "Thank you. Not just for the necklace, but for coming here, for spending time with me." Rising up on her toes, she pressed her lips to mine.

Tell her, I thought as I slanted my mouth over hers and slid my hands down over her ass. *Tell her*, I thought as I walked backward toward the bed, bringing her with me. *Tell her*, I thought as I turned her around, laid her back on the bed, and lifted up the long white dress.

But I didn't. Instead I knelt down between her legs, pushed her white lace underwear aside, and devoured her like a starving man, her hands fisted in my hair, her hips bucking beneath me. After she came, she begged me for more, and I couldn't stop myself from fucking her in that pretty white dress, her legs over my shoulders, her honey-colored hair spilling over the blankets, her fingers clawing the sheets.

With my hands wrapped tightly around her calves, I was rough with her, like I was trying to show her the truth about myself, so rough I hoped she'd plead with me to slow down. Tell me I was hurting her. Push me away. I wanted her to hate me like I hated myself.

But she didn't. She moaned and gasped and turned her face to the side, throwing her hands over her head, her angelic features contorted with pain or pleasure or both, and I rammed my cock deeper inside her, making her cry out with every vicious thrust, but she never asked me to stop. And it felt good, indulging the villain inside me— wicked and sexy and selfish and greedy and powerful, so powerful I was drunk with it.

I let go of her legs and leaned forward, pinning her wrists to the bed with one hand and taking her beneath the jaw with the other. "Look at me," I demanded, forcing her head in my direction. "I want you to watch me fuck you. I want you to see who I am. I want you to know exactly who you think you love."

She tried to say something and I stopped her by sliding my palm up over her mouth. I didn't want to hear her tell me she loved me. She couldn't possibly. Not now and not ever. I wouldn't accept it. "Shh," I told her, driven even closer to the edge by her helplessness, by my audacity. "Just watch. And feel. How hard you make me. How wet you are. How deep I am."

Her fingers curled into fists and she whimpered beneath my hand, but she did as I asked, and the prolonged eye contact as I pounded mercilessly into her body sent me hurtling toward ecstasy. The muscles in my lower body tightened as unimaginable heat unfurled inside me. It was lust and anger and need. It was lies and truth, past and present, betrayal and devotion. It was love and it was hate and it was rushing, rushing, surging, cresting, erupting over and over again as my body stiffened and I poured myself into her in hot, uncontrollable bursts.

When it was over, I took my hands off her and braced them on the bed above her shoulders. I could hardly believe

I was still standing. "Fuck," I said, closing my eyes. I wouldn't have blamed her if she'd hit me. "I'm sorry, Maren."

"Why are you sorry?"

I opened my eyes. "I was rough with you. It was selfish."

"Did it seem like I wasn't enjoying it?"

"I have no idea. I was only thinking about myself."

She shook her head. "No, you weren't. You were watching me the whole time."

"I shouldn't have put my hand over your mouth. You could have been trying to say no."

"But I wasn't." She smiled. "I might be sore tomorrow, but I actually thought that was really hot."

"You did?"

"Yeah." Her smile turned a little shy, her eyes adoring. "You were all manly and dominant and strong. Power is sexy. I mean, I don't want to be pushed around anywhere else, but you can get a little aggressive with me in the bedroom. I'm tougher than I look."

"I know you are."

She took my face in her hands. "And I'm crazy about you. All of you. Don't feel like you have to hold back with me, okay? You can be your real self. That's what I want."

I swallowed hard. "Maren, I have to tell you something."

"You can tell me anything. But can I have one second? I'm afraid of getting something on this dress, because I don't have anything else to wear to dinner." She squirmed, trying to make sure her dress wasn't underneath her.

"Oh, sure. I'm sorry." I carefully pulled out and watched her ease off the bed.

"I'll be right back," she said, giving me a sheepish grin as she headed for the bathroom.

"Take your time." I pulled myself together and sat down on the edge of the bed, elbows on my knees, head in my hands.

Could I do this? Was I really going to admit everything? Was I ready for what her reaction was going to be? Tears and pity and sorrow and pleading with me to have the surgery—and that was *if* she forgave me for keeping it from her all weekend. She'd be a mess at dinner, unable to explain why, and our last night together would be ruined.

Then there was the thing she'd said about power. *You were all manly and dominant and strong. Power is sexy.* If she knew the truth, she'd never see me that way again. She'd see me as sick and weak and at the mercy of other people. Smarter people. Like Finn.

The bathroom door opened, and she came out looking as perfect as she had when she'd walked in. "All good," she said, her smile fading as she got closer to me. "You okay?"

I stood up. "I'm fine. Ready to go?"

Her head tilted to one side. "Wasn't there something you wanted to tell me?"

"It was nothing," I lied. The disappointment in her face gutted me.

"It didn't sound like nothing. Come on, tell me." She slipped her arms around my waist.

"I just—wanted you to know how much this weekend has meant to me. That's all."

She smiled up at me. "Me, too."

"Should we head out?"

"Yes." But she hesitated. "There's nothing else you want to tell me?"

"No." I could hardly meet her eyes. "That was it. I'll just use the bathroom real quick, and then we'll go."

"Okay." She let go of me, and I hurried into the bathroom, closing the door behind me. I avoided the mirror.

What the fuck was I going to do?

———

DINNER WAS A STRUGGLE.

Not because of the company—Maren's sisters seemed great, and everyone was making an effort with me, but my head was not in the game.

"So, Dallas, I hear you're a tattoo artist?"

I blinked at the guy who'd asked the question. Walter, his name was, although it was hard not to think of him as Buzz after Maren's stories. He was tall and thin and professorial-looking, clean shaven with neatly combed sandy blond hair and wire-rim glasses. "Yes."

"That must be interesting work."

"Yeah." When I didn't go on, Maren spoke up.

"Dallas is amazingly talented. He used to draw things on people with a Sharpie at parties in high school. He once did this incredible design on my arm I never wanted to wash off."

"I remember that." Emme nodded enthusiastically. "Mom was *so* mad at you."

"She was." Maren laughed. "Every time she saw it, she would groan and tell me to go put long sleeves on."

"Ever do any tattoos of bees?" Walter asked. "I've sometimes thought about getting one."

"Can't say that I have."

The conversation stalled.

"Nate, do you have any tattoos?" Maren asked Emme's fiancé. He was dark-haired and thicker through the chest and shoulders than Walter, and he had a little bit of facial hair, but I was willing to bet he was not the type to have ink under his expensive suit. I hadn't tattooed a lot of lawyers in my life.

"I don't," he said. "I'm actually not a huge fan of needles near my skin."

Emme looked at him. "You're afraid of needles? I didn't know that."

"I said I wasn't a *fan* of needles, not that I was afraid of them. Big difference."

She rolled her eyes. "Right."

The oldest sister, Stella, tried to draw me out a different way. "So you're in Portland, I hear? How do you like it out there?"

"I like it."

"I've never been there," she went on, "but I've heard it's really nice."

"I'd like to visit Oregon wine country," said Emme. "I love Willamette Valley pinot noir. Have you ever done any winery tours or anything?"

"No." From my right I could sense Maren's unease with my failure to make conversation, so I tried to think of something else to say but couldn't.

My appetite wasn't good, so when the food came I took a few bites, but mostly just pushed it around on my plate.

"Do you not like the lamb?" Maren asked quietly. "I can share my gnocchi with you if you'd like."

"No, thanks. The lamb is good. I guess I'm just not that hungry."

"Are you feeling okay?"

"I'm fine." I tried to give her a reassuring smile.

Everyone else at the table chatted easily, and it was obvious the three sisters were very close. They teased each other without being mean, and were quick to praise one another's talents and accomplishments. Stella spoke glow-ingly of Emme's knack for taking an empty space and turning it into a bride's dream come true, even on a budget, and Maren blushed when Emme complimented her volun-teer efforts at schools in underserved communities in rural areas. "Those kids would never have the opportunity to take a yoga class at a studio," she said. "And did she tell you about how she got one company to donate mats to a women's shelter?"

"No." I looked at Maren, whose cheeks grew even pinker.

"She did. And then she went there and taught classes for free, not just yoga but mindfulness and meditation and—what was the other one, Mare?"

"Affirmations."

"Oh, right." Emme laughed. "I still remember my affir-mation from when you dragged me to that class." She sat up taller and recited it proudly. "I am deserving of a support-ive, loving, awesome relationship."

"And see? It worked." Maren gestured at Emme and Nate. "Once you said it enough, it created the right kind of energy for the relationship to happen."

"The right person helped, too," Emme said, patting Nate on the arm.

The right person. I looked at the other guys at the table —a college professor and an attorney, neither of whom, presumably, had a brain tumor or a gigantic secret he was keeping from the woman next to him—and felt like a fucking disaster. These were good guys. They had every-thing to offer. They'd done everything right. They were smart and honest and played by the rules, and life had rewarded them for it.

Why can't you be more like your brother? my parents

used to ask me. I'd hated it. I didn't *know* why I couldn't be more like him. I just wasn't. But sitting there at that table, I wished more than anything I had been.

Maybe then I wouldn't be stuck in this lie, stuck in this impossible situation where I had to either forfeit the love of my life or drag her down a dark, miserable road.

I looked over at her, and she smiled at me. She was so beautiful it hurt. So good to people around her. So loyal to everyone she loved. If I didn't set her free, she'd waste all her time trying to take care of me.

I wasn't worth it.

FOURTEEN

MAREN

"He's really cute, Maren," Stella said to me in the restaurant bathroom where the three of us stood in front of the mirror. "But he's so quiet. Not at all what I was imagining."

"Same," said Emme, pulling the cap off her red lipstick. "I thought he was more outgoing."

"He normally is." I shook my head. "I don't know what's going on with him. He's not acting like himself at all."

"Maybe he doesn't feel good," Stella suggested, fussing with her hair. "Does he have a headache today?"

"He did this morning. Maybe that's it." My eyes filled with tears. "But there's something he's not telling me, you guys. I can feel it."

"Like what?" Stella turned to me, concern in her eyes.

"I don't know." I took a shaky breath. "But I think it might be what you said—epilepsy."

She blinked. "Really?"

"I mean, I'm not sure, but I looked up some of the symptoms online, and—"

Stella groaned. "Don't do that. The Internet is a cesspool of misinformation."

"I'd have done the same thing," said Emme, putting her lipstick in her purse. "Can you ask him directly?"

I bit my lip. "I could, but I don't want to. I want him to tell me. I want him to trust me."

"Trust takes time," said Stella, squeezing my shoulder. "It's only been a couple days."

"I know, but we have history. It doesn't *feel* like it's only been two days."

"Well, then ask him, if it will make you feel better." Stella shrugged. "What's the worst that can happen?"

"Would it bother you if it were true?" Emme asked.

"No! Not at all." I shook my head. "I'm only bothered by the thought that he feels like he can't tell me."

"I get it." Emme gave me a sympathetic look.

"We should get back to the table," Stella said. "Are you okay?"

I took a deep breath, and then another. "Yes. Maybe I'm imagining this whole thing. He could just have a headache or be thinking about seeing his brother. That relationship is complicated."

"Okay. Call me tomorrow if you want to talk more."

I smiled at her. "Thanks."

ON THE WALK to the car, Dallas didn't hold my hand.

"Thanks for coming out tonight. I probably shouldn't have asked you to. I knew you weren't feeling well." I crossed my arms over my chest.

"It's okay."

I glanced at him. "Are you sure about that? You didn't seem to enjoy it too much."

He kept his eyes on the ground. "Sorry."

Great. Now I'd made him feel bad for feeling bad. "Does your head hurt?"

"Yeah."

I pressed my lips together. "Can I do anything for you?"

"No."

We reached the car, and he opened the passenger door for me, waited for me to get in, and closed it. Then he walked around to the driver's side and got in, but he didn't start the engine right away. He gripped the wheel with both hands and exhaled audibly.

"What's going on, Dallas?"

"Nothing. I'm just tired." He paused. Reached out and put a hand on my leg. "I'm sorry, Maren."

"For what?"

"I wasn't much fun tonight."

"You don't have to apologize. I just wish you'd talk to me."

He closed his eyes. "I know."

But without saying anything else, he started the car.

Neither of us said anything on the drive to my house, although my heart was pounding so loud, I was hardly aware of the silence. What the hell was going on with him? When we reached my house, he pulled into the driveway and put the car in park.

But he didn't turn it off.

"Are you coming in?" I asked, afraid of his answer.

"I don't think I should."

"Why not?"

"Because..." He rubbed his face with both hands before grasping the wheel again. "I can't do this. I thought I could, but I can't."

I shifted in the seat to face him. "Excuse me?"

He kept his eyes on his hands. "This. Us. It's not going to work."

"Are you kidding me?"

"No."

I stared at him, too shocked to cry. Then I switched on the car's interior lights. "Look at me, Dallas."

His jaw twitched, but he turned his face toward me. It was stony and cold.

"You're serious?" I demanded.

"Yes."

"Why?"

"I'm leaving. And a long-distance relationship isn't what I want."

The tears were coming, I could feel the sobs building in my chest, but I did my best to stave them off. "Since when? Last night, you said you loved me. You promised to give us another chance. Was that all bullshit?"

He swallowed. Opened his mouth and closed it again.

"Answer me! Tell me you were lying. Tell me you didn't mean a word you said."

"I was lying," he said. "I didn't mean it."

"I don't believe you." I started to cry. "You said those words and you meant them. I know you did. You had to this time. You had to."

"Look, I know it's hard to understand, but—"

"You're right, I don't understand," I cried. "Give me one good reason why we can't give this a shot."

"Look, Maren. I thought coming here was the right thing, and I was trying to do the right thing for once in my life, but I fucked it up."

"What do you mean?"

"I mean, I was only supposed to see you and apologize. None of this other stuff was supposed to happen."

"So why did it?" I demanded. "Why ask me to dinner? Why ask me to spend the night with you? Why tell me you love me? You could have made your apology and left without hurting me again."

"I made a mistake, okay? At least this time you got your goodbye."

"Fuck you, Dallas," I wept. "How could you do this to me?"

"Because I'm a selfish asshole, okay? And you're better off without me, so just go in the house and forget this weekend ever happened."

I tipped my face into my hands. Feelings churned and swelled in me like boiling lava. Sorrow. Frustration. Hurt. Anger. Humiliation. Was he really just a selfish asshole incapable of an adult relationship? Should I have seen this coming? It had felt so right, and now he was saying it was all a mistake. I didn't want to believe it, but what other reason would he have for breaking this off?

Unless he was doing it to avoid telling me his secret.

Sniffling, I picked up my head. "I don't believe you."

"What?" He looked at me.

"I don't think you're selfish. I think you're stubborn. I think there's something you don't want me to know, and you're shutting me out rather than telling me what it is."

"That's crazy."

I took a risk. "I know about the seizure, Dallas."

He stared at me. Seconds ticked by. "What seizure?"

"The one you had yesterday morning at the hotel."

He looked away again. "I don't know what you're talking about."

"Yes, you do." Suddenly I was convinced I had it right.

"I had a bad headache. I got dizzy."

"It was a focal seizure, wasn't it? I saw the pills you take." I took a deep breath, reminded myself to be kind and patient. "If you have epilepsy, you can tell me."

His head turned sharply toward me, but he didn't say anything.

"Dallas, it's okay." I wanted to touch him, but I didn't. His hands were gripping the steering wheel so tight his knuckles were white. He was breathing hard through his nose. "I don't care what ... conditions you might have. I just want to be with you."

"But you would care," he said bitterly. "You'd feel sorry for me. You'd have to take care of me, and I don't want that. I don't want anyone's pity."

His words were familiar. He'd just used them last night, hadn't he? When he was talking about—

It hit me.

"Oh, Dallas." I covered my mouth with both hands.

He still hadn't moved, but I could see how taut the muscles in his neck were.

I spoke softly. "It's not your dad with the brain tumor, is it?"

"Get out of the car, Maren."

"Dallas, don't do this." I put my hands on his arm. "Don't push me away because of your pride. Let me be here for you. Let me—"

"No!" he roared, shaking me off. "No. I'm sorry I hurt you, okay? I'm sorry for what I did then, I'm sorry for what I'm doing now, I'm sorry about my entire fucking existence on this earth, but this ends here. Now."

"Don't say that," I begged, crying again. "Please, can't we talk about this? I want to know what—"

"No, Maren. No. I don't want to talk about it with you. Now go inside and forget about me."

"What if I can't?" I sobbed. "What if you're the only man I'll ever love?"

He closed his eyes and swallowed. "You'll find someone better."

"But I love *you*!"

"No, you don't." His voice had gone wooden. "You love the idea of me. And I loved the idea of you. We were trying to recapture something from the past when life was simpler."

"You don't mean that." I cried harder, wiping my nose with my hand.

"Yes, I do. I didn't want to say these things to you, but you're not giving me any choice." He was looking at me with hard eyes. I barely recognized him. "I don't love you, Maren. I don't love anyone."

"Then why did you come here?"

He didn't answer me right away. Then he looked out the windshield again. "I wanted you off my conscience."

I sat there crying, trying to let it sink in that this was it—he didn't want to see me again. He didn't love me. As it turns out, I *was* just an item on his bucket list.

And he had a brain tumor.

Panic eclipsed my broken heart for a moment. My mind raced, desperately trying to recall what he'd told me about his father. "The surgery, Dallas. Everything you told me about your dad's treatment options. That was all about you?"

He didn't answer.

"Please. Please have the operation." I put my hands on his arm again, and he let me. "If you don't want me, fine, but don't throw your life away because you don't want anyone's pity. Please, Dallas, if you *ever* loved me. Listen to the doctor. Have the surgery."

He swallowed and spoke quietly. "I'll think about it."

"Will you ... will you let me know what you decide?"

"No. A clean break is better, Maren. For both of us. Now go."

Fresh tears spilled over. He was rejecting me. Again. My heart was crushed, my soul shattered.

"Okay, Dallas. You win. I'll go." I put my hand on the door handle and pulled.

Stop me. Tell me you're lying. Wake me up from this nightmare.

But he let me go without saying another word, and I got out of the car, slammed the door, and ran inside my house.

I locked the front door behind me and ran back to my bedroom in the dark, where I threw myself on my bed and cried into my pillow.

This couldn't be happening, I kept telling myself. There was no way. How could anyone's life take as many zig-zag turns as mine had in the last two days? I didn't know which end was up.

I sobbed and sobbed, my body shuddering, my eyes burning, my voice going hoarse. I couldn't remember the last time I'd cried so hard—probably when Dallas had disappeared the first time. After that, I swore I'd never let anyone hurt me that way again.

And here I was. Heartbroken and alone and desperately afraid for Dallas. Would he be okay? Would he have the operation? Would I ever see him again?

And *why* didn't he love me like I loved him?

I screamed into my pillow, pounded my fists into the mattress, kicked my feet like a child throwing a tantrum. Anger worked its way beneath my sorrow.

Fuck him! Fuck his lies and his careless words and his broken promises! Fuck him for kissing me like he meant it! Fuck him for making me think we had a chance! Fuck him for making me love him again and then breaking my heart! And fuck me for trusting him again—what was wrong with me?

I was so furious I wanted to smash something. I sat up and looked around. What could I throw? What could I shatter? What could I destroy so that I wouldn't feel so fucking helpless and feeble? I quickly untied one of my shoes and threw it as hard as I could at the wall. It felt good, so I did the same thing with the other one, too, grunting as I hurled it with all my might.

"Fuck you!" I yelled. Then I put my hands over my ears and screamed as loud as I could, trying to drown out all the voices in my head telling me I was stupid, gullible, weak, insignificant, not deserving of real love.

Then I flopped onto my back, squeezed my eyes shut and tried to calm myself with some deep breaths. It took a while.

When I was in control again, I got out of bed, found my laptop in the kitchen and took it back to my bedroom. Sitting up against the headboard, I opened it up and googled Finn Shepherd, Harvard University.

I found an email address easily enough, and immediately began composing a message. Dallas might be a selfish asshole, but I would care about him forever. I had to know he was going to be okay.

Dear Dr. Shepherd,

We have only met once or twice, a long time ago, but I am a friend of your brother Dallas.

We went to school together and dated seriously, but lost touch in the years between then and now.

I was surprised to see him on my doorstep two days ago, but we spent the weekend getting reacquainted, and I was very upset to learn about his medical condition.

I couldn't write *brain tumor*. I just couldn't.

We parted ways earlier this evening under difficult terms.

I stopped and took a breath as my eyes filled again.

I know about the surgery. I begged him to have it, but he says he hasn't decided yet and won't tell me what he decides. He wants a clean break.

I'm writing you tonight for several reasons. One, PLEASE do whatever it takes to convince him to have the surgery if that is the best option to save his life. I'm begging you.

I choked back a sob and kept going, although the screen was blurry.

Two, please be kind to him. I know he can be stubborn and difficult, but he won't respond well to insults or demands.

Three, could you please let me know what he decides? He doesn't want any contact with me, but I don't think I will be able to sleep peacefully until I know what he has chosen. I need to know he will be okay.

I did not tell him I was reaching out to you. Of course, I understand if you feel you have to

tell him about this email, but I would still ask that you consider my requests. He will probably be very angry about what I've done, but in all honesty, I love him too much to do nothing.

Feel free to reply to me at this address. I wish you luck with him, and I wish you well.

Sincerely,

Maren Devine

I hesitated for only a moment, during which I closed my eyes and searched my soul. Was this what I wanted to do? I risked alienating Dallas even further by going behind his back and contacting his brother when I knew there was tension between them. In the end, I decided I had no choice. I loved him, and I wanted to save him even more than I wanted him to love me back. If he never forgave me, so be it. I hit send and felt no guilt.

Setting my laptop on my nightstand, I opened the drawer and took out the sketch he'd made of me at seventeen. The sight of it and the memory of what he'd said to me last night brought fresh tears. After tucking it away again, I dragged myself from bed, undressed, and put on my pajamas. In the bathroom, I washed my face, brushed my teeth, and frowned at my puffy eyes. Back in my room, I took off the necklace he'd given me earlier, hid it at the bottom of my underwear drawer, crawled beneath the covers and curled up in a ball. My sheets smelled like him.

I closed my eyes and inhaled, wondering if he was lying in his hotel bed missing me as much as I missed him. I thought of his body beneath the sheets, pictured the warm bare skin, the firm muscles of his chest, the ink on his arms and shoulders and back. I thought of his blue eyes and the dimple in his chin. I thought of his hands. The sound of his laugh. The taste of him. How was it possible I'd never see him again? Or touch him or kiss him or hold him or feel him inside me? The ache of loneliness spread from my heart throughout my entire body.

I cried myself to sleep.

FIFTEEN

DALLAS

On the drive back to the hotel, I turned the radio on, putting the volume up as loud as it would go. I already had a headache, and the blasting rock music made it worse, but as long as I was distracted by the noise and the physical pain, I wouldn't have to deal with the emotional upheaval I'd just caused—mine or Maren's—or the voices in my head telling me I'd just walked away from the best thing that had ever happened to me.

Back at my hotel, I threw all my shit in my suitcase and crashed on the bed, slamming my eyes shut and praying sleep would come quickly.

It didn't, of course.

All I could do was picture the look on Maren's face when I'd told her I didn't love her. Hear her sobbing. She'd been devastated, as I knew she would be. Goddammit, it wasn't supposed to happen!

But I wanted her to be happy, and the only way that could happen was without me in her life. She'd realize that in time. She was smart—smart enough to put everything together about what was going on with me. Groaning, I rolled onto my back and stared at the ceiling. It was exactly as I'd suspected—the tears and sadness, the pity and fear. Why the hell would she want any of that in her life?

I loved her too much to put her through it. Better to disappoint her in the short term than sentence her for life. But fuck—*fuck*—it hurt me, too.

I grabbed the pillow from behind my head and put it over my face. It smelled like lavender.

My throat closed. My chest tightened. My heart ached at the thought that I'd never kiss her goodnight or sleep next to her or wake up with her again—and *someone else would*.

But that was the price I had to pay.

I LANDED in Boston around one o'clock the following afternoon. I hadn't slept well, the flight had been bumpy, and my stomach was upset, probably because of the Depakote combined with the lack of food. To say I was grumpy was an understatement.

I barked at someone in baggage claim for standing too close to me, I was a dick to the guy at the rental car agency when the SUV I wanted wasn't available, and I ignored Finn's texts asking if I was on my way. I'd never even told him which flight I was on or when it would arrive.

Instead, I put his address into my GPS and drove to his house, cursing and grumbling the entire way that I should have stayed in a hotel. How the fuck was I going to even breathe with four people in my face all the time?

Bree answered my knock on the front door, and her face lit up when she saw me. "Hey, Dallas!"

"Hey."

She held the door open for me, and as soon as I was

inside, she let go and threw her arms around me. "It's so good to see you."

The hug felt good, and I found my temperamental mood easing up a bit. "You too."

She released me and stepped back, eyeing me at arm's length. "You look good."

"So do you." My brother's wife was pretty and petite, with shoulder-length dark hair that was pulled off her face and a generous smile. It was a warm day, and she was dressed in cut-off shorts and a tank top smudged with dirt as if she'd been working outside.

"Oh Lord, I'm a mess. I've been in the garden already this morning. But come on in. Finn's at work—I don't think he knew exactly when you were arriving—but the kids are running around here somewhere. Oly! Lane!" she called out. "Uncle Dallas is here."

A second later, they came barreling toward me, Oly flying down the stairs in a bathing suit and Lane zooming in from the direction of the kitchen. "Yay!" one of them cried as both of them wrapped around my legs like monkeys. "You're here!"

"I'm here." The sight of them lifted my spirits even more. "And I have presents for you somewhere in my bag."

The kids cheered while Bree parked her hands on her hips. "You send them too much stuff already. They're still eating all the Easter candy you shipped here."

"What are uncles for?" I ruffled Lane's hair and tweaked Olympia's ear.

"Want to go swimming with me?" she asked. "We have a pool now."

"I know, I heard about it. I'd love to. Got a diving board?"

My niece nodded happily. "I can dive off it."

"I'll teach you how to do a backflip," I told her.

"Dallas Shepherd, don't you dare." My sister-in-law swatted at my shoulder.

I smiled. "Let me take my bags upstairs and I'll find my suit, okay, Oly?"

"Okay."

"Are you hungry?" Bree asked. "I have some pasta salad and some deviled eggs."

"That sounds good. I haven't eaten yet today." My stomach was feeling a little better, and food actually sounded good.

"I'll fix you a plate. You can take your things upstairs. You remember where the guest room is?"

I nodded. "Thanks."

Upstairs in the guest room, I dug my swimsuit and the kids' gifts out of my bag. The Tigers merchandise reminded me of being at the game with Maren, and a pit opened inside me. How was she today? I'd had no calls or messages from her, which surprised me. Was she too hurt and angry? Or was she trying to forget me already?

It doesn't matter. A clean break, remember?

I did my best to put her out of my mind and spent the afternoon with Bree and the kids, who loved their Tigers gear and had fun showing off their swimming and diving skills. I dazzled them all (plus some other neighborhood urchins) with my backflip and thunderous cannonball off the diving board, participated in underwater tea parties, diving for pennies, and about a million games of Marco Polo.

For dinner, I grilled cheeseburgers and hot dogs, and Bree brought out corn on the cob and broccoli salad, which the kids complained about but ate after their mother told them there would be no ice cream if they didn't.

Finn arrived home while we were eating on the patio, kissed his wife hello, ruffled each of the kids' wet heads, and offered me his hand. I thought for sure he'd make a comment about my ignoring his texts or failing to let them know when I would arrive, but he didn't. "Glad you made it," he said.

"Thanks."

He changed clothes and joined us at the table, and I found myself looking at him differently as I watched him interact with his family. I wasn't sure why. Was it because I knew he was seeing a therapist? Or because I kept waiting for him to harangue me about the surgery and he wasn't? Was he different somehow, maybe a little less intense and more relaxed? Was it because I knew he was interested in mending our relationship, maybe hearing me out before he dismissed my side of things as irrational or foolish or reckless?

Whatever it was, it helped to put me at ease. I didn't feel as on guard or defensive as I usually did around him. I liked watching him with his wife and kids, and for the first time, I envied what he had. Home. Family. Security. Belonging. I felt a part of it too, which was nice, but it wasn't mine. It never would be.

Later, after the ice cream had been eaten and the dishes were cleared and the kids had been dragged off to the bathtub by Bree, Finn asked if I wanted to have a beer with him out by the pool.

I hesitated. "The meds."

"No pressure, but I think one beer is okay."

"Okay, then. I'll have one with you." I was feeling better than I had this morning, at least physically.

Finn brought out two uncapped bottles and handed one to me, and we stretched out in two adjacent deck chairs.

The sky was streaked with pink and orange, and the crickets were chirping noisily. From an upstairs window I heard Lane protest, "But I don't need to wash my hair! I washed it three days ago!"

Finn chuckled. "That kid never wants to wash his hair."

I smiled, tipping up my beer. "They're getting so big."

"They are. And I'm getting old."

But you're lucky, Finn. So fucking lucky.

He drank too. "Nervous about tomorrow?"

"Should I be?" I looked over at him.

He shrugged. His shoulders were less broad than mine, but we had similar builds and coloring, although he wore his hair shorter and was slightly thicker through the middle. "I don't think there will be any surprises. He'll just go over the surgery with you."

I nodded, and we were both silent for a minute.

"I want to ask you what you're thinking, but I don't want to pressure you."

"You can ask. I don't have an answer, though."

"Fair enough." He paused. Drank. "How was your weekend in Detroit?"

I crossed my ankles. "Fine."

"You said you saw Maren Devine?"

"I did."

"How was that?"

"It was..." The muscles in my lower body clenched. "Interesting."

"Oh? Care to elaborate?"

I sipped my beer and gave it some thought. *Fuck it. Might as well.* "I went there to apologize for leaving without saying goodbye when Mom and Dad sent me away. It was a shitty thing to do to her, and I only did it because I was embarrassed. I hadn't talked to her since and always felt bad."

"So you wanted her forgiveness?"

"Yeah."

Finn nodded slowly, and I knew he understood why I'd gone. "What did she say?"

"She was pretty frosty at first, but she warmed up eventually. Said she forgave me." I started peeling the label off the beer bottle. "I asked to take her to dinner that night, and she said yes. We had a nice time."

Finn paused with his beer halfway to his mouth. "How nice?"

"She came back to my hotel and spent the night."

"Damn. That's pretty nice."

"Yeah." I inhaled and exhaled, fighting the memory of my body on hers. "So nice I didn't want to leave when I was supposed to. We spent the next day and night together, and things got sort of intense."

"Yeah?"

I took another drink. "I told her some things I probably should have kept to myself."

"What kind of things?"

"That I'd never forgotten her. That I thought of her every day." I paused and shut my eyes. "That I still loved her."

"Well, fuck."

"Yeah."

"What did she do?"

"She said she'd never gotten over me either and made me promise to give us a second chance."

"And you did? Make the promise, I mean?"

I nodded. "I did. But I can't keep it."

"Why not?"

I sat up taller in my chair. "Because, Finn. She doesn't want to be with someone defective like me."

"You're not defective, Dallas."

"I could be. The risks of that surgery scare the fuck out of me."

"I know, they're scary. It's brain surgery, no way around it."

"I don't want her to see me like that. And if they didn't get it all and I needed chemo and radiation ..." I shook my head. "No fucking way. I've seen the photos. I've read the stories."

"What stories?"

"On the Internet," I said, getting defensive, because I sensed a scolding ahead. "And don't tell me those aren't real, because they are. Chad was real and now he's dead."

"Who the hell is Chad?"

"He was a guy with a brain tumor, and he tried to fight it and lost."

"Oh, Jesus. Look, Dallas." Finn swung his feet to the ground and leaned forward with his elbows on his knees, his beer bottle dangling between them. "I won't pretend this isn't serious. Yes, you have a brain tumor. Yes, there are risks to the craniotomy. Yes, you may need additional treatment depending on what the biopsy shows. But this isn't a death sentence. Dr. Acharya thinks he can get it all."

"If I lost the use of my right hand, I'd never be able to work again. It would *feel* like a death sentence."

"Learn to tattoo with your left hand."

I gave him a look. "You can't be serious. I'm not the slightest bit ambidextrous."

"You're smart and talented. And the human brain is an amazing thing. I think you could learn. You could give me my first tattoo."

I had to laugh. "With my left hand? Why not just ask Oly to tattoo you? It would probably look better."

"I want it to be you."

"Are you serious?"

He shrugged. "I've been thinking about it."

"Since when?"

"For a while now. I was going to talk to you about it next time we saw each other."

"I thought you hated my tattoos."

He sighed. "I didn't hate them. I envied them."

"What? Why?" This made no sense.

"Because they stood for something about you that I've always been jealous of. You do what you want and you don't give a damn what anyone thinks."

"True."

"And you get along with everyone. Everyone likes you." He ran a hand through his hair. "Anyway, I'm working on caring less what people think as I get older. And getting a tattoo is a step in that direction. I mean, I don't want it on my neck or anything—I *am* still a professor at Harvard—but maybe on my back or chest or something."

"Sure," I said, amazed by these revelations. Finn envied me? He wanted a tattoo? "We can talk about it. Do you know what you want?"

"Not yet. Maybe you can help me decide."

"Okay."

He cleared his throat. "Anyway, we were talking about Maren."

I stared at him another moment and then looked straight ahead again. Time ticked by. "I want her to remember me like I was."

"I understand."

"And she deserves better than me, Finn. She always has.

I'd be a disappointment to her no matter what, tumor or not."

"That's your own self-pity right there, not anyone else's."

"Excuse me?" My tone was sharp.

He held up a hand. "No offense, but it seems like that's a handy excuse not to take a chance on letting her see you be a little vulnerable. You don't know what would happen in the future."

"A little vulnerable?" I sat up and pointed at him. "Fuck you, Finn. When have you ever let anyone see you as something less than perfect? As someone weak or vulnerable? Oh, that's right, *never*."

"Not true."

"Since when."

"Since Bree had an affair."

That stopped me cold. My jaw dropped. "What?"

"Bree had an affair," he said quietly. "Last year."

"How do you know?"

"She told me. It was someone she'd met through work, a consultant in the school district where she teaches."

"Did you kick his ass?"

He grimaced. "Uh, no. Number one, because I've never been in a fight in my life. Number two, because it wouldn't have solved the problem."

"What was the problem?"

"Bree was lonely. I wasn't listening to her. I was married to my work and took her for granted."

"Shit," I said, lying back again. "Is that why you're seeing a therapist?"

"That's what prompted me to get one. But the therapist is helping me with all kinds of issues, most of which stem from my need for control and perfection."

I scratched my head. "What about Bree and the guy?"

"It was very short-lived. I think only a couple weeks. She felt like she was getting something from him I couldn't give her—not physically, but emotionally—but eventually she felt so sick about it, she couldn't take it. She confessed to me and begged me to go to counseling, something I'd refused to do in the past, because one, I don't like talking about feelings, and two, it meant admitting I wasn't perfect."

"Well, fuck."

"Yeah. It wasn't a happy place around here for a few months. But we went to counseling, I found a therapist, Bree found a therapist."

"Did Oly have to get a job to pay for all the therapy bills?"

Finn laughed a little. "Not yet. But when she's old enough to need therapy, she might have to."

"Nah, she'll be fine."

"I hope so, but no one can fuck up a kid like a parent."

I looked at him, but didn't say anything.

He lay back in the chair again. Crossed his legs. "You know, I've got plenty of success stories too. To balance the scary Internet ones. If you want to hear them."

I finished off the last of my beer. "Maybe."

We lay there in silence for a while before Finn spoke again. "She emailed me last night."

"Who?"

"Maren."

I looked over at him. "Maren emailed you last night? Why?"

"Because she loves you." That was all he said.

I was still processing it when Bree came out of the house and asked if she could join us. We said yes, but because I didn't want to get into everything about Maren in front of my sister-in-law, I didn't ask Finn for any more details about the email. But it stayed at the back of my mind while the three of us sat around chatting. When the mosquitos chased us into the house, we sat in the family room for a while, but eventually I started yawning, and they said they were tired, too. Bree shooed us upstairs and said she'd turn off all the lights.

Finn and I went up, and I waited in the hall while he snuck into the kids' rooms to check on them. It was the kind of thing that made being a dad seem kind of nice, checking on your sleeping children. That had to feel good, knowing they were safe and sound and peaceful. I thought about how much fun I'd had in the pool with them today and wondered what kind of a father I would have been if I'd ever had the chance. It made me a little sad to think it would never happen.

Finn came out of Lane's room, leaving the door open a crack. "Out cold," he whispered. "That kid sleeps hard."

"Good." I hesitated, feeling awkward but wanting to say something. Finn had made an effort with me tonight that he hadn't made in the past. It didn't fix everything, but it made me feel a little less alone. "Hey, thanks for talking tonight."

"Anytime. Thanks for listening." He stuck his hands in the pockets of his shorts. "If you don't want me to reply to Maren, I won't."

Every time I heard her name, it was like a stab to the heart. "You can do what you want. She wrote to you, not me."

"Would you reply to her if she wrote to you?"

"No. There would be no point. My mind is made up."

"Do you love her?"

I hesitated, but decided to be honest. "I'll always love her."

He exhaled. "Okay. Goodnight."

"Night."

He disappeared down the hall toward the master bedroom and I let myself into my room, closing the door behind me. I got ready for bed and slid beneath the covers, exhausted but unable to sleep.

She'd written to him. I swallowed hard. She must have gone into the house last night and looked him up online. What had she said? Knowing her, I could pretty well guess she'd pleaded with him to talk to me about the surgery.

I thought about what Finn said about self-pity, that I was using my feelings of inadequacy, my certainty that I would disappoint her, as an excuse not to let her see me at my worst. But that was bullshit! How could he think that I wouldn't be a disappointment to her, when I'd been a disappointment to everyone else in my life who'd loved me?

He was wrong.

I'd done the right thing in setting her free.

FINN TOOK the morning off and accompanied me to the consultation with Dr. Acharya. I told him he didn't have to, but he insisted. Part of me was glad to have him there, and part of me felt like I was being treated as if I wasn't smart enough to ask the right questions or make my own decisions, but I kept my mouth shut for once.

I liked Dr. Acharya, a dark-skinned man in his fifties with a gentle voice, a serious demeanor, and hands that looked graceful and steady. He outlined the risks of the surgery, explained the procedure, and fielded my questions.

I was a little alarmed to learn that I would be awake while someone sawed out a portion of my skull, but he assured me that the brain doesn't feel pain. "And the drugs they give you will help you forget everything when it's done," he said.

I still hadn't agreed to anything, but I was glad I'd gone to the appointment. I thanked the surgeon for his time and told him I'd be in touch. "The sooner the better," he told me.

Afterward, Finn and I went for lunch, and I was grateful he didn't launch into a high-pressure sales pitch. I wanted the chance to think about everything on my own. I was more inclined than I had been yesterday to have the surgery, but still not convinced.

While we ate, I was tempted to ask Finn if he'd replied to Maren. Half of me was dying to know, the other half recognized that the sooner I got her out from under my skin, the better. In the end, I decided it was better not to know.

After lunch, Finn dropped me off at the house while he went in to work. I spent the rest of the day hanging out with Bree and the kids by the pool, grateful that none of them asked me about my head.

But a thousand times that day I wanted to pick up my phone and call Maren, tell her about the appointment, ask her what she thought. I wanted her to do the chakras thing —not just the blowjob (although I wouldn't have turned it down)—but the whole routine, because it was so calming, and I was feeling so mixed up. Was this operation worth the risk of losing my whole identity? Because that's what it felt like. Everything I valued—my work, my independence, my pride—would be on the table with me, at the mercy of the surgeon's knife.

I was also worried about her. I wanted to know how she was feeling and if she'd slept at all, if she'd had the nightmare, if she missed me. I wanted to tell her how badly I wished I could turn back time and do everything differently, do everything *right*, so she and I could have ended up together.

Later that night, when I was lying in bed, I checked my messages for the millionth time, but there was nothing from her.

I hardly slept.

The next morning, I was up early and decided to go for a run. I threw on running clothes and shoes and moved quietly through the house so I wouldn't wake anyone. Leaving the front door unlocked, I took off down the street at an easy pace, my stiff muscles groaning as they loosened up. I ran for about twenty minutes and turned around, heading back to the house. While I ran, I tried to keep my mind focused on the pros and cons of the craniotomy, but I kept circling back to Maren. I started to get angry.

At myself, for going to Detroit. At her, for making me fall in love all over again. At the universe, for giving me this shit luck. At Chad, for giving me hope and then crushing it. At Finn, for ignoring his wife. At Bree, for cheating on Finn. Jesus, if those two could fuck up a good thing, what hope was there for anyone else? Nothing made any sense.

I missed my old self. Suddenly I wanted nothing more than to go back to Portland and get my life back. Work. Hang out. Hike. Take a road trip now and then. Be alone when I felt like it and around friends when I didn't. Fuck a random girl on a Saturday night if I wanted to, one that wasn't going to matter to me.

But even that held no appeal. The only girl I wanted was Maren, and I couldn't have her.

Back at the house, I ran straight for the yard, where I did some pushups and planks, sit-ups and stretches. Then I ditched my shoes, socks, and shirt, and jumped into the pool. I stayed under the surface for a long time, and when I came up, Finn was standing near the edge, dressed for work and holding a cup of coffee.

"Morning," he said.

"Morning."

"Sleep okay?"

"Not really." I swam to the edge and rested my elbows on it, setting my chin on my forearms.

"Sorry to hear it."

"I think I might head back home."

"What? Dallas...why?"

"I'm wiped out, Finn. I can't even think. I just want to feel normal again."

"That's not going to happen." Finn sat on the end of a deck chair. "The reason you don't feel right is because there's something in your brain that doesn't belong there. Let's get it out."

I shook my head. "No."

"I talked with Dr. Acharya's office last night. They can get you in for surgery in ten days, and you can stay here as long as you need to."

"No, Finn. I want to go home. I feel like I need to be by myself for a while."

"For how long?"

"I don't know."

Finn opened his mouth to say something, then closed it.

"What?" I asked.

"How much of this is about Maren Devine?"

"What do you mean?"

"I mean, how much of this feeling sorry for yourself is because you talked yourself into believing she's better off without you?"

"That's the truth," I fire back.

"You're miserable, Dallas. She's miserable, too."

"She'll get over it."

"What about you?"

I said nothing.

"You should reach out to her. She's worried sick about you."

"She'll forget about me sooner if I don't. Talking to her will only make things worse."

My brother exhaled and ran a hand over his hair. "I don't know what to do with you, Dallas. I think you're making a mistake. Several mistakes."

"What else is new?" I heaved myself out of the pool.

"It's not like that, so don't get all worked up." He stood up and faced me. "I don't think you're making mistakes because you don't know better—I think you're choosing to suffer. I just don't know why."

"Yeah, well, you wouldn't." I went over to the fence where I'd hung the beach towel I'd been using the last couple days and wrapped it around my waist. It was no surprise to me that Finn didn't know what it was like to feel you weren't worthy of something. For fuck's sake, his problem was that he'd assumed his wife would *never* leave him.

"Look, don't go." He checked his watch. "I have to get to work, but let's talk this over some more, okay?"

"Did you write her back yesterday?" I had to know.

He paused. "Yeah. I did. I told her—"

"It doesn't matter," I said, changing my mind and walking over to where I'd taken off my running clothes. "It's between you and her. I don't need to hear it."

"But it's about *you*."

"I don't need to hear it," I repeated, angrily piling my sweaty things in my arms.

"You're acting like a stubborn child, Dallas! "

"Fuck you! I'm acting like a man who wants to make his own decisions and have his family respect them for once." I stormed toward the house.

Finn followed me. "I'm sorry, Dallas. Don't go. Please. Let me help you work through all this."

"You can't," I said, sliding open the patio door. "It's too late."

SIXTEEN

MAREN

Despite the fact that I'd barely gotten any sleep Sunday night, I got up and went to the studio on Monday in time to teach a six a.m. class. What I really wanted to do was stay curled up on my couch all day and cry over a box of strawberry Pop-Tarts, but I knew that wouldn't help me. I needed to get back to my routine in order to get through this.

Allegra took one look at me and opened her arms, and I went into them, glad to have a shoulder to cry on. But when she asked what was wrong, I found myself unable to go into it. I just didn't have it in me. Instead, I told her I was still having the nightmare and didn't know what I was going to do.

"If I point you in a certain direction, do you promise to have an open mind?" she asked.

"Of course." I grabbed a tissue from the box on the studio desk.

"Okay." She grabbed a pen and Post-It note and wrote something down. "Call this woman."

I looked at the paper. "Madam Psuka? Is that how you say it?"

"Yes. Like Puh-suka."

"Who is she?"

"She's a lot of things. Psychic, medium, intuitive, dream interpreter. She's a little odd, but I consulted with her all the time when I lived up north." She shrugged. "That's the only problem. She's not local."

"Where is she?"

"Traverse City."

"Oh." Something clicked in my head. "You know what? My sister invited me to go up north with her this week. To Old Mission Peninsula."

"Oh my God, that's like right there. You should go!"

I bit my lip. "But it would be Wednesday to Friday. And I already took the weekend off."

Allegra shook her head. "You worry too much about unimportant things. This is your health, your well-being. It matters the most."

"I know, but—"

"Listen, are you gonna go broke if you have to pay a sub and someone to cover the desk for a few days?"

"No," I admitted.

"Then go. I think she might be able to help you." She touched her chest. "If I'm wrong and she can't, I will take full responsibility. I'll cover the sub with my own paycheck."

"Stop. You are not doing that."

"So will you go?" she asked hopefully.

I sighed and looked at the name on the paper. It seemed a little out there—I believed people could intuit things about their own consciousness, but I wasn't sure a stranger could read anything into mine just by looking at my palm or whatever—but I was exhausted and unhappy and willing to try anything. "I'll look her up."

Allegra rubbed my shoulder. "Good."

I CHECKED my email repeatedly throughout the day Monday, but never got a reply from Finn Shepherd. Had he seen my message? Was he ignoring it? There was no way I'd gotten the wrong Finn Shepherd, Associate Professor of Neurology, was there?

I was just as obsessive about my texts, thinking maybe Dallas would come to his senses and reach out to me, or at least let me know he'd arrived in Boston safely and was going to do what the doctors said.

But he never did.

After work, I called Emme and asked her if I could come over.

"Sure," she said. "Everything okay?"

"No," I told her, fighting tears. "I'll tell you when I get there."

Nate opened the front door to their house and looked at me strangely. "Maren?" he said, almost like he didn't recognize me. Admittedly, I was looking pretty haggard from the lack of sleep and all the crying, and I was on the verge of another meltdown right there on their front porch.

"Yes," I squeaked, trying to hold it in.

"Are you okay?"

I nodded and squeaked again. "No."

Emme appeared behind him, her eyebrows rising. "Maren! What's wrong?"

One look at my big sister and I burst into tears, and I stood there wailing on their doorstep for a few seconds while they stared at me in shock. Nate recovered first and took me by the arm. "Come in, come in."

I stumbled into their front hall and threw my arms around Emme. "He's gone. He has a brain tumor and he's gone."

Emme gasped and embraced me. "What are you talking about?"

"Did someone die?" Nate asked.

I realized what I'd said. "No, no. He's fine. I mean, he's not fine—Dallas has a brain tumor—but he's alive."

"Oh my God." Emme hugged me tightly and let me go. "Come sit."

I went into their living room and sat on the couch. "Do you have any tissues?"

"I'll get some," Nate said, heading into the kitchen.

Emme sat next to me. "So what happened? Are you serious about this brain tumor thing? *That's* what was going on with him?"

I nodded, trying to compose myself so I could at least get through the story. Nate returned with a box of tissues and handed it to me before taking a seat across from us in a leather and chrome chair.

"Okay if I'm in here?" he asked.

"It's fine," I said, blowing my nose. "Embarrassing, but fine."

I told them about the conversation Dallas and I had had last night—how he'd attempted to break things off without telling me the truth, how I'd figured it out and confronted him, how he didn't want anything to do with me going forward.

"He s-said he d-doesn't love m-me," I blubbered. "He said it w-was a m-mistake."

"My God, you poor thing." Emme rubbed my back. "That had to be so hard."

They let me cry for a while without saying anything,

but Emme made soothing noises and kept a hand on my back.

When I'd calmed down enough to talk, I grabbed another tissue. "God. I'm such a mess."

"He seemed distracted at dinner," Nate said. "I'm usually pretty good at reading people, and I had the impression he was really uneasy about something."

"Maybe the fact that he was about to dump me? Or his brain tumor. Take your pick."

"God, this is horrible. And so sad." Emme looked like she might cry too. "I'm really sorry, Maren."

"What's the prognosis on the tumor?" Nate asked, leaning forward with his elbows on his knees. "Can it be removed?"

I lifted my shoulders. "I don't know for sure, because he wouldn't talk to me about it. He said he doesn't want my pity. I *think* there's a surgery he can have, but there are risks he's worried about."

"What kind of risks?"

I thought back to the conversation when Dallas had led me to believe it was his dad with the tumor. "I think he said something about potential loss of mobility on the right side."

Nate's expression was grim. "That has to be a particularly horrible prospect if you're a tattoo artist."

"I know, but not as bad as—as..." I couldn't even think it. A fresh round of tears welled, and I sobbed into a tissue.

"So now what?" Emme asked.

"Who knows?" I cried. "I emailed his brother in Boston, the neurologist, but he didn't email back."

"Have you reached out to Dallas?" Nate asked.

I shook my head. "He told me not to."

Nate looked surprised. "You're just going to do what he says?"

"What choice do I have? He rejected me, Nate. He doesn't want me." Pain wrenched my heart all over again.

Emme spoke up. "First of all, I don't think that's true. He might not have been himself at the table last night, but I saw the way he looked at you. He adores you."

"Then why would he push me away?"

"I don't know for sure, but if I had to guess, I'd say he doesn't want you to have to deal with his medical problems." Nate shrugged. "He probably thinks he's doing you a favor by cutting you loose."

"That's ridiculous," Emme said angrily. "He told her he loved her the night before."

Nate shrugged. "All the more reason to set her free."

"That makes no sense at all." Emme refused to budge. "If he loved her, he'd want to be with her."

"Not if he thought sacrificing her was for her own good."

"He said he doesn't want anyone to have to take care of him," I told them.

"Typical man," Emme huffed. "That's what you *do* when you love someone. You take care of them."

"He said I should forget him and find someone better. He's all fucked in the head because of how his family treated him. They favored his older brother," I explained to Nate. "So he grew up thinking he's not good enough, but he is. Oh, God, you guys. This is hopeless." I tipped over onto Emme's lap, and she stroked my hair.

"I'm sorry. Men can be so stubborn."

"Look, guys sometimes think they're being heroic by shutting down their emotions," said Nate, a little grudgingly. "Feelings scare us."

"I don't get that," said Emme. "Feelings are not scary. Brain tumors are scary!"

"Admitting you have feelings makes you vulnerable, though," Nate went on. "It's like you're giving someone the opportunity to hurt you."

"He sounds like Stella," I said to Emme.

"So he's protecting himself by breaking things off?" she wondered.

Nate shrugged. "Essentially, yes. But he doesn't see it that way."

"A man's brain is a frightening, frightening place." Emme looked down at me. "So now what will you do?"

I sat up and blew my nose again. "Try to get over him again, I guess. There's nothing else to do."

"Why not give it a little time and then reach out to him? Tell him how you feel. Tell him you still want to be with him, if that's what you want."

"It is, but ..." I shook my head, wondering if the tears would ever stop. "I'm afraid I'd only make a fool of myself. He flat out said he doesn't love me."

My sister put her arm around me and tipped her head onto my shoulder. "I'm sorry. I know it hurts."

It did. And I couldn't help thinking that somehow it was my own damn fault. I took a shuddery breath. "Hey Emme, is that invitation still open to go with you to Abelard this week? I could use some time away."

"Absolutely."

Nate exhaled and rose to his feet. "Let me know if there's anything I can do. In the meantime, how about some pizza?"

"Maren doesn't eat pizza," said Emme.

"What? Who doesn't like pizza?" Nate stuck his hands on his hips.

"I like it, I just don't eat gluten," I explained. "But you know what? I'll eat it tonight. I'm in the mood for it."

Emme squeezed me and stood up. "Pizza makes everything better. Come on, let's go open a bottle of wine."

"Okay." I grabbed the tissue box and followed her to the kitchen. "And do you happen to have any strawberry Pop-Tarts?"

THAT NIGHT when I got home, I lay in bed with my phone in my hand, my stomach in knots. I wanted to do what Emme said and fight back, but the truth was, I was too scared. I didn't want to hear him say he didn't love me again. But what if what Nate said was true? What if he really did love me, and breaking things off was his way of protecting himself?

What was the right thing to do?

I curled into a ball and hugged my knees to my poor belly, which had been upset *before* I'd eaten four slices of Meat Lovers Delight and two strawberry Pop-Tarts. (Nate actually went to the store to get them for me. He is a good man.)

In the end, I was so tired, I fell asleep without doing anything. The nightmare woke me around four, and I was so worked up, I couldn't fall back to sleep. I got out of bed and dug the Post-It note Allegra had written on out of my bag. *Madam Psuka,* it said.

I grabbed my laptop and googled her.

She had a website, psychicpsuka.com. On the All About Psuka, I learned that she was a "moonchild" who'd always had a special talent for premonitions, intuitions, and receiving messages from beyond. Her services included palm readings, numerology, dream analysis, house blessings and smudgings, aura cleansings, and spiritual channeling. The first visit was free.

Some of the things she did I believed in and some I didn't, but the testimonials were all good (Madam Psuka had cured one woman of her fear of chins, predicted another woman's big inheritance, and helped a gentleman connect with his beloved cat beyond the grave), and I figured it couldn't hurt to go see her.

I scheduled an appointment for Thursday afternoon and went in to work, miserable and exhausted.

———

LATER ON TUESDAY, I got a reply from Finn Shepherd.

Dear Maren,

Thanks for reaching out. I don't think it will betray my brother's confidence to let you know that he is here in Boston, he saw the surgeon this morning, and the appointment went well. He hasn't told me of his final decision regarding treatment yet, but I assure you, my family is doing everything possible to convince him to listen to the surgeon's advice.

However, as you know, Dallas is his own man.

I hope that you and my brother can mend your friendship. I know you are very special to him.

Don't give up.

Sincerely,

Finn Shepherd

I read through it three times. *Don't give up.* Why would he say that? What did he know? Had Dallas said something about me? I probably would have continued to obsess over it, but I was working the desk at the studio and evenings were always busy. At least I knew for sure that he'd met with the surgeon and was considering the operation. I hoped things were going well enough within the family that Dallas would listen to them, but it wasn't clear from Finn's letter whether that was the case.

Later that evening, I had dinner with Stella and told her what had happened. I was only slightly less emotional than I had been at Emme and Nate's house the night before, but I at least managed to get through the story without getting in her lap.

"I feel so stupid," I said, squeezing my eyes shut. "How could I have fallen for him again?"

"Don't be so hard on yourself, Maren. We can't control our feelings."

"I know, but ..." I set my fork down and covered my face with my hands. "I feel like I put myself right back where I was at eighteen. Like I've learned nothing. Like I'm doomed. God, I feel so stupid for trusting him. For trusting anyone that much."

"Stop." She reached out and tugged at one wrist. "It doesn't do any good to blame yourself for the actions of someone else. Yes, you trusted him, and he hurt you. That doesn't mean you shouldn't trust again, Maren. It means you have a big heart."

"Maybe."

She smiled. "Listen, I know Emme was the one we always teased about falling in love easily, but it can happen to anyone. Don't be ashamed of having those feelings."

"Okay. I'll try." But deep down, I vowed I would never

put myself in this position again. I would be more careful, more guarded. If men could turn off their feelings to protect themselves like Nate said, then I could, too.

And no matter what Finn Shepherd said, I had to give up on Dallas.

He'd given me no choice.

SEVENTEEN

DALLAS

In the biggest dick move ever, I left Finn's house Wednesday morning without even saying goodbye to Bree and the kids. Finn was already gone by the time I came downstairs, and there was no note or anything, no text or email from him, which I took as a sign that he didn't really care whether I left or not.

I went to the airport, turned in my rental car, and booked a flight to Portland. While I waited for departure, I felt guilty enough to send a message to Bree.

Hey, I felt like I needed to go home for a while. I left early, before you guys were awake. Please say goodbye to the kids for me. Thanks for everything.

I hit send, and then a minute later sent another text.

I'm sorry.

Then I turned off my phone and shoved it in my bag. The calls from my mother would start soon, no doubt, and Finn would be on my ass, too.

I didn't look at it again until I was sitting at the gate in Denver. As expected, I had missed several calls from both my mother and Finn. He'd also sent a text.

Bree said you left without saying goodbye.

I braced myself for the lecture. Instead, I got an apology.

I'm really sorry about what I said this morning. I shouldn't have pushed you. It's very frustrating for me to be in this position. I want to save your life, but you don't necessarily want it to be saved. I wish I could convince you that you've got a lot to live for, and that needing help doesn't make you less of a man. It takes courage to face something like this, and to admit you can't do it alone. We're your family, and we love you. We're here for you, no matter what you decide.

There was one more message.

Also, Mom is going nuts wondering what is going on. Do you want me to explain it to her? I promise to do it without criticizing your need to take a little time and think things over on your own. That is your right, and I will make sure she and Dad understand that. And respect it.

In reply, I simply said, **Yes. Thank you.**

In some ways, it was the nicest thing he'd ever done for me.

———

THAT AFTERNOON, I returned to the house I was

renting and flopped onto my couch. I lay there for a while, grateful for the peace and quiet. I'd almost dozed off when my phone vibrated. I looked at the screen, expecting it to be another text from one of my family members, but it was from Evan.

It was a picture of him holding a newborn baby wrapped in a blanket. A series of messages followed.

It's a boy

Hunter William Brawley, born 6:02 A.M.

7 lbs, 8 oz

Holy fuck, I'm a dad

Help

I grinned and replied.

Me: Congratulations, asshole! How's Reyna?

Evan: Who?

Me: Your wife? The person who just gave birth?

Evan: Oh her. Yeah she's fine.

Me: Tell her congrats from me.

Evan: Will do. You in Boston? How did it go with the surgeon?

Me: I'm in Portland. It went fine and I'll fill you in soon. I'm happy for you.

Evan: Thanks man.

I set my phone aside and crossed my arms over my chest. Holy shit, Evan was a dad. He was the first one of my friends to hit that milestone, and it seemed crazy that I could be that old. As a kid, and by kid, I mean from age one to twenty-nine, I'd never really given much thought to the future—I'd lived for the moment and sought out as many extreme experiences as I could. I'd figured that was all we had control over—the moment we were in. You couldn't change the past, and you had no fucking clue what the future would bring. For all I knew, I'd be dead by twenty-five, so why not get the tattoo, buy the Porsche, swim with the sharks, dive off the cliff? And I'd thought for sure that was the way I'd go—doing something reckless but fun. Something worth it.

A brain tumor?

Not worth it.

But what could I do?

You know what you could do. Fight it. Push back. Refuse to go quietly. Stand up and say, "Not like this, universe. No fucking way."

I frowned. And if it wasn't enough?

Then you make the most of the time you have. Mend the relationships that matter. Live fully. Love hard.

There was no one I wanted to love harder than Maren if my time was short. But suddenly I had other regrets—I'd never been to Bali. Never seen my artwork in a gallery. Never done anything to really make my grandfather proud.

I'd never get married, be a father, raise a family. It wasn't something I'd ever had my heart set on before, but it had never been off the table, either. It was always there, like that shirt in the closet you never wear but you can't bring yourself to throw out, because maybe someday you'll want to wear it. If and when you do, it's there.

I didn't like the notion that fate was taking away all my maybe somedays.

Eventually, I nodded off, and when I woke up, it was dark. My stomach was growling, and I thought about calling Evan and asking if he wanted to grab something to eat with me, but then I remembered—he had a new baby.

Impromptu meet-ups were probably off for a while. In the end, I ordered takeout and spent the evening alone, ignoring my family's calls and texts, eating Chinese food, watching old movies on Netflix, and wishing Maren was here with me. We'd stretch out on the couch, my arms wrapped around her, her head beneath my chin. One of those vivid memories struck me—dancing with her on the rooftop at the hotel. I could smell her hair, see the lights in the city, feel the breeze on my face, hear her gentle weeping. I closed my eyes and melted into it.

But as intense as the memory was, it couldn't compare to the real thing. Breaking things off, putting distance between us, refusing to talk to her—none of these things had alleviated the ache of losing her. If anything, it had only gotten worse. I loved her so much I had to do something about it, or I was going to lose my mind. I was full of this raging, pulsing, physical urge. If she'd been here, I would have ravaged her body all night long, worshipped every inch of her skin, made her feel so good she'd never want to leave. I'd have told her over and over again how much she meant to me, how sorry I was for hurting her, how I was going to spend the rest of my days making it up to her. I'd have made promises to her and kept them.

But without giving in, what could I do?

By the time the sun came up, I had an idea.

———

"WHAT? NO." Beatriz sat back and folded her arms.

"Come on, Bea," I said angrily, laying my forearm on the table in front of her. "Don't give me any bullshit."

"Who's Maren?" she asked, looking at the letters I'd stenciled on my inner left forearm.

"A girl."

She rolled her eyes. "For fuck's sake, Dallas."

"Just do it, okay?"

"Why? You've never talked about this person before, and now you want me to put her name on your skin? Have I not taught you anything?"

"Look, it's not like that. She's not my girlfriend."

"What is she then? You don't have a sister, and I know you well enough to know you wouldn't tattoo your mother's name on your body. So what gives?"

"She's someone from my past."

Beatriz arched one brow. "I'm listening."

I went through the story, grateful it was early enough that only the two of us were in the shop. I'd called her and asked her to come in before we opened. She heard me out without interrupting, keeping her face impassive and her arms folded over her chest, even when I admitted the truth about the tumor in my brain. "Yesterday, I flew back here. That's it."

She was wide-eyed. "Wow. You really fucked that up."

"Thanks for your sympathy," I snarled.

"Oh, I have sympathy about the brain tumor. That is a shitty fucking piece of rotten luck, and I hate that you're going through it. My brother had a tumor removed from his pituitary. The doctor got it all, and it turned out to be benign, but it was really hard on the entire family." Her eyes misted over—something I'd never seen before. "I am sorry, Dallas."

"I'm sorry about your brother."

"Thanks. He's fine now, by the way. Married with a kid and another on the way."

"Good."

"You're going to be fine too, you know."

"Bea. Can you just put her name on my arm please?"

"Not until you agree to have the surgery."

I banged my fist on her table. "Fucking hell! Is it too much to ask that I be allowed to make my own decision?"

She thought for a second. "Yes. Because you're not thinking clearly. You've got all this"—she moved her hands around in front of my face—"baggage that's weighing you down, influencing your decision. Your aura is totally clogged with it. You need to let it go."

I clenched my jaw and took a breath for patience. "I'm working on it."

She tilted her head. "Are you? Or are you using this whole refusal to have the surgery thing to get back at your family? Maybe even to punish yourself for hurting Maren?"

"Jesus, Bea. All I wanted was some ink. Not a therapy session."

She smiled. "Lucky you, it comes free with a tattoo today."

"Does that mean you're going to do it?"

"I'm deciding." She leaned her elbows on the table. "What is getting this tattoo going to do? If she won't see it, it won't help you get her back."

"It's not for her," I said quietly. "It's for me. I want her with me, Bea. I'll always want her with me."

She sighed, her eyes tearing up again. "You're starting to get to me, Dallas."

"Good."

Pulling on her disposable gloves, she shook her head. "I'm only doing this because I believe in my heart that you do love her, and that someday you're going to take your head out of your ass so you can be with her."

I didn't say anything while she worked, and I welcomed

the sting of the needle. It was a fraction of the pain I would have endured for her, and it made me feel like I was doing something about my feelings. As I watched Beatriz's hands, I thought about Dr. Acharya's, how capable they'd looked. I thought about how Finn had said the surgery could be done in ten days. I thought about the abrupt way I'd left my brother's house, angry and resentful, when I knew he was only trying to help.

And I thought about what it would be like if the tables were turned, and it was Finn with the tumor—or God forbid, one of the kids. Or Maren. I'd want them to have the surgery, too. I'd fight them if they argued. I'd tell them it was worth the risks.

When it was done, Beatriz covered it with a bandage and tried to send me home. "You look like shit. Have you even slept since you left here?"

"Very little in the last few days," I admitted.

"Go home and sleep. And don't come back here until you've scheduled that surgery. I mean it. I will fire your ass if you don't."

I gave her a tight-lipped smile.

She gave me a hug and sighed. "Maybe you should come back later so I can cleanse your aura. It's all kinds of fucked up."

That reminded me of something. "Maren cleared my chakras while I was in Detroit."

"She did?" Beatriz looked surprised. "How was it?"

"It was ... mind-blowing."

She rolled her eyes. "Something tells me it devolved into another activity entirely."

I paused. "Yeah. It did."

She patted me on the shoulder. "It happens. I wish I could meet this girl. She sounds amazing."

Closing my eyes, I swallowed the tightness in my throat. "She is."

I went home and tried to take a nap, but failed. After an hour or so, I gave up, took the bandage off my tattoo and washed it off. The skin was pink and tender, and the sight of her name on my body made me both happy and sad. I applied some ointment, put on some hiking shorts and a long-sleeved shirt to keep my arm covered, grabbed a bottle of water, and drove to Powell Butte. I was nearly ready to make the call to my brother, but I felt like I needed a little more time. I needed to do this for me, not because Finn or my parents or Evan or Beatrix or even Maren wanted me to.

While I hiked, I thought a lot about my childhood—my parents, my relationship with my brother, my behavior. The way I purposefully defied my parents to make a point. The way I refused to try my best at school so that no one could tell me my best wasn't good enough. The way I sought solace in art but never felt like I was taken seriously. The kind of parent I would be if I ever had the chance.

Finn was a good dad, I'd give him that, but I'd work way less than he did. I wanted to be there swimming in the pool with my family and putting the hot dogs on the grill, not coming home after dinner was already on the table. Our dad, a corporate attorney, had worked a lot too.

At one point I stepped off the trail for a water break, and stood for a moment looking at Mount Hood in the distance. Its snowy peak never failed to take my breath away. I'd climbed it once and had always wanted to do it again—the view from the summit at sunrise was stunning, the kind of view that made you glad to be alive.

A few hours later I drove back home, sweaty and famished and tired, but certain of what I should do. When I pulled into my driveway, I was shocked to see Finn sitting on my front porch.

Not once had Finn ever come to see me anywhere I'd lived.

I got out of the car and walked toward him slowly.

"Hey," Finn said, rising to his feet.

"Hey." I thought about offering my hand, but while I was doing that, he came forward and hugged me.

It was a little awkward—he and I weren't huggers—but kind of nice too. "Sorry for showing up like this," he said as he released me.

"It's okay." I scratched my head. "What are you doing here?"

"I came to talk to you."

I probably should have told him right then I'd decided to have the surgery, but I didn't. Some part of me wanted to hear what he was going to say first. "Want to come in?"

"Sure."

We walked to the front porch, where I noticed he had a small carry-on bag. "This is quite a surprise."

"I know." He picked up the bag and slung it over his shoulder. "Bree said I should call, but I wasn't sure you'd have let me come. And I wanted to say some things in person."

"Okay." I unlocked the front door and we went in. "Can I get you anything to drink?"

"No, thanks. I'm fine." He set his bag down while I turned on the living room lamps, then took a seat on a chair adjacent to the couch. "I'm here to apologize."

I sat on the couch. Folded my arms over my chest. "For what?"

"For not being a better older brother. If I had been,

you'd still be at my house, and you'd have an easier time taking my advice."

"Fair enough."

"You had it rougher than I did growing up, and I don't think I understood that until I had my own kids. Being a dad has made me rethink some things." He leaned forward, elbows on his knees. "I want the chance to be better, Dallas. I came here to say I'm sorry and also to say ..." He sat up taller and sort of puffed out his chest. "I'm—we're, Bree and the kids and Mom and Dad—not giving up on you. We're your family, dammit, and we want you around."

"You do?"

"Yes. Has Mom been calling?"

"Yes. And Dad."

"I told them what was going on, and I also told them that if we expect you to care what we want, we have to show you we care about *you*. I don't think we've shown it enough." He paused. "I talked to them about the past, asked them to imagine what it was like for you. I hadn't done that either until now."

I wasn't sure I liked the idea of the three of them all sitting around talking about me like that, but maybe it's what had to happen. "What did they say?"

Finn sat back. "What you'd expect, at first. Claiming they never favored me, they treated us both the same, it was you who forced them to be hard on you. But the more we talked, the more they saw things from your perspective. I think they should hear it from you—I can only really guess from things you've said how you felt—but I think they're willing to listen to you."

I sighed. "I don't even know if there's a point to that. The past is past."

"The point is to take responsibility for the way we treat

others. Actions have consequences. I should have stuck up for you, Dallas, and I didn't. And if the consequence of that is losing you, I—" A strange choking sound erupted from his throat and he dropped his head.

I was shocked. Finn was *crying*.

Maybe there was hope yet. Maybe it wasn't too late.

"I'm going to have the surgery."

He looked up. "You are?"

"Yes. I'll call Dr. Acharya's office in a minute."

"Oh, thank God." Finn closed his eyes, and a tear slid down his cheek.

Embarrassed, I got off the couch, went into the kitchen and grabbed the tissue box. Then I tossed it onto the table next to Finn. "Here."

"Thanks." He pulled one from the box and blew his nose.

I sat down again. "Do Mom and Dad know you're here?"

He nodded. "They wanted to come out here too, but I said no. I thought that would be too much."

"Thank you. It would have been."

"God, I'm so relieved." Finn exhaled. "I can't tell you how scared I was that you were going to say no or just shut the door in my face."

That sounded familiar. "I know the feeling."

"Have you spoken to Maren?"

I shook my head.

"Are you going to let her know what you decided?"

"No."

Finn looked like he wanted to say more, but decided not to. He pulled out his phone instead. "Here. I've got Dr. Acharya's office number. Can I call?"

I shrugged. "Sure."

He tapped the screen a few times and handed the phone to me. His expression was pure relief. "Here you go. You're doing the right thing."

AFTER I FINISHED the call with Dr. Acharya's office— my craniotomy was scheduled for next Friday, one week from tomorrow—I took a quick shower, being careful not to get my new ink wet. I couldn't wait for it to heal so I could look at it every day. I was hoping that being able to see it would ease some of the ache in my heart.

Finn and I went out for something to eat, and for maybe the first time in our lives, really enjoyed each other's company. We talked openly about all kinds of things, and he asked a lot of questions. For once, I didn't feel like he was judging my answers. We were two brothers on equal footing who had taken different—and somewhat distant—paths in life, but who wanted to change that. It was nice.

He accepted my offer to stay the night in my guest room, and when we got back to my house he looked around at some of the art I had hanging on the walls. Moving closer to a sketch I'd done of a barn and rural landscape while working on the ranch, he pointed at it. "Did you do this?"

"Yeah."

He turned around and looked at me, as if in awe, then turned to the sketch again. "Dallas. This is amazing."

I shrugged, but I was pleased. "Thanks."

"And these?" He moved on to a trio of portraits I'd done of a friend a couple years ago. Each one showed her face from a different angle. She wasn't particularly beautiful, but her face had interesting angles.

"Yes."

He stared a little longer, then shook his head. "Incredible. Maybe you can draw the kids sometime. I'd love to have something like this."

"Of course."

"You're really fucking talented."

I laughed, a little embarrassed now. "Thanks. So how about that tattoo? Have you thought more about it? I could do it tomorrow," I offered. "After that, it might be a while."

He faced me. "That's not a bad idea. I don't have to fly back to Boston until Saturday."

"Cool. We'll go into the shop tomorrow. I'd like you to meet Beatriz, the woman who owns it, and maybe my friend Evan, if he's working, although his wife just had a baby this week, so I'm not sure if he's back yet."

"Sounds good."

We went upstairs, and I showed him the guest room where he could sleep. "Towels are in the hall closet here. Bathroom right across the hall."

"Thanks." He paused before going into the room and looked at me. "I can't tell you how relieved I am, Dallas. Everything is going to be different from now on. Everything is going to get better."

For once, I wanted him to be right.

Later that night, I lay in bed listening to a summer storm and thinking about Maren. Was she okay? Did she hate me? Would she even care that I'd scheduled the surgery? I spent an hour obsessing over her Instagram account, but seeing her photos only frustrated me—I couldn't smell her or taste her or touch her or hear her. I needed something more. Even the tattoo on my arm wasn't enough.

I typed a message to her.

Are you awake?

My heart beat fast as I waited for a response. When I didn't get one after a full minute, it sank in my chest.

Probably not. It's late here, so it's even later for you. Even if you were, you probably wouldn't reply. I don't blame you.

I closed my eyes, fighting back tears. There was so much I couldn't say and so little I could.

Anyway, I just wanted to say once more that I'm sorry about what happened. I never meant to hurt you. I promise I won't contact you again.

I hit send and watched the blue bubble with my bullshit words appear on the screen. They made me so angry, I felt like throwing my phone out the bedroom window just to hear the sound of breaking glass. A moment later, my jaw dropped.

Three gray dots were fading in and out, indicating she was answering my message.

Maren: I'm awake. I can't sleep.

Me: The nightmare?

It took her a long time to reply, so I was surprised to see only one word appear.

Maren: Yes.

I pictured her in her bed, the bed I'd shared with her less than a week ago. My chest tightened. My arms twitched. I wanted to hold her so badly.

I wanted to tell her I hadn't lied, I did love her, I always would. I wanted to beg her to forgive me so we could have that second chance. I wanted to tell her that Finn had come to see me and we'd had a really good talk. I wanted to bring *her* to Portland and ask her to climb Mount Hood with me, snuggle with her in a sleeping bag to keep warm, rise before the sun to make the final ascent, and hold her hand when we made it to the top and took in the view. I wanted to show her my new tattoo and say, *This is forever, you and me. I know it.*

But in the end, all I had were the same two inadequate words.

Me: I'm sorry.

I waited hours for a reply that never came.

EIGHTEEN

MAREN

"Are you sure about this?" Emme eyeballed the sign on Madam Psuka's door.

MADAM PSUKA: *Psychic, Medium, Clairvoyant, Intuitive*

Palm Readings, Dream Analysis, Spiritual Channeling, & Numerology
FIRST READING FREE*

*does not include Spiritual Channeling

It was Thursday afternoon, and we were slightly early for my three o'clock appointment. "No, I'm not sure. But I'm desperate. I haven't gotten a good night's sleep in forever. I have to do something, and Allegra said this woman is really good."

Emme shrank back a little and sniffed. "Smells weird in here. Like something's burning." She glanced down the stairs we'd just come up like she might make a run for it. We were standing on the second floor landing of an old Victorian building that had two storefronts on the ground level and apartments above. Madam Psuka was in 2A.

"I told you that you didn't have to come with me," I said irritably.

"I know, I know. But people are crazy. You shouldn't go to a stranger's house alone, and this place feels creepy." She sighed. "But if you think this will help, I will fully support you."

"Thank you." I rapped on the door three times. After a moment, it opened and a woman I presumed was Madam Psuka appeared. She was in her fifties, I guessed, with lots of curly dyed blond hair showing a good solid inch of brown and gray roots. Her face was buried beneath layers of makeup, and her eyebrows had been almost completely plucked but penciled in thick and black. She wore jeans, a brightly colored blouse, and no shoes.

She paused dramatically, drawing herself up. "Velcome."

"Hello," I said. "I'm Maren Devine."

"Yes." She nodded like she'd known this already. "And this is your sister?"

I glanced at Emme, wondering if the resemblance was so strong it was obvious we were siblings or if this woman was actually psychic. "Uh, yeah. Is it okay if she stays with me for the reading?"

Madam Psuka didn't answer right away. Instead she looked back and forth between the two of us, like she was trying to figure something out. "You have very different energies."

"Yes," I said, tucking my hair behind my ears. "I'm here because—"

"You are restless," she finished. "You are in chaos. You seek peace and cannot find it."

Emme and I exchanged a look.

"And you." The madam looked Emme up and down. "You are in balance. Is unusual for you."

"Yes," Emme said, beaming. "I think it's because—"

"But," Madam Psuka interrupted, holding up a finger to silence her. "Great change is coming."

Emme's smiled grew even bigger. "I'm getting married."

"No." Madam Psuka dismissed my sister's matrimony with a wave of her hand. "Is not that."

Emme grabbed my arm. "You mean I'm not getting married?"

"Listen," I said, getting a little nervous. "I'm here to—"

"Yes, you are getting married," said the madam with a slight roll of her eyes, like it wasn't that important. "But there is a greater change coming."

"Greater than that?" Emme shook her head. "I can't imagine what it could be. We already moved into a new house. I'm not looking for a new job."

"Change is vithin," said Madam Psuka smugly.

"It is?" Emme looked confused. "I can't imagine what it is, unless..." She glanced down at her stomach and put a hand over it. "Oh, no."

Great, now Emme was going to get dramatic. Did everything always have to be about her?

"It can't be." She continued to stare at her stomach.

"Oh, I think it can." Madam Psuka nodded knowingly. "Vould you like to come in?"

Emme was silent and frozen.

"Yes, please," I said, guiding my stunned sister inside the apartment. "Thank you."

Madam Psuka shut the door behind us, and I had to

squint as I looked around. Very little light filtered through the windows, which were all covered in multi-colored panels of fabric. Tapestries, paintings, and blankets covered the walls, and the floors were covered with faded rugs as well. She had no couch or chairs, but large pillows in every hue lined the walls or sat in heaps in the corners. It was sort of like being in a very colorful padded cell. She had stacks of books everywhere, beaded rope hanging from corner to corner, and several giant green plants. How they survived with so little natural light, I had no idea.

"Come. This vay." Madam Psuka led the way over to a low round table covered with a Moroccan print cloth. She walked with an air about her, almost like royalty. Then she lowered herself grandly to the floor. "Ve sit."

Emme followed suit, slowly and carefully like a nine-month-pregnant woman would do, still cradling her belly.

"Emme, for God's sake," I whispered as I dropped down next to her.

"I have to be careful," she hissed back. "There could be a baby in there."

"So." Madam Psuka folded her hands on the table. "Who vants to start?"

"Oh, she's not here for—" I started to say, but Emme broke in.

"Me," she said. "Start with me."

I rolled my eyes as Madam Psuka nodded. "Give me your hand."

Emme did as requested, and Madam Psuka held it in both of hers, closed her eyes, and hummed softly. After a moment, she opened her eyes and spoke. "You are confident and outgoing. A leader. A planner. When you want something, you go for it. People are drawn to your positive energy and admire your motivation. You work hard and value beautiful things. You always turn heads in a room."

Emme looked at me and I shrugged. It was pretty spot on.

"Now, your veaknesses."

Emme's smile faded. "Oh. Do you have to?"

"Yes. Is important." She hummed again. "You can get too wrapped up in details. You can be vorkaholic. You have tendency to overreact sometimes and it can make troubles for you."

My sister cleared her throat. "Right."

"You must remember to take time to relax and unvind. Is important for you."

"Is there anything about ... you know." Emme looked down at her stomach.

Madam Psuka closed her eyes for a full minute, then opened them. "No."

"No?" Emme gaped at her.

She shrugged. "Sometimes the spirits are stingy." Dropping Emme's hand, she gestured to me. "Next."

I cleared my throat. "Okay, well, I'm here because of a nightmare I keep having. I'd like a dream analysis if that's okay?"

She nodded. "Yes. Is right for you. Yes. Give me your hand and tell me the dream."

I took a breath and described the entire thing in detail, from the crowded room to the snake and the clock and the door. While I talked, Madam Psuka kept her eyes closed, but she didn't make the humming noise. "That's it," I said when I was done. "I can't get out of the room and the snake is going to bite me."

Madam Psuka said nothing but kept my hand in hers. The humming began. After a few minutes, I got impatient and spoke up again. "I think I know what it is. At least, I thought I knew."

"Oh?" The madam opened one eye and looked at me. "Tell me."

"Well, I think the snake is my ex-boyfriend from a long time ago. I never really got over him, and he hurt me really badly. Then out of the blue, he showed up on my doorstep six days ago to ask my forgiveness. Stupid me, I let him in, to my house *and* my heart, and he hurt me all over again. I feel like I can't escape the cycle of heartbreak with him. Like I'm trapped in it. That's the locked door."

"And the clock?" Madam Psuka challenged.

"The clock is probably some kind of biological thing reminding me that I'm not getting any younger and I need to stop trusting people who hurt me."

"Hm." She shut her eyes and the humming began. Emme and I exchanged glances.

"Do you think you can help her?" Emme asked, but the madam held up a hand to silence her.

"Hush." After an interminably long time, she finally opened her eyes and looked at me. "You are wrong."

"I am?" I stared at her. "How?"

"Snake is not him. Snake is you."

I shrank back. "Me!"

"Yes. Snake is often symbol of evil or temptation in dreams, but not in your case. Snake can also be sign of transformation because it sheds its skin. Your dream snake is you letting go of the past so you can move forward. It is you choosing love and not fear."

"But I had no choice!" I protested. "He left me—again!"

"You are still having this dream, yes?"

"Yes."

"Then the moment the dream is preparing you for has not yet come. The story is not done."

"Great," I snapped. "More trauma to look forward to."

Emme rubbed my arm.

"Okay, the clock," I challenged. I wasn't convinced this woman knew better than I did what my own dream meant. "What's that about?"

She shook her head. "Is not a clock you hold in your arms."

"It's not?"

"No. Is your heart. The ticking is your heartbeat."

Emme looked at me. "That makes sense to me. You were guarding it."

"She guards it still." Madam Psuka spoke quietly, but her words struck a nerve.

"I have to, okay? I'm protecting myself from being hurt again." I shook my head. "I should have seen this coming, especially since it wasn't the first time."

"This is vhy you are still trapped." Madam Psuka's voice was maddeningly calm. "Is not that you don't trust man. You don't trust yourself."

"So what do I *do* about it?" I asked. "And don't say fall in love again, because that is *not* going to happen. I am done with love. The universe was clearly trying to teach me a lesson, and I learned it."

"Let me ask you another question."

"Fine," I said irritably, ready to leave.

"How do you know there is only one door in the room?"

I gave her a blank look. "What do you mean? That's the only one I saw."

"Did you look around? Perhaps there are other doors."

"There are no other doors," I insisted, pulling my hand

away. "Nothing in the dream is a choice, okay? Nothing in real life was a choice either—I was misled, lied to, and cast aside. The End."

Madam Psuka shook her head. "Is not the end. All is not lost."

"Well, it feels that way to me." I stood up. "Come on, Emme."

But the madam wasn't done with me. "Be stronger. Be braver. Trust yourself. Open yourself up to all possibilities. Stop seeing yourself trapped in a cycle of heartbreak, and a way out will present itself to you—but not if you refuse to let it. Not if you refuse love."

"Fine." At this point, I was ready to say anything just to get out of there.

She was wrong.

The story was over.

AFTER WE LEFT Madam Psuka's, Emme made me go with her to the drugstore, where she bought a pregnancy test.

"Have you even missed a period yet?" I asked her on our way back to the cabin we were staying in at Abelard.

"No. But I'm expecting it any day now. The test might work!"

"Aren't you on the pill?"

"I am," she admitted, pulling into the Abelard drive, "but there have been a couple times I forgot."

"Didn't you double up the next day?"

"Yes, *Mom*, I did everything right, and I'm probably not pregnant but if there's a chance, I want to know."

"Okay, okay." I held up my hands. "Sorry. Let's

find out."

When we got into our cabin, Emme disappeared into the bathroom and I sank onto the bed. I was disappointed that the session with Madam Psuka had made me feel worse, not better. Flopping onto my back, I threw an arm across my eyes. I felt hopeless. Helpless. Deceived and defeated.

A moment later, Emme came out of the bathroom and I sat up. She was holding the capped stick in her hand and staring at it as she walked slowly toward me.

"Well?"

"I don't know yet. It's thinking." She froze. "Wait. It's doing something."

I jumped off the bed and walked around so I could see. Slowly, a bright pink line appeared on the right, but there was also a faint one coming in on the left too. I gasped and grabbed her arm. "Emme. Oh my God."

She didn't speak.

The line on the left wasn't as vivid as the one to the right, but the stick clearly had two lines, and two lines means Emme was—

"Ahhh!" Emme screamed. "Maren, I'm pregnant!"

We turned to each other and hugged and squealed and jumped up and down, both of us tearing up.

"You're having a baby!" I wiped my eyes. "I don't believe it."

"Me either." She stared at the test again. "This is crazy."

"I feel bad I know before Nate."

Emme gave me a look. "No, you don't."

"Not really." I smiled, so glad to have some good news. "Oh, Em, this is such great news. How do you feel?"

"Incredible! It's just ..." She turned around and sat on

the bed, looking a little pale and dazed. "Sooner than planned. We're not even married yet."

"Well, look, you've only been pregnant for like, what, two weeks or something? You have time. You said yourself, you could put together a wedding in no time. And Mia said lots of Friday nights are open this fall."

Emme nodded. "Right." She put a hand on her stomach and looked at it. "Nate's gonna die."

I sat next to her and put my arm around her shoulders. "He's gonna be thrilled. He's crazy about you." An unwelcome knot of envy lodged in my stomach. I'd never have this.

She giggled. "He's going to have two kids under the age of two."

I shoved the uncomfortable reality of my jealousy aside and refocused. "So they'll be close, like you and me. We're only fifteen months apart. Sure, we fought like cats and dogs growing up, but I loved having a sibling close in age."

"Me too." She tipped her head onto my shoulder. "I'm so glad you made me go to that Madam Whoever. I never would have guessed."

"Me either. At least the visit was helpful for one of us."

"I'm sorry. Are you feeling any better?"

"Not about myself. But I'm happy about your news. Are you going to call Nate?"

"No, I should tell him in person. But I have to tell someone—let's call Stella!" She hopped up and grabbed her phone from her purse.

"You're telling everyone before you tell the dad," I said. "He might be upset to be the last to know."

Emme's eyes were huge as she put the phone to her ear.

"I know. That's why you guys can *never tell him*." She held out one pinky finger.

I hooked mine through it, grateful to have the support of my two incredible sisters. They'd always be there for me. "My lips are sealed."

———

I DIDN'T HAVE the nightmare that night, probably because I barely slept. I lay awake for hours listening to Emme's deep, restful breaths and contemplating my life. Did I need to make a change? Move somewhere new? Start over? I didn't necessarily want to, but I was clearly vibrating at the wrong frequency and needed to recalibrate. But how?

I could sell the studio. It was doing well enough that I didn't think that would be a problem. But where would I go? What would I do? I was trying to puzzle it out when my phone buzzed. I reached over and picked it up from the nightstand, and my heart began to pound.

Dallas: Are you awake?

I stared at the screen. What the hell was this? I was still open-mouthed in shock when another message arrived.

Dallas: Probably not. It's late here, so it's even later for you. Even if you were, you probably wouldn't reply. I don't blame you. Anyway, I just wanted to say once more that I'm sorry about what happened. I never meant to hurt you. I promise I won't contact you again.

Reading his words, I was angry. How dare he text me in the middle of the fucking night with his lame apology! It didn't matter that he never meant to hurt me—the damage was done. Part of me was tempted to text back something sarcastic and bitchy, but then I realized there was no point. Sadness overwhelmed me. I didn't want to fight.

Me: I'm awake. I can't sleep.

Dallas: The nightmare?

No, you damn fool. It's you. I'm still in love with you. Do you care? Do you know how many tears I've cried for you? Do you know how miserable I am thinking I'll never see you again? Do you know how terrible I feel about myself? Do you know how worried I am about you?

Me: Yes.

It was just easier that way.

He took a few minutes to reply, and—stupid me—I let myself get a little hopeful that his response might make me happy. Maybe he would admit he lied. Maybe he would say he loved me. Maybe he would tell me he'd scheduled the surgery and wanted me there when he woke up. With every fiber of my being, I willed the words to appear. *Give me a choice, Dallas. Give me something.*

Dallas: I'm sorry.

Tears blurred my screen, and I set the phone aside, screen down. I didn't want another apology.

Sorry didn't mean anything anymore.

THE NEXT MORNING, Emme and I grabbed breakfast at a cute little bakery called Coffee Darling in downtown Traverse City. It was pretty early, barely seven, since Emme was eager to get on the road and home to Nate.

Sitting at the counter sipping herbal tea (Emme wanted

to avoid caffeine now), I told my sister about the late night messages.

"See? He still cares."

"No, he doesn't," I said irritably, wondering how badly my stomach was going to protest if I ate another cinnamon roll.

"Maren, why would he text you in the middle of the night if he didn't care?"

"I have no idea. To torture me." I grabbed a second pastry from the basket we'd ordered.

"And what's he doing in Portland? I thought he was in Boston."

"I don't know that either. I thought he was too. Seems like he can't stay in any one place for too long."

"Well, I still don't think he'd bother to reach out to you if you weren't still on his mind. I think Madam Psuka was right and this isn't over."

"Madam Psuka was right about *you*," I said, reaching for my teacup. "Not about me."

The woman behind the counter approached with a smile and the teapot. "Can I pour you fresh tea?" she asked. "I just brewed more."

"Sure," I said, sliding my cup closer to her.

"So I couldn't help overhearing," she said as she poured. "Did you say you saw Madam Psuka?"

Emme and I exchanged a surprised look. "We did," I said. "Do you know her?"

The woman smiled. "Yes. And I just wanted to tell you that she sounds a little crazy, but she's really good."

"Tell me about it," said Emme. "She pretty much told me I was pregnant. I had no clue. I took a test yesterday, and boom—she was right."

"Congratulations! That's so exciting. I'm Natalie, by the

way. The owner of the shop." She smiled brightly at both of us.

"It's so cute," Emme said, looking around.

"Thanks. It's funny, she knew I was pregnant too when I went there. And I wasn't showing yet or anything."

"Same!" Emme exclaimed.

I let myself be irritated with them both for just a second.

"She also predicted I would fall in love with my husband," Natalie went on, shaking her head. "It will always baffle me how she knew, but she did."

"That's amazing," Emme said. "We went there because Maren needed her to interpret this nightmare she's been having."

Natalie nodded and looked at me. "Was it helpful for you?"

I sighed. "Not really, unfortunately. There's this ... situation in my personal life. I messed up and trusted someone who hurt me." I picked up my napkin and dabbed at the corners of my eyes. "Madam Psuka thinks I need to let it go for the nightmares to stop. I don't know how I can."

"I'm sorry," Natalie said sympathetically. "I've been there, and I remember how it hurts. I remember feeling powerless in my situation too, like there was nothing I could do. But there was—I just had to see things differently. I remember she said to me, 'You must be villing to see things not as they have been or as they are, but as they could be.'" Natalie imitated Madam Psuka's accent perfectly.

It probably would have made me smile if I'd been in a decent mood. "Sounds like something she'd say."

"And you nailed the accent." Emme nodded enthusiastically.

"Thanks." Natalie smiled. "Anyway, she was right." She reached out and touched my arm. "You'll find your way."

I appreciated her kindness, but clearly our situations had been totally different.

We finished breakfast and got on our way. Emme drove, and I spent most of the nearly five-hour ride listening to her chatter on about the wedding and the baby, which best she could figure would be due in March. I nodded and commented when appropriate, but my mind wandered. I kept thinking about what Natalie had said. *You must be willing to see things not as they have been or as they are, but as they could be.*

I chewed my thumbnail and looked out the window.

I had no trouble seeing how things could have been for us. We could have been happy together. I could have seen him through his surgery and recovery. I'd have gone anywhere and done anything for him. It had been *his* decision to destroy all that. And with that future in ruins, what was left but the past and the present? I saw those perfectly clearly, and I'd learned from them.

You couldn't trust your heart.

Love could be a lie.

FRIDAY NIGHT, I went online to look for options for a yoga or mindfulness retreat and noticed I had an email from Finn Shepherd. Heart racing, I opened it up.

Dear Maren,

I thought you would like to know that Dallas has agreed to have the craniotomy, and it is scheduled for a week from today. He gave me permission to tell you when I asked.

I have full confidence in the surgeon and

know Dallas will pull through.
   Sincerely,
   Finn

My first reaction was relief. I closed my eyes and took a huge breath, letting gratitude fill me. But the positive vibe was short-lived, because my second reaction was a crushing wave of sadness. He'd changed his mind about the surgery, but not about me. He couldn't even be bothered to tell me himself.

It confirmed everything he'd said in the car Sunday night. He didn't feel what I felt. He didn't want me in his life. I'd been only a thing to cross off his list. Why he'd texted me in the middle of the night, I could only guess. His conscience again? Well, fuck that. I didn't want to be anyone's regret.

I exited my email and went back to my search results, deciding to book a five-day stay at a silent meditation and yoga retreat center on the coast of Maine, starting on Monday. I needed to slow down, unplug, and unwind. I needed to be alone with myself in order to heal and rebalance. I needed to hear that inner voice, the connection to my soul, and I couldn't do it surrounded by all this noise.

I was desperate for peace, inside and out.

Over the weekend, I talked to Allegra about taking over for me next week and offered her a raise to compensate her for the increased hours and responsibilities. I wasn't happy with how absent I'd been from my business and my employees lately, but I needed this time to reconnect with myself, contemplate my journey in life and what I wanted to accomplish, and center myself on the right path moving forward.

Love had knocked me way off course.

NINETEEN

DALLAS

On Friday, Finn and I went into the shop, and I introduced him to Beatriz. I told her I'd scheduled the surgery and really would be gone for a while this time. "I can't be alone, so Finn invited me to recover at his house."

She hugged me tightly. "I'm so proud of you."

"Thanks."

It was a long time before she released me. "So when do you leave?"

"I haven't booked a ticket yet, but probably Tuesday or Wednesday. And I have a ton of shit to do before then, so I'm not sure how much I can work." Besides getting my house in order and packing up, I had to make a will, something I'd never even thought about. Finn had suggested it, although he assured me it was just a precaution, and actually, I hadn't even freaked out.

Much.

Beatriz waved a hand in front of her face. "Don't even think about work. Take time to do what you need to do."

"Thanks. I'll stop in before I leave and clean out my

station. But if it's okay with you, I was going to give my brother here his first ink."

She looked at Finn in surprise. "Really?"

He shrugged, a little color coming into his face. "I've been thinking about it for a while. Seems like a good time, since I'm here."

Beatriz nodded. "Absolutely. And you can't go wrong with Dallas. He's the best." She lowered her voice to a whisper. "But don't tell anyone here I said that."

Finn laughed. "Never."

She looked at me. "Let's have a drink before you go, okay? Maybe we can even drag Evan out of the house."

"Sounds good."

I took Finn over to my station, and we looked through a book of stencils I had for other tattoos I had done. He didn't want anything too big and only had one idea—his kids' names and their birthdates. Nothing wrong with that idea, and I'd have done it, but I thought it might be a little more meaningful if it had more personality. I happened to have some of the artwork Olympia and Lane had sent me taped on the wall in my cubical, and we decided to do their first names in their own handwriting along with their birthdates. Finn liked the drawing I did, and I suggested it might be nice to put it on the left side of his chest.

"Let's do it," he said.

I created a stencil, cleaned and shaved the area, and applied the design. Both Beatriz and I thought it was the perfect placement, and Finn gave the go ahead.

"You nervous?" I asked as I finished prepping.

"A little," he admitted, lying back in the chair. "But I trust you."

"Good." Then I pulled on my gloves and got to work.

FINN and I hung out all day Friday, and he helped me make a list of things I should take care of before leaving for Boston, which I'd booked for Wednesday. He loved his new tattoo and said he couldn't wait to show Bree and the kids. I could tell he felt pretty badass about it, and it made me happy. The only tense moment between us came when he asked if I planned to tell Maren about the surgery. I said no, and he asked my permission to let her know.

"She cares, Dallas," he said, tipping back his beer at dinner Friday night. He glanced at the ink on my forearm, where the skin was still healing. "And if you care about her—"

"You know I do," I snapped. "Caring about her isn't the issue."

"Then call her." He set the bottle down hard. "She'd want to know."

"*No.*" I focused on my right hand, which was spinning my water glass around. There was no fucking way I could handle hearing her voice.

"Dallas."

"No, Finn. I promised her I wouldn't contact her again." And I could keep that one promise, at least, couldn't I? For fuck's sake, I'd broken every other one I'd ever made to her.

He sighed. "Any objection to my telling her?"

I shrugged. "Suit yourself."

When I took him to the airport on Saturday, he hugged me goodbye and told me how much he'd enjoyed spending time with me—it was the first time we'd ever done that without his family or our parents around, too. "We should do this again sometime. A guys' weekend."

"We should." Although these days, I wasn't counting on anything in the future.

"See you in Boston."

"See you. Safe trip home."

I spent the next few days cleaning my house, clearing out the fridge, and packing my bags. I got a haircut, checked in with my neurologist, who was happy to hear I'd elected to have surgery, set up auto-pay for my monthly bills, and asked my next-door neighbor to bring in the mail. On Monday, I saw my lawyer, who had created a will according to my specifications. If anything happened to me, my inheritance, and anything else left over after settling the estate, would be split equally between Olympia and Lane. I was only renting my house, so I didn't have to worry about that, and anything in it, I wanted donated. Two other attorneys in his office served as witnesses while I signed it.

All day, every day, I thought about Maren. Missed her with an intensity that rivaled the pain in my head. My house had never felt so fucking lonely.

But it was nothing less than I deserved for what I'd done.

On Tuesday night, I met Beatriz and Evan for a drink at the Teardrop Lounge. We congratulated Evan again and asked to see pictures of his son, and he happily obliged. He had dark shadows under his eyes and said nights were rough, but I could tell he was happy. I envied him.

Our drinks arrived—since Beatriz had offered to pick me up and drop me off, I'd indulged in some whiskey—and we raised our glasses.

"To Hunter William," Beatriz said. "May he take after his mother as much as possible. And to Dallas's speedy and full recovery."

"I'll drink to that," said Evan.

Evan finished his cocktail quickly and had to get home, but he shook my hand before he left and told me both he and Reyna were pulling for me, and asked me to let them know how everything went as soon as I could. I said I would.

As soon as we were alone at the table, Beatriz lit into me.

"You look miserable," she said.

"I feel worse than I look."

"Still haven't talked to the girl?"

I shook my head.

"Why not?"

"Because if I hear her voice, I'll fall apart," I said quietly.

"Dude." She lifted her drink to her lips and sipped. "You're a fucking mess. I'm not trying to tell you what to do, but let me tell you what to do."

I frowned at her.

"I've been thinking about this a lot, ever since you conned me into giving you that tattoo. You need to come clean with her. It's got you all fucked in the head. Your aura is, like, choking on this pain."

"It's all I have of her."

"Christ, Dallas. Do you even hear yourself? You're clinging to the pain and guilt instead of the woman you love. She could be there by your side getting you through this. She'd make you stronger, you know. I bet you'd fight harder."

Her words made sense, but I'd already done too much damage. "I fucked things up too much. They can't be fixed. It's too late."

"You haven't even tried!"

"She probably wouldn't even talk to me."

Beatriz shrugged. "Guess you'll have to find that out."

I sat there for a few minutes, staring into my whiskey. "I miss her, Bea. I really fucking miss her."

"I know, babe."

"I thought coming back here and burying my head in the sand would make me feel better, but it didn't."

"It never does."

"And I'm scared." It felt good to say it aloud.

"Of what?"

"Of dying. Of losing feeling in my right hand. Of needing people to take care of me. Of not being enough for her." I looked up at her and admitted the truth. "But I can't keep living like this. It's only been ten days, and I'm going crazy."

"So *do* something about it, Dallas." She reached out and touched my wrist. "We all make mistakes. We're all human. What sets one man apart from the next is what happens afterward."

Exhaling, I closed my eyes. "I don't even know what to say to her. How to explain myself. I told her a bunch of lies. She won't know what to believe."

"Can I offer a suggestion?"

I nodded.

"What do you think she wants more than anything in the world?"

"A second chance," I said without hesitation.

"And what do you want?" She held up one hand. "Wait, let me rephrase. What do you want that you have control over getting?"

"To make her happy. If I can."

"What would make her happy?"

I sighed. "She wants to be there for me. Take care of me."

"Are you comfortable with that?"

"No. Fuck no." Frowning, I rubbed the back of my neck. "But if that's what it takes …"

"If it were me," Beatriz said, touching her tattooed chest, "that's what it would take. Knowing that you were willing to let me see you at your most vulnerable. Because with you, she's at her most vulnerable too."

"Yeah," I said miserably, picturing her sobbing into her hands after I told her I was leaving. "You really think letting her see me all out of it and half-bald and stapled together is the way to go?"

"Yes." She leaned forward, elbows on the table. "Because it says, This is the real me. Yes, I'm the big, strong tattooed hottie with the eyes and the hair and the chiseled jaw, the guy who makes everyone laugh and all the girls swoon and never shows a sign of weakness, but I'm something else with you. I let you see all of me, because I love you."

"Damn." I blinked. "That's pretty good."

"Thank you. Now go make it happen. You're one of the lucky ones, Dallas. You found it. Don't let it pass you by." She reached for my hand and squeezed, her eyes misting over. "Then get better, and bring that girl back here so I can meet the one woman amazing enough to steal your heart."

I took a breath. "I'll try."

I TEXTED HER THAT NIGHT.

Maren, can we talk?

No answer.

I don't blame you for ignoring me. But if you have it in your heart to give me a few minutes, I'd really love to talk to you. Call me when you can.

I waited and waited and waited. Nothing.

It was late in Detroit, after midnight, so she was probably already asleep. Was she teaching an early morning class tomorrow? If she was, she'd be up within a few hours. I set my phone down, got ready for bed, and checked my phone once more. Nothing.

I plugged it in to charge and got in bed, but slept only fitfully throughout the night. Every so often, I checked to see if she'd written me back, but was disappointed every time.

By the following morning, I had to consider the possibility that she'd seen my messages and had decided against replying. After I finished packing and was ready to leave, I decided to try calling her. I got her voicemail. The sound of her voice on the outgoing message made my pulse quicken.

"Maren, it's me. You've probably seen my messages by now. You haven't called, which means you're either too upset with me to talk or you need more time to think about it. I get that. I'll be on a plane to Boston most of today, but you could reach me in the next couple hours or later tonight. I'll be on your time zone by then." I paused. "I don't know if Finn told you or not, but I decided to have the surgery. It will be on Friday. I'd really like to talk to you before then, if possible. I ... hope you're well. I miss you." Then I hung up before I started breaking down.

TWO HOURS LATER, I was checked in and waiting to board the plane, and I still hadn't heard from Maren. Frowning at my phone, I heard my zone get called, but I ignored it, wanting to stay at the gate as long as possible just in case she called. Finally, I couldn't delay boarding any longer, and I was forced to get on the plane without a word from her, not even an acknowledgment that she'd gotten my texts. I reluctantly switched my phone to airplane mode and dropped it into the carry-on bag at my feet.

What was I going to do if she didn't call? Keep trying? Leave her a longer voicemail telling her the truth about why I'd broken things off? It wasn't the kind of thing I wanted to do over voicemail, but she might not leave me a choice. Or would the right thing to do be to leave her alone? If her silence continued, didn't that mean she didn't want to hear anything from me? At this point, she was probably thinking, *Fuck him and his apologies. I don't need them.* How could I get her to listen?

I tipped my head back and closed my eyes. This hole I'd dug for myself was deep, maybe too deep to climb out of.

But I wouldn't give up.

TWENTY

DALLAS

I arrived in Boston and spent the evening with Finn and his family. Seeing the kids cheered me up a little, but later, when it was just the two of us, Finn asked me what was wrong. "You seem upset," he said, his expression concerned. "Are you nervous?"

"Yes, but it's not that." We were still at the dinner table, but Bree had taken the kids up for their baths. Finn said that he would take care of the dishes.

"What is it?" He stacked a few plates.

"I reached out to Maren and asked her to call me, but there's just silence on her end."

"Ah." He piled forks and knives on top of the stack. "I'm sorry."

I shrugged. "I get it. She's hurt. Why should she call me? She thinks she's heard everything I have to say."

"But she hasn't. She just doesn't realize it."

"I can't force her to listen to me. I don't know what else to do."

Finn didn't answer, and after a few minutes, he stood

and started carrying dishes into the kitchen. I did the same. When everything from the table was in the sink, I took a seat at the island and watched him load the dishwasher. "Want help?"

"Nah. I got it."

I looked around the big, beautiful kitchen, with its gray-painted cabinetry, black stone counters, and polished wood floor. It was clean but lived-in—kids' artwork on the fridge, shoes piled over by the back door, the clutter of everyday life all around. "You're really lucky," I said.

"Damn right I am." He looked back at me. "But it's not just luck."

"What can I do, Finn? She won't talk to me."

"Maybe email her? She seems to check email often enough."

"Did you tell her about the surgery?"

"Yes. And she replied the next day that she was glad to hear it and thanked me for letting her know. She said she wished us all the best."

I swallowed hard. "Okay. I'll email her. Can you forward me her email address?"

"Of course."

LATER THAT NIGHT, I lay in bed with my laptop trying to find the perfect words to say, the words that would undo all the damage I'd done and bring her back to me.

It wasn't easy. I wrote, deleted. Wrote, deleted. Wrote, deleted. I'd never been a confident writer, and the pressure in this situation was almost unbearable. Finally, after three hours and a hundred different drafts, I gave up on perfect and just wrote from the heart.

Dear Maren,

An email is probably the worst way to say everything I want to say to you, but it's the way I'm stuck with because I'm stubborn as fuck and waited too long to have the chance to do it in person. I haven't been able to reach you by phone, not that I blame you for not wanting to speak to me. I've put you through too much already, and part of me thinks I should leave you alone even now. But I need to tell you the truth about my feelings for you, and this might be my last chance to do it.

Everything I told you the night we went to the baseball game is true.

Everything.

I never stopped loving you. I fell in love with you all over again the weekend we spent together, and I love you still. I said it was a lie only to make you hate me, so that leaving wouldn't hurt so much.

Of course, it hurt anyway. More than I can say.

When I made the decision to come see you, it was because leaving you the first time has always been my biggest regret, and after getting the news about the tumor in my brain, you were all I could think about. I had to make things right with you. I never intended to fall for you again.

But being with you was like coming home to a place where I was more loved, more alive, more *me* than anywhere I've ever been. I should have told you about the tumor right away, but I couldn't bring myself to ruin those perfect, happy hours we had—and I knew they were numbered. My future was so uncertain, and I didn't want to drag you into it. I didn't want you to feel burdened by your feelings for me. I didn't want your pity. In my head, the only way to spare you from having to see me at my worst was to hide the truth from you.

And because I want to be honest, I will also admit that I wanted to spare myself the pain of losing you. The truth is that I don't think I'm worth your love or all the trouble it will take to care for me. Maybe that's because of my childhood, or maybe it's just because I know I can be a selfish, stubborn prick and you shouldn't have to put up with my bullshit, but there it is. So I tried to protect both of us by breaking things off.

I was wrong, and for that I am deeply sorry.

What I should have done was tell you the truth and give you the choice to be with me or walk away.

Which brings me to now. As you know, I am having the surgery on Friday, and the surgeon is hopeful he can remove the entire tumor. After that, we will wait for the biopsy to tell us if it is benign or cancerous. If it is cancer, I will likely need additional treatment like chemotherapy and radiation. It would be a long, difficult road to travel.

I don't know what's going to happen, and I'm scared.

I'm scared of losing feeling in my right hand. I'm scared of losing speech and memory. I'm scared of being dependent on someone else to take care of me. I'm scared of waking up and not feeling like myself anymore. And although I've never felt this way before, I'm scared of dying—not because I don't want to face whatever reckoning awaits me, but because I don't want to leave this earth yet. For the first time in my life, I'm looking ahead and thinking to myself, *I'm not done.*

I'm not done living, and I'm not done loving you, Maren Devine. Not by a long shot.

Granted, I'm not much of a catch right now, but I swear to God if you'll give me that second chance, I'll spend the rest of my life making you the happiest woman alive.

You once asked me to let you love me, and I promised I would. Let me keep my promise.

Now, then, always and only yours,

Dallas

I read it over a million times, took a deep breath, and hit send.

Then I closed my laptop, lay back, and prayed she would have it in her heart to forgive me. To accept me. To be mine.

It was going to be a long night.

I WAS AWAKE FOR HOURS—FRANTICALLY checking my email every five minutes—but eventually fell asleep sometime after three a.m. When I woke up, it was nearly eight, and I quickly looked at my inbox again.

Nothing.

Sighing, I closed my eyes and tried not to feel like this was a hopeless cause. But my head was pounding, my stomach was upset, and I had a horrible stiff neck from the awkward way I'd slept. Dragging myself out of bed, I followed the smell of coffee downstairs.

"Morning," Bree said cheerfully, pulling clean plates from the dishwasher. "How are you feeling?"

"Not great," I admitted.

She gave me a sympathetic look. "I'm sorry. Can I get you some coffee?"

"I can get it." I took a cup from the cupboard and filled it with coffee from the pot. "Finn at work already?"

"Yes. He went in early today, and he said he'll be late tonight. But he's taking off tomorrow and a few days next week."

That was because of me, and I felt guilty about it as I sat down on a stool at the island. "I wish I didn't have to inconvenience you guys."

"You're not an inconvenience, Dallas." She gave me a look. "You're family. This is what we do for each other."

I nodded. "Thank you. I appreciate everything."

"You're welcome." She paused in her work and sipped from a mug on the counter that said *There is a good chance this is vodka* on it. "Finn told me you guys had a nice time in Portland."

"We did."

"I'm really glad. I think it really bothered him, more than he realized, that you two didn't have a very close relationship. It bothered *me*, that's for sure. I was always on him to do something about it, but he was just so darn stubborn."

I gave her a half-grin. "Runs in the family."

She laughed. "True. Anyway, I'm so happy about it. I've always been so close to my sisters, I can't imagine what my life would be like without them."

Her comment got me thinking about something. Maren was close to both her sisters. If I didn't hear back from her by this afternoon, could I reach out to one of them?

"So what are your plans for today?" Bree asked.

"Uh, not sure, exactly." *Stalking my ex-girlfriend's sisters* seemed like a bad answer.

"Just let me know if there's anything you need or if you want to go somewhere. I'm happy to take you. And is there anything special you want for your last ... for dinner?" She caught herself, but I could see the slip had made her uncomfortable.

I wanted to put her at ease. "You know what was really fun? The night last week when we grilled hamburgers and hot dogs and hung out by the pool."

She smiled, relieved. "Pool party it is!"

I drank some coffee, ate the toast Bree insisted on making for me, and checked my email again—nothing from Maren. After a quick shower, I unpacked my suitcase, putting clothes in dresser drawers and hanging a few things in the closet, although I hadn't brought very much. When the kids got up, they wanted me to swim with them, so after checking my inbox one more time—nothing—I put on my suit, and followed them out to the pool.

"Hey, Oly, can I use your sunscreen?" I asked, spying some Coppertone near her pink unicorn towel.

"Sure," my niece said, watching as I gently put some on my new tattoo, which had healed nicely. "Why do you have to do that?"

"To protect it."

She looked closer. "What does Maren mean?"

Everything, I thought. "Maren is a name. She's a friend of mine."

"In Oregon?"

"Actually, she lives in Detroit. But I hope she comes to see me in Portland sometime."

"Can I come to Portland sometime, too?"

"You better," I said, giving her a threatening look.

She flashed a gap-toothed grin my way and went running for the pool. "Last one in's a rotten egg!"

I pretended to hustle but let both her and Lane jump in before me.

"You're a rotten egg, Uncle Dallas! You stink!" Olympia taunted, holding her nose. I retaliated by hoisting her up over my head and throwing her into the deep end. When she surfaced, she was laughing. "Do it again!"

I spent the day at home with the kids, and Finn surprised us all by coming home early. While he went up to change, I checked my email on my phone again, but there was no message from Maren. At this point, it was hard not to feel despondent—she had to have seen it by now, and she'd replied fairly quickly to Finn, hadn't she? I'd texted and called and emailed. She had to have seen one of those attempts on my part. It was becoming increasingly clear that the issue wasn't communication—the issue was that she was choosing to walk away.

But even if that was the case, I wanted to know for sure.

"Be right back, guys," I said, wrapping a towel around me and heading into the house.

Upstairs in my room, I searched "Emme Devine wedding planner" on my phone. From what Maren had told me, Emme was the most romantic of the three sisters, so I figured she was my best bet. The website for Devine Events came up in the search results, and I clicked it.

Then I called the phone number.

"Good afternoon, Devine Events. Amy speaking."

"Hi, I'm looking to speak with Emme Devine, please."

"She's not in the office right now, can I take a message?"

Fuck! I frowned at the water I was dripping on the carpet. "Is there any way I could get hold of her? It's sort of urgent."

"Can I have your name?"

I cringed. Emme was not going to want to speak with me. "Dallas Shepherd."

"And what event is this regarding?"

"It's not regarding an event. It's about her sister, Maren."

"Oh." Amy sounded alarmed. "Is everything okay?"

"Yes. No. I mean—there's no emergency or anything, I just really need to speak with Emme about her, and I'm running out of time. Maybe." God. I sounded like a fucking lunatic.

"Can you give me your number, please?"

I recited my cell number for her, and she said she'd get back to me. I wondered if it would be a while and contemplated going back outside, but it was only about thirty seconds before my phone vibrated. The number on the screen was not the one I'd just called.

"Hello?"

"Hi, Dallas? This is Emme."

"Hey, Emme. Thanks for calling me back."

"No problem. My office called and said something about an urgent matter regarding Maren?"

"Yes." I exhaled. "I'm trying to contact her."

"Can I ask why?"

"Because I made a horrible mistake, letting her go."

Silence. "I'm listening."

I closed my eyes. "I want her back."

"Why did you do it?" she asked. "Why did you break her heart like that?"

"Several reasons, all of which seemed valid at the time, but none of which matter to me anymore."

"They matter to me," she said. "So if you want me to help you get in touch with Maren, you better spill them."

"Okay," I agreed, and launched into the story. I told her everything, taking her on the journey from Portland to Detroit to Boston and back again. It was embarrassing and uncomfortable and really fucking awkward at times, but she was right—if I expected her to help, I had to make it clear what this meant to me.

"So the stuff you told her in the car last Sunday night was all bullshit?" she asked.

"Yes."

"And you really have loved her all this time?"

"Yes."

"And you want to be with her now?"

"More than anything."

"Wow, Nate was right."

I had no idea what she meant by that. "I'm sorry?"

"Never mind. But Dallas, do you think she should trust you again, after what you did to her?"

I sighed, my eyes closing briefly. "I know it's going to be hard. But yes, she should. I'm going to do everything I possibly can to earn it back."

"Good." Then she surprised me with a long sigh. "This is so romantic. I really want it to happen."

"Do you think it can? Has she gotten my calls and messages the last two days?" I asked desperately.

"No. That I can tell you for sure. She's been at some yoga retreat place where you have to completely unplug and live like forest nymphs or something."

Relief, pure and powerful, washed over me. "When will she be back?"

"Not until tomorrow."

"Oh." I was due at the hospital at six in the morning. Disappointment pressed heavily on me, and I lowered myself to the bed. "Okay."

"You said the surgery is tomorrow too, right?"

"Right. I was kind of hoping to talk to her before I went in, but ... that might not be possible." I felt like crying.

"I'm sorry, Dallas."

"It's my own fault."

Emme was silent for a moment. "When she gets back, I'll talk with her. I can't promise anything, because she was so angry and heartbroken, but I'll try."

"Thanks." I swallowed hard. "Is she ... okay?"

"No. She's a mess, Dallas. She blames herself for falling for you. She thinks she deserves a broken heart for trusting you again."

It was like a knife to the gut. I had no words.

"She went to this retreat place to recover some sense of self-worth, I think. Find her balance again. You really wrecked her." Then she sighed. "But I do love a second-chance romance. And for what it's worth, I think you're being sincere about your feelings for her. So I'll do what I can."

"Thank you." I barely got the words out.

"You're welcome. And good luck tomorrow, okay?"

"Thanks."

We hung up, and I flopped back on the bed. My head ached, and my heart was in a million pieces, but I'd done all I could.

Now it was up to her.

TWENTY-ONE

MAREN

The knock surprised me.

It was Thursday evening at the retreat center, my last night there, and not once all week had anyone disturbed me in my room. I'd returned from the evening guided meditation session and was getting ready for bed when I heard the soft knock. I opened the door and found a retreat employee, a young woman, standing there.

"Yes?" My throat was scratchy and I cleared it. I hadn't had a real conversation with anyone in four days. The silence was supposed to make it easier to find clarity and hear your inner voice, and although I was feeling slightly calmer than when I'd arrived, my inner voice had stayed quiet. I didn't feel as though I'd resolved anything. I still cried myself to sleep, I still missed Dallas, and I was still having the nightmare almost every night.

"I'm so sorry to bother you," the employee said quietly, "but there was an urgent message for you to call your sister, Emme."

I panicked. "Okay, thank you. I'll call right away."

I shut the door and flew to my suitcase, where I dug out

my phone. I hadn't looked at it since I got off the plane in Bangor on Monday, and frankly, I hadn't even missed it.

Quickly I plugged it in, and when it came on, I called Emme. She answered right away.

"Maren?"

"Is everyone okay?" I asked frantically. "What's going on?"

"Everyone is okay," Emme said. "And I'm sorry to disturb you on your retreat."

"What's wrong?"

"Oh jeez, now I don't know if I did the right thing."

"Emme." I touched two fingertips to my temple. "Please."

She sighed. "Okay, but if you're mad at me for this, I only did it because I thought you'd want me to. Well, and because it's romantic, but—"

"*Emme.* I'm really not supposed to be on the phone or talking at all here."

"You can't talk there? That's weird. Why not? I mean, I get the thing about unplugging from technology, but talking? Human to human? What's wrong with that?"

Suddenly I appreciated the atmosphere of silence more than ever. "Because it encourages us to spend time within ourselves."

"Is it helping you?"

"Some."

"Well, good. Before you go back inside yourself, though, I just thought you might want to know that Dallas is trying to get in touch with you."

My heart stopped. "He is?"

"Yes."

"How do you know?"

"Because he called me at work."

"He did?" A wave of dizziness came over me, and I sat on my bed.

"Yeah. He said he's called and left messages for you."

"But why?"

"I think you need to hear it from him."

"*Tell me.*"

"Gah, I didn't want to do this. But I'm afraid if I don't, you won't talk to him."

I took a deep breath.

"He loves you, Maren."

"No, he doesn't. He doesn't love anybody. He told me that, remember?"

"He lied to you."

"What?" The room was spinning. "Why?"

"Because he's a man, and when men get feelings with a capital F, they act like idiots with a capital I. They make terrible decisions and do all the wrong things. In their caveman minds, it all makes sense somehow. But he loves you. He told me so."

"He told me a lot of things. Doesn't make them true."

"Look, just talk to him. Or at least read his messages."

"You know what, I don't even want to read his messages, Emme. Like you said, he lies. And I've fallen for too many of them already."

"Okay, then don't. I only thought you might like to know because he's having that surgery tomorrow. I felt like if there was anything you wanted to say to him, you might want to say it now."

"I've said everything I want to say to him already," I said bitterly. I wouldn't be guilted into playing the fool again. He'd made his choice. "And I've heard all I need to hear."

"Okay, Maren." Her voice was quieter. "I'm sorry if I upset you. I thought I was doing the right thing."

I took a breath and softened my tone, too. "I'm sorry, too. I'm not upset with you. I'm upset with myself. I'm having a really hard time getting past this."

Silence. And then, "Do you still love him?"

I closed my eyes, felt my chest tighten. *Of course I do.* "It doesn't matter."

"If it makes a difference, Mare, when I talked to him, I felt like he was being sincere."

"I did too, Emme—that's the problem! He's a master at sincere. He can make you trust him so easily it's criminal." I started to cry. "But it's not real. And it doesn't last. He always leaves."

"Oh, honey, I'm sorry. I shouldn't have told you. This is all my fault."

"No, it isn't." I sniffed and wiped my eyes. "I'm sorry, I'm being bitchy and you're trying to help. How are you feeling?"

"Great. I saw the doctor yesterday and everything is perfect so far. I'll have an ultrasound at ten weeks to confirm the due date."

"Has Nate recovered from the shock?"

Emme giggled. "Almost. I've only seen him faint one other time in his life, and that was the night he found out about Paisley."

"So he's consistent at least."

"Yeah." A pause. "Are you going to be all right?"

I swallowed. "Eventually. I hope."

"Home tomorrow, right?"

"Right."

"Travel safe. Love you."

"Love you, too." I ended the call and buried my phone in my suitcase again.

HOURS LATER, I was still tossing and turning in the dark. It was almost worse than the nightmare. Sleep absolutely *refused* to come, and the thought of my phone in my suitcase was killing me.

Should I do what Emme said? Should I listen to his messages? Should I risk whatever healing I'd done this week, put what little peace I'd found with myself in jeopardy? Did I want to trade that in for another apology? Because I didn't believe for one second that he actually loved me. He couldn't.

But something in me would not rest. As if I were compelled by an outside force, I got out of bed and dug out my phone again.

Just the texts, I told myself as I plugged it in. I'd read his texts and then put my phone away.

There were two, both from late Tuesday night.

Maren, can we talk?

And then:

I don't blame you for ignoring me. But if you have it in your heart to give me a few minutes, I'd really love to talk to you. Call me when you can.

I frowned at the screen. That did *not* sound like a man in love. That sounded like someone who wanted a favor. Or a man who was selling something.

Well, I wasn't buying any insincerity today, thank you very much.

Then I noticed he'd left me a voice message on Wednesday morning. Convinced it could only reinforce my belief that Emme had been fooled just as I had been, I listened to it.

"Maren, it's me. You've probably seen my messages by now. You haven't called, which means you're either too upset with me to talk or you need more time to think about it. I get that. I'll be on a plane to Boston most of today, but you could reach me in the next couple hours or later tonight. I'll be on your time zone by then. I don't know if Finn told you or not, but I decided to have the surgery. It will be on Friday. I'd really like to talk to you before then, if possible. I ... hope you're well. I miss you."

The sound of his voice sent chills up my spine and blanketed my arms with goose bumps, but I still hadn't heard anything that suggested he'd changed his mind about us. To me, it sounded like he just wanted to apologize again, and he wanted me to offer my forgiveness before he went into surgery.

If that was the case, a text back would suffice. A simple *I forgive you, good luck tomorrow*. There was no way I could call him, like he'd requested—I'd break down and cry, and I was so tired of tears.

I typed out the message and hit send. A few seconds later, I got a Failed to Send text. I tried again, but it failed a second time. Sighing, I gave up on the text and decided to send an email to Finn. Dallas would probably hate that, but I had no other option. It was either Finn passing the message along or nothing. I didn't have an email address for Dallas.

I opened my inbox. And there it was—a message from Dallas.

Subject: **Those who understand us enslave something in us.**

I recognized the words right away—they were from his

tattoo, the first one I'd asked him about—and my breath caught in my lungs.

Before I could stop myself, I read through the email, my heart pounding faster with every word. I covered my mouth with my hand.

Was this *real*?

I read the entire thing over and over again.

My God, no wonder Emme had called me. If he'd sounded half as sincere on the phone as he had in this email, I'd have believed him too.

But should I?

My head said no.

My heart said yes.

My gut ... I wasn't sure yet. My inner voice was still silent.

Setting the phone down next to me, I pulled the covers up to my chin and lay there, shivering and scared and wide-eyed in the dark.

I wanted more than anything for his words to be true, for his feelings to exist as he'd described them. I'd never heard him so forthright about his fears or talk about the future like that.

I picked up my phone again and reread the ending.

FOR THE FIRST **time in my life, I'm looking ahead and thinking to myself, *I'm not done*.**

I'm not done living, and I'm not done loving you, Maren Devine. Not by a long shot.

Granted, I'm not much of a catch right now, but I swear to God if you'll give me that second

chance, I'll spend the rest of my life making you the happiest woman alive.

You once asked me to let you love me, and I promised I would. Let me keep my promise.

Now, then, always and only yours,
Dallas

MY EYES FILLED. My stomach churned. What if this was just his fear and adrenaline talking? What if he woke up after the surgery and said, *Sorry, changed my mind.* What if I showed up at the hospital and he refused to see me?

But ... what if he meant these things? What if my head was wrong? What if my heart knew the truth? Which part of myself could I trust?

I closed my eyes. I breathed deeply, in and out, aware of each breath, turning my focus inward. Somewhere inside me was the answer, I was sure of it.

I heard Madam Psuka's voice. *Then the moment the dream is preparing you for has not yet come. The story is not done.*

I drifted deeper.

Still the voice was hers. *Be stronger. Be braver. Trust yourself. Open yourself up to all possibilities. Stop seeing yourself trapped in a cycle of heartbreak, and a way out will present itself to you—but not if you refuse to let it. Not if you refuse love.*

And deeper still, until I'm in a room full of people, but they can't see me.

I keep trying to talk to them, but I can't speak. I can't even open my mouth.

I look down and notice I'm naked.

That's when I see the snake.

Slithering through the crowd along the dark wood floor, it's heading straight for me.

Panicked, I start running for the door at the end of the room, carrying the clock. It's ticking loudly.

Eventually, I reached the door but discover there is no handle. And it won't budge.

For the first time, I turn around and face the snake. It stops short of me.

I hear a voice. It is my own, not speaking aloud, but inside me. It says, *I am not afraid to love.*

The snake hisses, as if it heard me.

I welcome the voice, and it speaks again. *I am not afraid to love.*

The snake begins to vanish.

I am not afraid to love.

The room is empty now; the people have disappeared. I look at the snake again and discover it's gone.

I am not afraid to love.

I walk to the center of the room and set the clock on the floor, where it continues to tick loudly, neither fast nor slow, but with a steady, reassuring rhythm. Then I turn and look around. The closed door is still there. But there is another door as well, on the opposite side of the room. It has a handle.

I am not afraid to love.

I move toward the door, slowly at first, but eventually start to run. When I reach the door, breathless and exhilarated, I grab the handle and pull hard. It's heavy and does not open easily, but I don't give up. I grasp harder and pull with all my strength, will it to give with all my might. I don't know what's on the other side, but I know I have to get there.

With one final heave, the door swings open.

"I am not afraid to love," I whisper.

And I run through.

I WOKE UP WITH A START, my eyelids flying open. Immediately it all comes back to me—the phone call with Emme, the messages and email from Dallas, the dream.

"Shit!" I hadn't meant to fall asleep. I look at the clock on the bedside table and see it's after seven already. "Shit, shit, shit!" Was Dallas in surgery already? I'd never replied to his email!

I jumped out of bed and frantically got dressed, brushed my teeth, and braided my disheveled hair, all the while throwing all my crap into my suitcase without even folding it. Thankfully, my phone had charged all night. My first call was to Emme.

"Hello?" she said sleepily.

"Hey, it's me. Listen. I'm not coming home today. I'm going to Boston."

"You are?" Suddenly she was wide awake.

"Yes. I read Dallas's messages."

She squealed. "You did?"

"Yes." My stomach was jumping around like mad. "And at first I wasn't sure what to believe, but now I think you were right and he is being sincere. At least, my gut is telling me that."

"Oh God, Maren. I'm going to feel really bad if I'm wrong."

"You won't have to." I shut my suitcase and zipped it up. "This is my choice. I know it's a risk, but I'm willing to take it. I can't be afraid of love, Emme. Madam Psuka was right.

Even if it means getting hurt again, choosing love is always the right thing to do."

Emme sniffed. "I'm going to cry."

"Don't cry. I need you."

"Anything. What can I do?"

"Can you book me a hotel room in Boston? I don't even know what hospital he's in, and I won't until I get hold of Finn, but any place will do." I glanced around the room one last time.

"Consider it done. How are you getting to Boston?"

"I don't know that either."

She laughed. "This is crazy, Maren. But I kind of love it."

"Wish me luck."

"I don't think you're going to need it, but good luck."

We hung up, and I rushed out of the room, dragging my suitcase behind me.

———

IT TURNED out the easiest way for me to get to Boston was by bus. I caught a taxi into Bangor in time to get on the nine a.m. coach, and sank into my seat with relief. I felt like I'd hardly stopped moving since I'd woken up this morning. Once I was on my way, I used my phone to send an email to Finn.

Hey Finn, it's Maren Devine. Dallas reached out to me, and I'm on my way to Boston. Can you please let me know which hospital he's in? Thank you!

I gave him my phone number in case he wanted to text back, then sat back and exhaled. My emotions were all over the place—anxiety about the operation, relief about Dallas's email, excitement about seeing him, uncertainty about the future. There were a lot of questions to be answered, but I told myself they could all wait. Right now, the most important thing was getting to his side. I felt terrible that he'd gone into surgery thinking I didn't want him back. Hopefully, I'd be there when he woke up.

Hurry, I willed the bus driver. *Hurry*.

IT WAS AFTER NOON, and I still had about an hour to go before reaching Boston when I got a text from Finn.

Maren, great to hear from you. Dallas is out of surgery, and the doctor said it went well. He was able to get it all.

I paused, dropping the phone to my lap, and tears welled in my eyes. I closed them in a silent prayer of thanks, and wiped beneath them when I couldn't stop the tears from spilling over.

"Would you like a tissue?" asked the woman next to me, pulling a travel pack of Kleenex from her purse. She reminded me of one of the little old ladies in my Yoga for Seniors class.

I smiled at her and took one. "Thanks. It's good news. I'm just a little emotional."

"I understand." She smiled back.

I dabbed at my eyes and went back to the text.

We are at Mass General. He's in ICU right now, but all vitals are good. Text me when you arrive and I will come get you.

I replied, saying I would, and thanking him profusely. I

wondered if he knew anything about the email Dallas had sent and what he thought about my coming to Boston. If he didn't know, he probably thought I was nuts. Then again, he'd told me not to give up.

I texted Emme and Stella and brought them both up to speed, then I fidgeted and sighed and shifted around in my seat, impatient with the last portion of the ride. I needed to be there already!

Emme replied that she'd booked me a room at a hotel called The Liberty, and the reservation was under her name and credit card. I could switch it when I checked in. Stella replied that she was happy to hear the surgery went well and wished me luck.

When the bus stopped, I practically mowed people down to get off it and plowed through the station to get to the taxi line. On the way to Mass General, I fidgeted some more, and my stomach growled like crazy because I hadn't ever stopped to eat anything.

At the hospital, I got out of the cab and rushed inside, where I texted Finn. He replied in seconds that he was on his way to get me. That was when I first stopped and thought about what I looked like. I hadn't even showered, I was wearing gray yoga pants, a backless, loose-fitting, mint green top with an orange sports bra underneath, I hadn't combed my hair before hastily whipping it into a braid, and a quick look at my feet revealed I'd worn *two different shoes*. I'd bought the same pair of mesh slip-ons in navy and brown because they were so comfortable, and I'd accidentally put on one of each this morning without knowing it.

I glanced at my suitcase and wondered if it would be terrible manners to open it up here in the lobby and dig out one or the other color. But before I came to a conclusion, I heard my name.

"Maren?"

I turned and saw an older, slightly less muscular version of Dallas walking toward me, holding a Styrofoam coffee cup. The resemblance was enough to make my belly flip-flop, although, as he got closer, I saw more differences. His hair was a little thinner and darker, his forehead had more lines, and his chin didn't have a cleft. But when he smiled, I saw Dallas again.

"Hi," I said, throwing my arms around him before I could stop myself.

He laughed and hugged me back a little awkwardly. "Hi. I'm glad you made it."

"Me too." I released him and stood back. "Although I'm a little mortified. I just realized I'm wearing two different shoes."

Smiling, Finn shook his head. "Dallas isn't going to care about your shoes, although that's pretty funny. Your mind must have been elsewhere this morning?"

"Uh, yeah. So everything went okay?" I asked nervously.

"Yes. Absolutely."

"Is he awake?"

"He's sleeping right now. Follow me."

While we walked to the elevators, Finn explained the surgery to me and said that even though he'd been awake, Dallas probably wouldn't remember much and hadn't felt any pain. "He's got to be in neuro-ICU for at least a day so they can monitor him closely for bleeding, infection, or seizure activity. Barring any issues like that, he'll be moved to the tenth floor tomorrow."

I nodded. "Okay. Did the surgeon say whether the mass was benign or malignant?"

Finn smiled. "Looks benign. We'll know for sure when the biopsy results are back."

"Oh, thank God." I touched my chest, breathing a huge sigh of relief.

"I didn't tell him you were coming," Finn said. "I wasn't sure you wanted me to."

I bit my lip. "Will the shock of seeing me hurt him?"

Finn laughed. "No. I think he'll be very glad to know you're here."

"Okay."

Finn studied the lid of his coffee cup. "He told me what happened."

"He did?"

"Yeah. We've ..." He cleared his throat. "We've been talking a lot more over the last week or so. Last night, he sort of spilled his guts to me about you." His cheeks went a little red.

"I'm glad. He probably needed someone to talk to."

"I think he did."

"I never got any of his messages until last night. I was at a silent yoga retreat center in Maine. No electronic devices."

Finn's eyes went wide. "Really? No wonder."

The doors opened, and I went out first, still pulling my stupid suitcase. "Yes, and I have a room at a hotel here in Boston, I just haven't checked in yet. I came straight to the hospital from the bus station."

"Don't worry about that. Bree or I can take you over to your hotel when you're ready. I imagine you're anxious to see Dallas."

I nodded quickly. My heart was galloping inside my chest. "Yes."

"It's one visitor at a time, so I'll wait out here. Bree has the kids in the cafeteria for lunch, so no one's in there now. I can keep your suitcase out here in the waiting area."

"Okay."

He pointed toward a closed glass door. "Right through there."

I turned toward it and took a deep breath. My legs felt shaky as I walked toward his room and slid the door open. They nearly gave out when I saw him lying there in a railed bed, eyes closed, oxygen tube in his nose, bandage on his head, an IV in his left arm and another in his right hand.

But his face was the same, and it took my breath away. The room was sort of dark—the blinds were closed—and I moved closer, careful not to wake him. My hands kneaded together. I wanted to touch him so badly. Stroke his hair, caress his cheek, hold his hand. His arms were lying on top of the blanket...

And that's when I saw it.

Maren, in beautiful script on the inside of his left forearm.

Tears dripped down my cheeks. When had he done that?

I sniffed, and his eyes opened. He blinked.

"Hi," I said softly, my heart spilling over with love.

"Hi." He paused. "Is this real?"

I laughed gently. "Yes."

"You're really here?"

"I'm here." Smiling through tears, I reached over the rail and took his hand.

He closed his eyes for a moment, almost like he was praying. When he opened them, they were shining. "You got my email?"

I nodded. "Yes. It made me so happy."

"Good."

"Finn said the surgery was a success."

"That's what I hear." He spoke slightly slower and more quietly than usual, but not enough to worry me. It was probably from the drugs. He had to be drowsy.

"How are you feeling? Any pain?"

"No. Not even a headache yet."

"That's wonderful." I stroked the back of his hand with my thumb. "I like your new tattoo."

"Yeah?" A shadow of his old smile.

I nodded. "When did you get that?"

"Last week."

"I thought it was against your rules to tattoo a name on someone."

"Not when the someone is me, and not when the name is yours."

My throat closed, and I squeezed his hand.

"I still won't do it for anyone else, because I don't know how they feel. But I know how I feel." His blue eyes looked dark and intense. "And I know it's forever."

I sniffed again, wiping at my eyes with the back of my hand. "I love you, too."

"No more tears, you." He closed his eyes. The talking was tiring him out, I could tell.

"No more tears," I promised, looking around for somewhere to sit while he slept. "And you need to rest. I'll just sit here in this chair, okay? I won't leave."

"No. Come here." He tugged on my hand.

"What?"

"Come here. In bed with me."

"Dallas, I can't—"

"Please?" His eyes opened again. "I missed you so much."

My heart couldn't take it. I glanced at the nurse's station. "Okay. But only for a minute."

Somehow, despite the rails and the oxygen and the IVs and machines, I managed to crawl into the twin bed next to him and cuddle up to his side.

"Much better," he said.

I kissed his scruffy cheek. "Yes."

"So you want to move to Portland?"

Smiling, I patted his chest. "Why don't we wait until after the drugs wear off to talk about that?"

"I'm not high, Maren. I'm just done wasting time. I want you to live with me."

"You do?" I could hardly breathe. Was this the same guy who told me he was too selfish to be a good boyfriend?

"Yes."

"Won't ... won't everyone think it's a little sudden? And maybe crazy?"

"Fuck everyone. I don't care what they think."

Yeah, it was him.

I snuggled closer. "I'd love to. Let's get you better first, and then we'll figure it out. Deal?"

"Deal." With effort, he shifted a little and kissed my head. "I'm just going to say it once more, and then we're leaving the past behind. I'm sorry for what I put you through. Can you forgive me?"

"Of course I can."

He kissed me again. "If you told me I died on the table and this was heaven, I'd believe you."

I smiled. "It's not, babe. This is your life. And it's only gonna get better."

He sighed contentedly. "Good."

I lay there with him for a few more minutes, listening to

him breathe, reassured by the solid warmth of his body and by his words.

We would have our second chance.

Maybe it was sudden. Maybe it had always been destined.

Maybe it was crazy. Maybe it made perfect sense.

Maybe love was a game of chance, played at the whims of Cupid, as random as the roll of the dice.

Or maybe it was a story written in the stars, about a boy and a girl whose hearts wouldn't rest until they were together again.

Either way, it was always and only him.

THREE MONTHS LATER

Dallas

THE SHOP WAS NEARLY EMPTY, and everything was in place.

Even so, I was still a little nervous. Not about what I was about to do, just about making everything perfect. Maren deserved perfection.

"You ready?" Beatriz came by my station with a grin.

"I think so." I wiped my sweaty palms on my jeans. "Fuck, I hope she says yes."

"Are you kidding me? This girl fell in love with you twelve years ago, you broke her heart—twice—she takes you back, moves across the country to be with you, nurses you back to health after brain surgery, says she'll move to bumfuck Oregon with you to live on a ranch she's never even seen and teach yoga to a bunch of angry teenagers, and you're wondering if she's gonna say yes?" She thumped me affectionately on the shoulder. "What's wrong with you?"

I laughed. "It seems too good to be true, that's all."

"Well, you deserve it. You've been through a lot."

"What if she thinks it's too soon?"

She rolled her eyes. "When you know, you know. And trust me—she knows."

"Thanks." I stood up and gave her a hug.

"Okay, I'm getting out of here. The champagne and cake are in the fridge and the food will be delivered as soon as I let them know to bring it, so text me when that ring is on her finger." Beatriz, Evan, and a few other friends were going to wait at a bar down the street, then come back to celebrate with us.

"I will."

She gave me one last smile as she headed for the front. "Good luck."

I double-checked my station to make sure I had everything I needed, then wandered up front to wait for Maren.

It was just after nine, and already dark outside. Autumn had come quickly—it seemed like we'd barely had time to blink, and summer was over.

After the surgery, Maren had remained in Boston for several days, and she hardly left my side while I was in the hospital. We agreed to table any major decisions about moving until after I got stronger, but having something to work for motivated me to follow all instructions and recover as quickly as I could.

I moved in with Finn's family for a month, and Maren visited every weekend. We all celebrated together when the biopsy results came back indicating the tumor was indeed benign. Subsequent scans showed that Dr. Acharya had been able to remove it all, and the seizures, headaches, and dizzying memories had ceased. Yes, I had a big bald patch and a bunch of staples holding my scalp together, and at first I couldn't even take a shower without help, but that was all temporary. I felt unbelievably lucky and grateful.

When I felt strong enough to go home, I asked Maren again about moving to Portland. My feelings for her had only grown deeper and stronger, Finn and Bree adored her, and even my parents—when I finally felt well enough to handle a visit from them—fell under her spell. My mother started hinting around about grandchildren as soon as she saw how natural Maren was with my niece and nephew, and even though I rolled my eyes and shut her down, it was in the back of my mind too.

We talked about it a lot, and although she loved Detroit and had a really hard time moving away from her sisters, she wanted to be with me and was up for starting a life somewhere new. I fucking loved that about her. She sold her studio to one of her instructors in August, got out of her lease, and moved out here right away—without even seeing the house. I asked her if she wanted to visit first, but she said, "I trust you. If you say the house is perfect for us, it is."

Waking up next to her every morning was better than a dream. She was patient and kind and forgiving, but she was tough on me too—she made sure I took all my medications, refused to let me skip checkups and therapy appointments when I tried to say I felt fine, and she calmed something in me that had been restless and unsettled without her in my life. She brought a sense of peace and clarity to my life that I'd never had before. And she made me excited about the future.

Together we'd decided to take Evan up on his offer to buy property adjacent to the ranch and build a home. All that would take a while, but she was as excited as I was about living in the country, working on a responsible, sustainable ranch (she and Evan were of similar minds on that), and teaching yoga and mindfulness as part of the youth program. In the meantime, I was back at the shop several days a week, and she was teaching yoga at a couple different studios. Life was good.

But I wanted more.

Every time I looked at the lotus necklace around her neck—which was often, since she rarely took it off—it gave me a thrill. I couldn't imagine how happy I was going to be when I saw a ring on her finger.

Maren wasn't the kind of girl who waxed poetic about big diamonds or poofy white dresses or having all eyes on her as she walked down the aisle, but I was hoping she wanted to be my wife as much as I wanted to be her husband. But I couldn't just come right out and ask her—not my style at all, and I knew how much Maren loved a surprise.

So I'd concocted a little plan.

When I saw her coming down the street, I pushed the glass door open. A cool October breeze blew in with her, carrying the scent of fallen leaves and her lavender oil. "Hi, beautiful."

Her face lit up. "Hi. How are you feeling?"

I kissed her lips. "Like a million bucks. You ready?"

"Yes! You've been promising me this tattoo forever. Since high school, I believe."

"You're right," I said, letting the door close behind her. "Let's do it."

I took her over to my station and had her sit in the chair. "Okay, put your arm up here."

She extended her left arm across the table, and I prepared her skin.

"Did you make the stencil?" she asked.

"Uh huh." From my desk, I pulled out the stencil of the

words she wanted inked on her forearm in script, going from her inner wrist toward her elbow.

I am not afraid of love.

I held it up. "Like this?"

She nodded happily. "Yes! I'm so excited."

"Okay, close your eyes."

"Why?"

"Because I want it to be a surprise."

She giggled and gave me a strange look. "You're goofy, but okay."

Eyes closed, she leaned back in the chair and I silently pulled a second stencil and a ring box out from my desk. I set the box in my lap and carefully applied the secret words to her arm. My pulse was racing.

When I was finished, I lifted the paper and saw the words I'd temporarily transferred.

Will you marry me?

"Okay," I said, closing my trembling hands around the ring box. "You can look."

She opened her eyes and dropped her gaze to her arm. Her smile faded. Her mouth fell open. "Oh my God." She stared at the words, almost like they didn't make sense. "Is this—are you—?" She looked up at me, an astonished expression on her face. "Is this for real?"

I took the ring box from my lap, moved the table aside, and got down on one knee. Then I opened it.

She gasped and covered her mouth with her hands as she stared at the ring.

"It's real. And maybe it seems a little sudden, but I feel like I've spent my entire life waiting for you. I thought it was too late for us, but you've shown me that it's never too late when you love someone the way I love you. Some things are just meant to be, some people are just meant to be together, and sometimes, love *is* forever."

"Oh, Dallas," she whispered, her eyes tearing up.

I took the ring from the box and slipped it on her finger. "I never want to be without you, Maren. You make me a better man. Will you marry me?"

She nodded as the tears began to spill over.

"Is that yes?"

"Yes. Yes!" Laughter bubbled out of her, even as she wiped her eyes. "I can't believe this." She held out her left hand and stared at it. "Oh my God, it's stunning. I've never seen one like it."

"It was my grandmother's," I said quietly, my throat feeling a little tight. "My grandfather left it to me. It's been in a safe deposit box at the bank for years. I never once thought I'd need it."

Her eyes met mine. "Oh, honey. I love it."

"Are you sure? I had it reset with a champagne sapphire because I know you like color, and the jeweler said that stone is perfect for rose gold. The little diamonds on the band are original to the ring—I liked that. But if it's not what you want, I'll get you a new one. I know it's not very modern."

She cradled her left hand against her chest as if I'd tried to take the ring from her finger. "You want this ring back, you'll have to pry it off my cold, dead hand. It's perfect. *Perfect*."

"Good."

She leaned forward, taking my face in her hands and pressing her lips to mine. "I've never been so happy in my entire life. My heart is going to burst right out of my chest."

"Mine too."

"So happy or so shocked!" She giggled and looked at her hand again. "I thought I was coming here for a tattoo!"

I laughed as I got to my feet. "You can still have your tattoo. I just couldn't wait to see that ring on your finger. And you know I love to surprise you."

She jumped off the chair and threw her arms around me, and I held her tight, lifting her right off her feet. "Never stop surprising me," she whispered as she clung to me.

"Never," I promised. I closed my eyes and breathed her in, feeling overwhelmed with love and luck and gratitude. "You know what?"

"What?"

"I've never been so thankful for that stupid brain tumor."

She laughed as I set her down. "Thankful? Why?"

"Because it brought me back to you." I cradled her beautiful face in my hands. "And it's exactly where I'm supposed to be."

"I love you," she said, her eyes filling once more. "I loved you then, and I love you now, and I'll love you forever."

I kissed her lips. "I'm counting on it."

———

MAREN

I COULDN'T STOP LOOKING at my left hand. Even in the dark, the ring sparkled and shone. Everyone at the impromptu engagement party at the shop had commented how gorgeous and unique it was, and when we had time, I was going to ask Dallas to tell me all about the woman who'd worn it before me. I loved that my ring had a connection to his history.

Dallas chuckled as he pulled into the garage at our house. "You really do like it, huh?"

"I love it." I hugged my left hand against my heart. "I can't get over how perfect it is for me. In a million years, I'd never have been able to describe it. I'm not like Emme, who had her ideal engagement ring picked out by the time she was sixteen. I wasn't even sure I'd ever get married."

"Me neither." He turned off the engine and we got out of the car. "I thought that ring would sit in the box forever."

"Can you give me the real tattoo tomorrow?" I asked. I hadn't wanted to wash off the stenciled proposal tonight, because it was such a fun piece of the story. I'd taken a thousand pictures of it, and sent some to my sisters, who were thrilled and weepy and sent their congratulations and hugs. I couldn't wait to show them the ring, which I'd be able to do next week when we went back to Michigan for Emme's wedding.

We held hands as we walked toward the house. It was an adorable two-bedroom place in a lovely old neighborhood that was perfect for a couple like us, but I was glad we'd have more space eventually. Already, I was thinking about a family, which was another thing I'd never been sure about. Now I wanted a whole tribe. "What do you think about kids?" I asked. "Or is it too soon to talk about that?"

He gave me a look as he unlocked the door. "You're not trying to tell me anything, are you?"

I laughed. "No. It's just a question."

"Okay. Good." He pushed the door open and let me go in first, then he closed it behind him and wrapped me up in his arms from behind. "Because I feel like I just got you all to myself and I'd like to enjoy that for a little while."

I smiled as he walked me from the shadowy kitchen into the living room, where we'd left one lamp on. "But after that?"

"After that we can talk." He kissed the side of my neck.

I spun around in his arms to face him. "How many can we have?"

His gorgeous blue eyes widened. "How *many*?"

"Yeah. Now that I've seen where we're going to live, I want a whole gaggle of kids."

"A gaggle?"

I nodded happily. "Yes! I'm picturing like eight adorable little hippie children running around the ranch, dirt on their faces, flowers in their hair, planting vegetables, picking fruit off the trees..."

He shook his head. "Oh my God. You are not putting flowers in my son's hair."

"I will if he wants me to. And who knows, maybe we'll have eight girls."

His eyes closed. "I'm in so much trouble."

"But you love me." I kissed his lips. "And I love you, and whether we have eight children or twelve or twenty or none—"

"Or two," he said, backing me toward the stairs. "Two is good."

I rolled my eyes. "Two isn't even enough for a game of hide and seek, let alone enough to tend a farm. Hey, can we have peach trees? I love peaches."

Groaning, he bent down, picked me up and threw me over his shoulder. "Me too." He bit my ass cheek through my long cotton skirt. "I'm in the mood for some right now, in fact."

I shrieked as he carried me up the stairs and into our moonlit bedroom, tossing me on the bed. "No! Don't eat me!"

"But I'm so hungry," he growled, reaching beneath my skirt and tugging down my underwear. "And you're so sweet."

I laughed as he disappeared under my skirt and buried his head between my thighs, but before long I was sighing with pleasure, my hands in his hair, his tongue and fingers working their magic.

Then he was sliding up my body, shrugging out of his clothes, lifting my shirt over my head. For the millionth time, I marveled that this was real—this man inside me, this love reborn between us, this future we had imagined. I held him tight as he brought me to a place where we were the only two people in existence, where we'd been made only for each other, and the whole world was ours alone.

I would cherish this feeling forever.

THE END

THANK you for reading Dallas and Maren's story. If you enjoyed this, you'll love Emme and Nate's story, Only You, available now! Stella's story, Only Love, is coming this November 26th.

Want more Dallas and Maren? For access to an exclusive (and steamy) bonus scene, go to the next page!

BONUS SCENE

Dear Reader,

Thank you so much for choosing to read Only Him! I hope you loved reading their story as much as I loved writing it. If you'd like a little more Dallas and Maren, sign up for my newsletter with the link below and the first thing you'll receive is a bonus scene you can't get anywhere else!

http://www.melanieharlow.com/onlyhimbonus/

Love,
    Melanie

NEVER MISS A MELANIE HARLOW THING!

Sign up here to be included on Melanie Harlow's mailing list! You'll receive new release alerts, get access to bonus materials and exclusive giveaways, and hear about sales and freebies first!

http://subscribe.melanieharlow.com/g5d6y6

To stay up to date on all things Harlow, get exclusive access to ARCs and giveaways, and be part of a fun, positive, sexy and drama-free zone, become a Harlot!

https://www.facebook.com/groups/351191341756563/

Follow me on Bookbub to be notified about freebies and sales!

https://www.bookbub.com/authors/melanie-harlow

Prefer text messages? Text HARLOT to 77948 for new release alerts only!

ACKNOWLEDGMENTS

I'm so grateful to the following people:

Melissa Gaston, Dima Gornovskyi, Kayti McGee, Corinne Michaels, Laurelin Paige, Sierra Simone, Jenn Watson and the Social Butterfly team, Rebecca Friedman and Friedman Literary, Flavia Viotti and Bookcase Literary, Nancy Smay of Evident Ink, the Shop Talkers, the Harlots and Harlot ARC Team, bloggers and event organizers, my Queens, my readers, and my family.

You lift me up.

ABOUT THE AUTHOR

Melanie Harlow likes her heels high, her martini dry, and her history with the naughty bits left in. In addition to ONLY HIM, she's the author of ONLY YOU, the After We Fall Series, the Happy Crazy Love Series, the Frenched Series, STRONG ENOUGH (a M/M romance co-authored with David Romanov), and The Speak Easy Duet (a historical romance set in the 1920s). She writes from her home outside of Detroit, where she lives with her husband and two daughters. When she's not writing, she's probably got a cocktail in hand. And sometimes when she is.

Strong Enough (A M/M romance cowritten with David Romanov)

The Tango Lesson (A Standalone Novella)

CPSIA information can be obtained
at www.ICGtesting.com
Printed in the USA
LVHW02s1959120718
583538LV00011B/471/P

9 781732 413801